The Second Empress

Michelle Moran's experiences at archaeological sites around the world first inspired her to write historical fiction. She is the author of *Nefertiti* and its standalone sequel *The Heretic Queen* as well as *Cleopatra's Daughter* and *Madame Tussaud*. She lives in California with her husband.

Please visit her at www.MichelleMoran.com

ALSO BY MICHELLE MORAN

Nefertiti
The Heretic Queen
Cleopatra's Daughter
Madame Tussaud

The Second Empress

MICHELLE MORAN

Quercus

First published in Great Britain in 2012 by

Quercus
55 Baker Street
7th Floor, South Block
London
W1U 8EW

A CIP catalogue record for this book is available
from the British Library

ISBN 978 0 85738 860 5

10 9 8 7 6 5 4 3 2 1

Printed and bound in Great Britain by Clays Ltd, St Ives plc

The Second Empress

"My family have done me far more harm than I have done them good."

—Napoleon Bonaparte

Cairo, July 25, 1798

You will see in the newspapers the result of our battles and the conquest of Egypt, where we found resistance enough to add a leaf to the laurels of this army.

Egypt is the richest country in the world for wheat, rice, pulse, and meal. Nothing can be more barbarous. There is no money, even to pay the troops. I may be in France in two months. I recommend my interests to you.

I have much domestic distress.

Your friendship is very dear to me. To become a misanthropist I have only to lose it, and find that you betray me. That every different feeling toward the same person should be united in one heart is very painful.

Let me have on my arrival a villa near Paris or in Burgundy. I intend to shut myself up there for the winter. I am tired of human nature. I want solitude and isolation. Greatness fatigues me; feeling is dried up. At twenty-nine, glory has become flat. I have exhausted everything. I have no refuge but pure selfishness. I shall retain my house and let no one else occupy it.

Adieu, my only friend. I have never been unjust to you, as you must admit, though I may have wished to be so. You understand me. Love to your wife and to Jérôme.

Nap.

A letter written by Napoleon to his brother, acknowledging acceptance of his beloved wife Joséphine's infidelity. The private correspondence was captured by the British and published in the *London Morning Chronicle*.

1809

CHAPTER 1

MARIA LUCIA, ARCHDUCHESS OF AUSTRIA

Schönbrunn Palace, Vienna
November 1809

I study Maria Ludovika's face in the fresh light of our studio, trying to determine whether I should paint her with or without the golden diadem in her hair. A few steps away, almost close enough to touch, she is holding up a paintbrush and studying me. The courtiers in my father's palace call us the Two Marias, since we share nearly everything together: our shoes, our hobbies, even our names. We are second cousins, but whereas I am tall and buxom, with pale gold hair and wide hips, Maria Ludovika is small and thin. Her dark hair falls in waves around her shoulders, and she has not inherited the Hapsburg lip as I have—full and slightly protruding. Anyone looking at the two of us would think that I am older, because of my significant height. But I am eighteen to her twenty-two, and while she is the empress of Austria now, I am simply an archduchess.

When she came from Italy, I imagined it would be strange to have a stepmother only four years older than me. She is my father's third wife, my mother having died two years ago. But since her arrival in Vienna we have been like sisters, laughing over foolish palace intrigue, arranging trips to the Christmas markets in the city, and painting portraits in our cozy artist's workshop overlooking the winter gardens of Schönbrunn Palace. I have never had another woman my age for entertainment, since I am the eldest. My sixteen-year-old brother, Ferdinand, is the closest in age to me, but he was born dull-witted, as was my little sister, Maria-Carolina. So even as a child, I was lonely.

"Shall I put Sigi in your picture?" Maria asks, looking down at the small spaniel sleeping at my feet.

"I don't know," I say. "What do you think, Sigi? Would you like to sit for a portrait?"

My little *Schnuckelputzi* opens his eyes and barks.

"He knows you're talking about him!" Maria laughs.

"Of course he does." I put down my paintbrush to pick up Sigi, cradling him in my lap. "There's not a dog in Vienna that's smarter than him. Isn't that right?" Sigi buries his head under my arm. In all of Austria, I have never seen another dog with ears covered in such long, fringed hair. He was a gift to me from Maria when she first arrived at Schönbrunn, and now he goes wherever I do.

"If you make him sit still, I'll paint him on your lap."

"Sigi, behave yourself," I say sternly. He rests his chin on his front paws and looks up at me.

"*Exactly.*" Maria dips her brush into the black oil, but before she can apply the paint to the canvas, he has already moved. "Oh, Sigi." She sighs. "What's the matter with you?"

"He's nervous," I say. "He's been like this since the emperor came," I whisper.

"I'm not surprised. Even the animals despise that man." She means Napoleon, who came to us last month with the humiliating Treaty of Schönbrunn, determined that my father, the Emperor Francis I, should sign it. Our English allies were bitterly against my father's surrender. But in his war against Napoleon, three million lives had already been lost.

The terms of Napoleon's treaty were harsh, demanding that we cede our city of Salzburg to Bavaria, Galicia to the Poles, East Galicia to Russia, and much of Croatia to France. So four hundred thousand citizens who speak only German, eat only German food, and know only German customs woke up to find themselves belonging to four different nations. Yet the rest of the kingdom remained intact, and for this, my father owes Prince Metternich. They say there has never been another diplomat like him in the world. That if not for Metternich, the great Hapsburg-Lorraine empire would have been reduced to nothing.

When the treaty was signed, I heard courtiers whisper, "Better to be a beggar in the streets than a coward." They believed my father had sold the Adriatic coast for the price of his crown. But they were not the ones with sons or husbands in the army. They did have not have to receive—week after week, month after month—the terrible lists of the dead. I did. I was there, in my father's Council Chamber, as one day I will be regent when Ferdinand takes the throne. I know the price Napoleon exacted on Austria. But the courtiers seem to have forgotten what the French are capable of. How only sixteen years ago they beheaded my great-aunt, Queen Marie-Antoinette.

There are few people who understand the true cost of this treaty to my father, but Maria is one of them. She was still a child in Italy when Napoleon's army appeared thirteen years ago. The soldiers swept through the streets taking whatever they pleased: carriages, villas, valuable china, women. Her father, who was the governor of the Duchy of Milan, gathered her family together, and they escaped with only the clothes on their backs. When they arrived in Austria, he was made the Duke of Breisgau. But Maria has never forgotten the loss of Milan, her childhood home, and it was with great unhappiness that she watched her husband sign the Treaty of Schönbrunn, surrendering to her family's most bitter enemy for a second time.

"And do you remember how small he was?" Maria asks, and I know she is about to continue with a familiar tirade.

"I only saw him from a distance," I remind her. I refused to enter the Council Chamber when my father was forced to sign away parts of his empire.

"Like a little gnome. Prince Metternich says that in France his enemies call him the King of Diamonds, a squat little emperor wrapped in red velvet and fur. Who is he?" she demands, and her voice is rising. "Where does he come from? And to think we had to bow to that man! A *Corsican*. Do you know what they do in Corsica?" She doesn't wait for me to answer. "They send their daughters to brothels to earn extra money. Even the nobles!"

I don't know if this is true, but Maria believes it.

"Just look at his sister, Pauline." She leans forward, and our painting is forgotten. "What sort of woman poses nude for a sculptor? *Nude!*" It was a scandal all across Europe, that the Emperor of France could control an army of three hundred thousand men but not his own family. First Jérôme Bonaparte married without Napoleon's approval and fled to America to escape his brother's wrath. Then Lucien Bonaparte took a wife without his brother's consent. Now, Pauline has left her second husband in Turin to pursue the life of an unmarried woman in Paris.

They are not a family fit for any throne. I think of my father's continuous sacrifices to be a Hapsburg king his people can respect: the nights he has stayed up balancing accounts, the mistresses he has refused in order to be a moral husband, and his vigilant oversight of the nation's treasury. It is not exciting work, and it is hardly glamorous. But a people are a reflection of their monarch, and we must provide a good example for them. My siblings and I have all been taught to keep records, so that we know exactly how much was spent keeping us in silk slippers and warm cloaks. For the month of November, I cost my father nearly twice as much as Maria-Carolina. Next month I will be more careful. "A king who rules without watching his treasury is a king who will soon be without a crown," my father says.

And it doesn't help that the Treaty of Schönbrunn has bankrupted our empire, forcing my father to make reparation payments to Napoleon of more than fifty million francs. Napoleon had wanted a hundred million, but no kingdom in the world can afford such a sum. So he settled for half, and my father has had to abandon silver coin and begin printing our money on paper. If there are hungry women and children in the streets, it is because of this treaty. It is because Napoleon could not be satisfied with Croatia, or Salzburg, or even Tyrol. He wanted the world to know that the Hapsburgs had been defeated, and now the German people must suffer for daring to believe they could stop him from consuming all of Europe. And even Europe was not enough.

Eleven years ago Napoleon marched an army of nearly forty thousand soldiers into Egypt. We were told he wanted to take control of the Indian Empire from the British. But the truth was something different. Prince Metternich lived in Paris as Napoleon's ambassador for more than three years, and he has told my father that the French emperor went to Egypt for one reason—glory—and that nothing is more important to him. He wanted to rule the land once conquered by Alexander the Great. He wished to hear his name echoing around the world.

To rise so high, so fast, you would think that God Himself was on his side, pushing him to even further greatness. But how can that be when his actions have deprived our people of food? When his treaty has impoverished the most benevolent empire in Europe? The Hapsburg-Lorraines have ruled for almost eight hundred years. Who is this man who thinks he can conquer the world before he's even forty?

I am about to reprimand Sigi for not staying still when a sharp knock on the door sends him jumping from my lap. I frown at Maria, since no one disturbs us in our artist's retreat.

"Come in," she calls.

Sigi growls at the door, but it is my father and Prince Metternich who enter, and immediately we rise. They are two of the most handsome men at court, with thick golden hair and slender waists. Even at forty-one and thirty-six, they are the picture of vitality, and both have the famous Hapsburg skin that made Marie-Antoinette so admired.

"The Two Marias," my father says in greeting, and although we are standing, he waves this action away. "Keep painting," he tells us. "That's why we've come."

"For a painting?" I ask.

"Your most unattractive portraits."

I am about to laugh, but there is no humor in his face.

Prince Metternich explains. "Napoleon has requested paintings from every noble house in Europe. He is particularly interested in Europe's unmarried princesses."

"But he's already married!" Maria exclaims.

"There is talk of a divorce," my father says quietly.

Maria and I exchange looks.

"It will likely come to nothing," Metternich says smoothly, "but he has made the request, and we cannot deny it." As usual, Metternich's voice is calm. If Napoleon had asked for nude statues of us, he would have passed this along in the same even tone.

"You are to choose your least attractive portrait," my father says.

My hands are shaking. "But I thought he loved Joséphine," I protest. After all, he forgave her even after all of Europe came to know of the affairs she conducted while he was in Egypt.

"Certainly he loves her," Metternich replies. "But the emperor needs an heir."

"And he has gotten a child on his mistress," my father says contemptuously, "proving he's not infertile."

"Do the scandals never end with this family?" Maria stands. "We shall send him the very first portraits we made of one another. Then he will *never* look to Austria for a bride." I follow her across the room to the wall where all our efforts at portraiture have been framed. "That one." Maria points. Aside from my blond hair and blue eyes, I am unrecognizable.

Prince Metternich clears his throat. "Mockery may be inadvisable," he says.

"This is no mockery!" my father shouts. "Does he think he can do away with his wife as easily as he did away with Egypt's mamelukes? The pope will not have it. Europe will never consider another wife of his legitimate!"

"Then he might choose to proceed without the pope," Metternich replies.

The three of us stare at him.

"He is a bold man, Your Majesty. Nothing can be discounted. I would consider sending that one," Metternich suggests, indicating a large, oval painting from three months ago. It is the best likeness of me: my wide-set eyes are a vivid blue, and in life they are probably my best feature. But it also captures my too-strong jaw, the length of my nose, and my Hapsburg lip.

"No," my father rules. "It is too pretty."

Metternich looks from the painting to me, and I flush. "He will want a good likeness" is all he says.

"And how should he know?" Maria demands. "He has never laid eyes on her!"

"Your Majesties, this is a man who may choose to visit Vienna tomorrow, or next week, or even next month. What will he think if he sees the archduchess and realizes that you have made a fool of him? Please, give him something that will not make him suspicious."

"Send whichever one you want," my father says. "Just do it quickly, so we may stop talking about this man."

Metternich bows. "There is still the matter of your wife, Your Majesty. He also wishes to see every member of the royal family. Is there a painting you prefer—"

"Yes. Whichever's cheapest. And do not send him anything in a gilded frame." My father pauses at the door, then looks around. "That one," he says, pointing to the unfinished canvas on my easel. I have already painted Maria's black eyes, her small, pretty lips, and the abundant curls that hang in dark clusters on either side of her head. Although her dress remains to be done, there is no one who will look at this without thinking that my father has chosen well.

"When will you be finished?" Prince Metternich asks.

I feel the heat creep back into my cheeks. "Another five days. Perhaps a week."

He crosses his arms over his chest, scrutinizing the painting. Then he looks up at me. "You have talent."

His sudden interest makes me uncomfortable. "Not much. Not like Maria."

"How long have you been painting?"

"Three years."

"And how many languages do you speak?"

"What is this about?" My father steps back into the room.

"Nothing." Prince Metternich is quick to add, "Just idle curiosity." But when he looks back at me, I feel compelled to answer.

"Six."

He smiles widely. "As accomplished as any Hapsburg arch-duchess should be."

CHAPTER 2

PAULINE BONAPARTE, PRINCESS BORGHESE

Fontainebleau Palace, south of Paris
November 1809

I stand in front of the mirror before he comes in, and as usual, I am shocked to see just how beautiful I am. I don't mean beautiful in the way that Joséphine is beautiful. All that woman has are her great cow's eyes and a head of thick curls. I mean *exquisitely* beautiful, like one of Bartolini's marble statues. At twenty-nine, you would think I would already be losing my looks. But my waist is long and slender, and because I only gave birth once, my breasts are still high and taut. I turn, so that I can admire the effect of my Grecian gown from behind. In the candlelight, it is perfectly transparent.

"Paul!" I shout, and my chamberlain appears. He is my staunchest ally, my fiercest guard. I named him after myself when I discovered him in Saint-Domingue seven years ago. Of course, now that our colonists have their independence, they are calling their island Haiti. But for the French, it will always be Saint-Domingue. "Is he here?" I ask him.

"In the hall, Your Highness."

"What does he look like?"

Paul tells me the truth. "Unhappy."

So Joséphine has arrived, and they have spoken. I am certain she threw herself at his feet, begging his forgiveness. And my brother no doubt felt sympathy for her. But this time he will not feel pity. This is not some affair with a young lieutenant—this is an unforgiveable lie. For fourteen years she has convinced him that he cannot father a child. That it's been *his* failure, not hers, that he would never have an heir. And then came Walewska. Pretty, blond, married Walewska, who eventually gave up her husband to bed my brother, and now everything has changed. My God, I could kiss her! In fact, I shall send her a diamond brooch. She should know what kind of service she has done for the Bonapartes, ensuring Empress Joséphine's disgrace at last, and the downfall of the Beauharnais.

"Shall I send him in, Your Highness?"

I return to the mirror, a gilded monstrosity my second husband gave me as a wedding present, and study my reflection. My hair is held by a simple pearl band, and I arrange it around my shoulders like a long black shawl. "No. Let him wait another minute."

Since we were children, Napoleon has admired my hair. In Corsica, I would ask him to braid it for me. He would only laugh and call my request a harlot's trick, adding that no man could resist a woman whose hair he had touched. But then, if you listen to the women at court, I *am* a harlot.

I know what the gossips say. That when my first husband took me to the Caribbean, I experimented with every kind of lover: black, white, male, female. I grin, thinking of my life in Saint-Domingue. The lazy nights eating sapodillas with two, sometimes three partners in my bed. And the mornings after when the sun would cast a golden net over the sea . . . But then my husband died of yellow fever, and it was back to Paris. I was the Widow Leclerc without even a title for my name.

"Tell him I am ready."

Paul bows at the waist and shuts the door.

My second match, however, changed everything.

I think of Camillo Borghese, doing whatever it is that he does in Turin. While it's true that he is the greatest imbecile ever to hold the title of prince, my marriage to him was my finest triumph. My brother granted both my sisters the rank of Imperial Highness, but I am the *Princess* Borghese, with a palazzo in Rome, a vast collection of art, and three hundred thousand francs worth of Borghese family jewels. Even my mother could not have envisioned such a match for me.

I wonder what the old women of Marseilles would think if they could see their "Italian maid" now. I was thirteen when our family fled Corsica and took refuge in their miserable seaside town. Everything we owned was left behind. We had nothing when we arrived, and that is how the French treated our family—as nothings. They believed that because we were born in Corsica, we wouldn't know French. "There go the Corsicans," they whispered, and, "What a shame they have nothing. That Paoletta is quite beautiful. She might have made a good marriage."

When my sisters and I were sent to be maids in the grand Clary house, the men assumed they had purchased our sexual favors as well. "Corsican girls," they said, "are only good for one thing." I never told Napoleon. He was a twenty-four-year-old general with a war at his back. But when he visited us in Marseilles, he knew. Caroline had grown as fat as a pig, and I had stopped eating. "What's the matter with them?" he asked my mother, and she pretended it was the food. "It's not like Corsica." But Napoleon saw my tears, and he knew.

"You and Caroline will leave that house tomorrow," he said. "You will both come to Paris. With me."

But Paris was a war zone. "It's too great a risk. We'll have nothing."

"We will never have *nothing*. We are Bonapartes," he swore, and something changed in his face. "And we will never be vulnerable again."

Today no one would dare whisper that a Corsican comes cheap. I turn to my little greyhound, who is lounging on the chaise across the room. "We are the most powerful family in Europe," I say, in the voice I reserve only for her. She thumps her tail with enthusiasm, and I continue, "We have thrones from Holland to Naples. And now, when they talk about us, it's with fear in their voices. 'Beware the Bonapartes,' they say. 'The most powerful siblings on earth.'"

The door opens, and Paul announces grandly, "His Majesty, the Emperor Napoleon."

I turn, but slowly, so that my brother may see the full effect of my gown.

"Thank you, Paul." He returns to the salon, and I face

Napoleon. We are similar in so many ways. We have both inherited the dark looks of our mother's Italian family, the Ramolinos, and like them, we are both hot-blooded and passionate. When he told me as a child that someday all of Europe would know his name, I believed him. "So you told her." I smile.

Aubree runs to greet him, and he pets her mechanically. "How could I?" He stalks to my favorite chair and sits. "She was hysterical and weeping."

"You *didn't* tell her you are seeking a divorce?" My voice sends Aubree scampering from the room.

"She loves me—"

"Half of Europe loves you! She is a *liar*." I cross the chamber to stand in front of him. "Think of the ways she has deceived you," I say quickly. "First her age, then her bills, now her fertility!" *My God*, I think, *she is six years older than you! A grandmother already. How could you spend fourteen years believing you were the one at fault?*

His eyes narrow. "It's true. She has always deceived me."

"She has undermined your manhood." I close my eyes briefly, and then play my best card. "Look at what she told the Russian ambassador."

His face becomes still. "*What?*"

I step back. "You didn't hear?"

"What did she tell him?" He rises from his chair.

I give him my most pitying look, then close my eyes briefly. "At one of her soirées, she told the Russians that you might be impotent." My brother is enraged. He rushes across the room, and I hurry to stand in front of the door before he can leave and confront her. "It's already done!"

"Step aside!" he shouts.

"There's nothing you can do! Be calm." I reach out and caress his face. "No one of importance believes these rumors. And with Marie Walewska carrying your child, who will give her words credit?" I take his arm and guide him to the chaise by the window. "Shall I open it? Do you need fresh air?"

"No. It's bad for your health." But he can't stop thinking about the Russians. "*Impotent!*" he seethes. "If I went to her bed and refused to take her, it was because I had just returned from a visit with Marie!"

My sisters would be scandalized by this, but there is nothing Napoleon and I keep from each other. I sit on the edge of the chaise and lean forward. "And so she spread this rumor . . . this *vile* gossip. She has always been devious." He can't possibly forget the bills she hid from him after they married. How he had to sell his stable—his precious horses—to pay for her extravagances, which still continue. He may be richer than the pope, but I will never forgive her for using him this way. And I will *never* forget what she has done to me . . .

"I am right in wanting to divorce her."

"Yes."

"I . . . I will tell her tomorrow."

But I know what he is thinking. He has an unnatural attachment to this woman. If these were different times, I would wonder if she had cast some sort of spell on him. "Perhaps you can have Hortense break the news," I say casually, as if this thought has just occurred. This way Joséphine can weep, but she can't change his mind. Then I change the subject entirely, as if we are agreed. "I have arranged a soirée for you tonight."

"So I hear."

By now, the guests must have arrived in my salon, filling the room with their laughter and perfume. "And I invited someone special for you."

"Another Greek?"

"No, an Italian. Blond and very discreet. Not like Beauharnaille." This is my favorite pun on Joséphine's name. It means "old hag." "Shall we?" I stand, and with the candlelight at my back, I know that I must appear entirely nude.

He recoils. "You're not leaving like that."

"No?"

"It is indecent!"

I look down. "I could put on different slippers."

"Your gown is transparent!"

"This is what they wore in ancient Egypt," I protest. His conquest of Egypt put all of France in the thrall of the pharaohs. The soldiers returned from the Battle of the Pyramids with unimaginable wonders: painted sarcophagi, alabaster jars, small figurines carved from bright blue stone. In my château in Neuilly, my collection of Egyptian artifacts fills nearly three rooms. And every birthday, as a gift, Napoleon gives me something new. Last year it was a statue of the Egyptian god Anubis. The year before that, it was a queen's gold and lapis crown. Someday, when I become too sick to host my brother's *fêtes*, I will dress myself in Egyptian linen and cover my wrists and chest with gold. Then I will die an honorable death, like Cleopatra. She didn't wait for Augustus Caesar to kill her. She was the master of her body.

"You take this love of the ancients too far." He stands,

though he cannot help but look. "Find something else."

I lift the gown over my head and let it drop onto the chaise. Then I cross the chamber and stand naked before my wardrobe.

"The gauze dress with silver embroidery," he says, coming to stand behind me.

"I wore that yesterday."

"The new one."

My brother knows everything that is purchased within his palaces, from the food for the kitchens to the dresses bought by court women. In this last matter, he takes a particular interest. We are to outshine every court in Europe, he says, and if that means every lady-in-waiting must buy four hundred dresses a year, then so be it. And if a woman should be foolish enough to appear at a gala in a dress she has worn to some previous *fête,* she will never be invited again. I adore my brother for understanding this. I hold out the gauze dress, and Napoleon nods.

He watches me dress, and when I reach for a shawl, he shakes his head. "It's a shame to cover such shoulders."

I turn to place the shawl on my dressing table, and a sharp pain in my stomach makes me wince. I glance at Napoleon, but he hasn't noticed. I don't want him to worry about my health. Although someday, no amount of rouge or shadow will cover my illness. It will show itself in lines on my face and the thinness of my body. "Have you ever imagined what it would be like to be the pharaoh of Egypt?" I ask him. I know Egypt makes him think of Joséphine, since it was there that he discovered her infidelities. But in Egypt, their rulers never die. In a thousand years, Cleopatra will still be young and beautiful. With every golden crown and faience ushabti discovered in Cairo, she will be remembered for eternity.

"Yes," he quips. "Dead and mummified."

"I am serious," I tell him. "There have always been emperors and kings. But there has not been a pharaoh for nearly two thousand years. Imagine if we could reign together."

He smiles.

"Why not? The ancient Egyptian kings anointed their sisters as wives. There would be no greater couple in the world."

"And how would I do this?" he asks. "Or perhaps you don't remember that the Egyptians rebelled?"

"You would reconquer them. If you could defeat the Austrians, you could defeat the mamelukes. How difficult could it be?"

"Not very."

I take his arm, and we head toward my salon. "Think of it," I say. And for the rest of the evening, his eyes follow me. Though I am sure he will be happy with the Italian I've found for his pleasure, I know I am the one who fascinates him.

CHAPTER 3

PAUL MOREAU, CHAMBERLAIN
TUILERIES PALACE, PARIS

"Of Napoleon's three sisters, Elisa, Caroline and Pauline,
the latter, famous for her allurements, was the one of
whom he was fondest."

—Joseph Fouché, Duc d'Otrante, Napoleon's
Minister of General Police

Only two things are honest in Pauline Borghese's world: her
mirror and me.

When she arrived with her first husband in Haiti, I was
the only person on my father's plantation to warn her of the
clap. The aristocratic *grands blancs* and *gens de couleur* were
all too afraid to speak the truth to the dazzling wife of the
General Leclerc. I was only seventeen, but if she continued
to bed men like my promiscuous half-brother, even I could
see how it would end: in cramping, then bleeding, and finally
fever. So I told her who I was—the son of Antoine Moreau
and his African mistress—and I described for her the risks
that she was taking.

She stood still at first, frozen as a carving made from

juniper wood. Then she smiled. "You're jealous of your brother, aren't you? Bitter that while he's French, you're just a mulatto, so I would never ask you."

Then she waited for my reaction. But I'd seen her try to bait men this way before. "Does this mean Madame has already forgotten Simon?" I asked. An *homme de couleur*, he'd been her lover for two months and was much darker than me.

Her cheeks blazed, and I wondered if I'd gone too far.

"What did you say your name is?"

"Antoine."

She stepped closer to me. So close that I could smell the scent of jasmine on her skin. "And what is it you do on this plantation?" she asked.

"I'm my father's chamberlain."

"At fifteen?"

"Seventeen," I told her. "But I was overseeing the plantation last year as well."

She studied my face, and I wondered what she made of my mother's high cheekbones and my father's strong jaw. No one in Haiti mistook me for French. But few believed my mother was African, either. My curls are too loose, my eyes too light. "Does your father know you speak so frankly to his guests?"

"I should hope so. He schooled me."

For the first time during our interactions, she smiled.

And for the rest of her days in Haiti, Madame Leclerc strolled the fields with me, watching the sheaves of wheat turn from winter's green to summer's gold. This is how we came to know each other, and she understood, long before I did, that neither of us belonged. The great Haitian warrior Toussaint had just started a revolution, boldly telling the French that he was declaring an end to slavery on our island. But we were the wealthiest colony in the world—growing indigo, cotton, tobacco, sugar, coffee, even sisal for the benefit of France—and Napoleon was enraged. This was truly the reason Pauline and I met: her brother had sent General Leclerc to subdue Saint-Domingue by any means.

When Pauline arrived, black did not trust white, white did not trust black—and no one trusted a *mulâtre*. I was a *mulâtre*. If Pauline's brother succeeded, my mother would be returned to slavery. My half-brother was fighting for Napoleon while my mother was secretly helping Toussaint. When I asked my father which side he was on, he said, "Freedom son. From France and from enslavement." Before my birth, he had owned more than two dozen slaves. But he told me that after he looked into my eyes, he freed every one. So I would always be free, but to whom would I belong? Increasingly, it seemed, I belonged with Pauline.

She understood what it was to live in a county torn apart by war, and the chaos it wrought on families. "You never speak with your half-brother," she once remarked.

I looked down at my shoes. It wasn't that she had bedded him. It was that she had once thought a man who was as handsome as a prince and as ignorant as a peasant was preferable company to me. What did they discuss? French politics? French conquest? "No," I told her. "We have little to say."

"Because of the war?"

"For many reasons."

But if I wanted to remain close to Pauline, I had to accept the other men. They might possess her body for a night, but I was the one who shared her heart. In those long summer nights, I taught her how to eat sugarcane and make fried plantains. In return, she taught me how to dress like a Parisian and dance.

"There's nothing more important to the ancien régime than their etiquette."

"Is that what keeps them rich?"

"No. It's what keeps them separated from the likes of us."

"But you're Corsican nobility," I pointed out.

She laughed sharply. "That's not good enough for them."

So we practiced ballroom curtsies and bows in my father's salon, pretending the lamps were chandeliers, and that the windows looked out onto vast castle gardens. Every day we met, and I was young enough to believe that we would live like this for the rest of our lives: picnicking on the banks of the Ozama River, reading to each other from Ossian's poems, *Deaths wander, like shadows, over his fiery soul! Do I forget that beam of light, the white-handed daughter of kings?* and listening to the birdsong from the mango trees. I was even foolish enough to ignore the sound of gunfire from the hills and, on the terrible nights, the screaming of women.

Then our fantasy ended when her husband died of the fever.

"Madame, you shouldn't be in my chamber," I warned her. "They'll talk." She had never come to my room before, and

I wondered how the small wooden armoire and thin cot appeared in her eyes. This wasn't how my half-brother lived, with his heavy teak furniture and long writing desk. But this wasn't how our workers lived, either.

She seated herself next to me on the cot. "As if they don't talk already?"

It was true. Though I had never touched her, even my half-brother assumed we were lovers. He confronted me one morning outside the stables, threatening to kill me and my whore of a mother if I didn't stop meeting Madame Leclerc. Before he lunged for my throat, I asked him, "Do you really think she'd bed a *mulâtre* like me?" It was a trick I had seen Pauline use on her husband once at dinner. He didn't know that Pauline didn't care about color, or that I would never take a woman without marrying her. After that, he smirked whenever he saw "the stunning Madame Leclerc with the pathetically, smitten *mulâtre* Antoine."

Now she buried her head in her hands, and tears slipped through her fingers like rain. "It's over, Antoine. I'm returning to France."

"*Forever?*"

"Yes. But you are going to come with me."

I pulled away from her. "You can't command me like one of your servants!"

"But you love me." She stood, pressing her chest against mine. "I'm a widow now. It's what you've been waiting for, isn't it?"

I searched her face to see if this was true. If it was . . . "Madame, you are grief-stricken," I told her.

"I know what I am! And I am devastated at the thought of returning home without you."

I closed my eyes and tried to think with her body against mine. "My father cannot run this plantation without me."

"He will hire someone. You're a *mulâtre*, Antoine. You don't belong here. The blacks won't have you in their army, and if you fight with the French, you'll be turning your back on your own mother."

It was true.

Pauline caressed my cheek. No woman had ever touched me like this before, and I wondered if this was how she had touched my brother when they were together. "Come with me," she repeated, but all I could hear was her breath in my ear. "They don't need you, and I do. We will go to Paris until this war is over. There will be food and peace and nights without gunfire. I'll hire you to be my chamberlain. In a few years, you'll be wealthy. You can return to Saint-Domingue and buy any plantation you desire. And who knows? Maybe I'd be ready to return here, too."

My heart beat wildly. I could return to my island with the most enchanting woman in the world, my fortunes great enough to buy a farm of my own. "You would return to Saint-Domingue?" I asked her.

"Why not? But we can't stay here now. My brother has called me home. Come," she implored. "Think of it as an adventure."

The ship we boarded for France was the *Janus*. I learned then what kind of adventure it would be: she took two lovers while we were at sea, and after that there were all the men she invited to her chamber in Paris. Then there was her second husband, Camillo Borghese, the short, fat Prince of Guastalla. "But not as fat as his accounts," she'd joked.

"Have you ever loved any of them?" I asked one night, watching her in the mirror as she brushed her hair—for this is what I am paid to do: watch, and wait, and listen, and advise. Two years had passed since we left Haiti, and when I glanced at my reflection in her husband's glass, I did not recognize the man who peered back at me. He wore a red velvet coat with gold epaulettes. His hair was cut short, just below the ears. And his name—the name Pauline insisted upon when she burned a path like the sun toward the Tuileries Palace—was Paul Moreau. I had abandoned Antoine somewhere in Haiti; in the mango groves, perhaps, with my mother's songs. I was named after the Princess Borghese, and as a member of France's imperial court, I spoke with princes and walked with kings.

If my family were alive, they would not know the man who chatted daily with the emperor in his study. They would think the well-dressed chamberlain quoting Rousseau, and arguing against slavery in France's colonies of Saint Lucia, Guadeloupe, Martinique, and Senegal, was the son of a highly educated diplomat. But then, my family isn't alive to see me. Like my name, I abandoned them in Haiti.

Pauline turned to face me, and I could see her thinking about my question. After sharing her days and heart with me, did she love the men she spent her nights with? "Of course not," she replied. "You know there are only two men in my life." She paused, waiting for me to ask. When I didn't, she said, "Napoleon and you."

Five years later she is just as wild, and selfish, and dazzling. This morning, she can barely contain her joy because the emperor has done it. He has told his wife, the woman who followed his star even when it was sinking low in the heavens, that their divorce will be announced in fourteen days.

"My God, Paul, I'm so happy I could weep! No, I'm so happy I could *dance*. In fact"—she rises from the mirror, and I know from the way her eyes have grown large that she has hit on something she considers great—"tonight I shall host a ball!"

I do not move from my chair. It is here, on this chaise at the far end of her boudoir, that I spend each morning listening to her plans while Aubree curls onto my lap and falls asleep. "And you think that is wise?"

But whenever this mood takes her, she is impossible to reason with. "He's my *brother*. Why shouldn't he know that I love him?"

"Because there are those who still love the empress as well. And she has just lost it all. This palace, her husband, the imperial crown—"

"Which should never have been hers to begin with!" She turns back to her mirror and brushes her hair frantically. If she continues this habit whenever she's upset, she'll be bald by forty. "I am hosting a *fête*, Paul, and not even you can change my mind."

"Your devotion to him is clear," I say. *It is also unhealthy*, but I do not add this. She craves his attention. In all of France, there have never been two siblings with such raw ambition. They goad each other on. "And the empress?" I ask. "What will become of her?"

She walks to the commode and considers her silk robes. "He will banish her," she guesses, choosing the red. "Then she will know how it feels to lose the man she wants."

Although she already has my attention, she drops her chemise to the floor. For all the prostitutes on the Boulevard du Temple, I have never seen another woman's body but Pauline's. And she is utterly without shame. After she married her wealthy Italian prince, she gifted him a statue by Antonio Canova, who sculpted her in the nude as the goddess Venus. When the emperor saw it, he flew into a rage, forbidding any future statues. So in the Château de Neuilly, her private residence in Paris, she has modeled the serving bowls on her breasts instead. I have seen her brother eat nuts out of them. "Why should I hide them away?" she told me, enjoying her little joke. "The ancient Egyptians were proud to bare them."

When she has fastened her robe, she crosses the bedchamber into the salon. "Are you coming? I have a story to tell you about Joséphine."

I follow her into my favorite room in the Tuileries. The doors to the balcony have been thrown open, and fresh light illuminates the gilded walls where an artist has painted scenes from the temples of Egypt. Women in white sheaths raise their arms to the sun, and strange gods with the heads of jackals and bulls carry powerful insignias: crooks, flails, a golden key to life—all symbols of rule. I sit across from her on a padded chair while she arranges herself on the divan.

"I was only fifteen when I met Fréron, but I knew what I

wanted. We were set to marry in Martinique until Joséphine
. . ." Tears redden her eyes, and I am shocked. I had no idea
she felt so strongly about Fréron, whose name she has
mentioned briefly in the past. "Until Joséphine told my
brother that Fréron would never be good enough for me."

I sit forward. "Then you loved him?"

"Of course! I was fifteen."

"But he wasn't a soldier," I point out. Nearly all of Pauline's
affairs have been with men in French uniforms.

"No." She closes her eyes. "I almost tied my fortunes to a
lowly deputy. Can you imagine? I would have lived in poverty,
clinging to the hope that the government might increase his
salary one day! But Joséphine was not to know that," she
adds heatedly.

"So she saved you from penury," I reply, and the look she
gives me is thunderous.

"I was a sensitive girl! He was going to save me. You don't
know—"

But I do. I know exactly how it is with Pauline Borghese, the
princess of Guastalla who was raised in poverty on the little
Italian island of Corsica and vowed with her brother to conquer
the world. I wish I had known her then, before the world gave
her so much pain and grief. She wipes away real tears with
the back of her hand, and this rare show of tenderness presses
at my heart. Then, as if on cue, Aubree arrives, curling herself
on the divan next to her mistress. There is nothing in the world
the princess loves as this dog. She is tiny, weighing only ten
pounds, but her eyes are filled with a world of expectation and
play. "Tell me what you've heard about the divorce," Pauline

says, tracing the delicate, folded ears of her Italian greyhound. *Tell me something cheerful* is what she means.

"I heard the empress fainted when he told her the news, and that the emperor had to carry her up to her chamber because she was too weak to walk."

"What an actress!" she exclaims. "I've never asked to be carried by the emperor, and *I'm* the one who's always in pain. Do you remember how terrible it was last week?"

"Your Highness couldn't move from the divan for two days."

"And did I ask my brother to come and carry me? Did I stand up and pretend to faint at his feet?"

"No, you are far more subtle than that."

She stares at me, but my face betrays nothing.

"I told him to have *Hortense* tell her," she continues. "He could have spared himself the theatrics. What else? I know my brother confides in you. Have you heard anything about how she's to be treated?" She sits up on her divan, forcing Aubree to readjust her position.

It would be easier for us both if I lied, but I will not. "The emperor has offered her a kingdom in Italy, including"—I exhale—"the city of Rome."

There is a tense moment of silence, and even Aubree knows what is coming; the little greyhound buries her nose in her paws.

"*Rome,*" she repeats, as if she can't believe it. "How can he offer her the greatest jewel in Italy without any thought for me?" And then she cries, "I am the Princess Borghese, and Rome should be *mine!*"

I spread my hands, as if it's a mystery. But the truth is,

her brother feels guilty. He has cast off a wife he still loves for a woman who will be able to give him sons. It is cruel. Especially since he has already gotten a child on his Polish mistress and might easily make the young boy his heir and keep his wife.

"And what did she tell him?" the princess demands.

What any woman of dignity would have said. "That love cannot be bought and sold," I reply. "The empress refused the offer."

She sinks back on the divan. "Thank God."

A knock on the door sends Aubree rushing across the salon. She is practically dancing in anticipation, twisting her charcoal-colored body back and forth. "Look at her!" The princess laughs. "Calm down, *ma chouette,* it's only a visitor."

I cross the salon to open the double doors, but when Aubree sees who it is, she hurries back to the divan. "Her Majesty Queen Caroline," I announce without enthusiasm.

The youngest of the Bonaparte sisters pushes past me, and I am in full agreement with the dog. I cannot imagine a less likely woman for the queen of Naples. She is short and ungainly, with eyes that are forever darting about and the complexion of someone stricken with fever.

"I have news." She seats herself across from her sister and arranges her velvet cap so that the feathers are tilting jauntily to the side. The emperor may have made her shifty husband, Joachim Murat, the king of Naples, but he can never buy either one of them style. She is a dim star to Pauline's sun, and there are a hundred petty jealousies between the sisters.

"I know," Pauline says smugly. "Paul's already told me. He's going to divorce her!"

But Caroline, who should look dismayed that I've gotten to this news first, keeps smiling.

"What?" Pauline presses. "Is there something else? Is he officially announcing it?"

Now her sister plays coy. "I don't know. Perhaps *His Highness* can tell you." Her eyes cut toward me. "He seems to know everything."

Pauline shrugs. "If you can't say—"

"He's drawn up a list of names!" she blurts. "All foreign princesses. And not a single one's French."

Pauline's voice rises. "For *marriage*?"

Caroline, satisfied with this reaction, nods sagely. "Including Maria-Lucia of Austria and Anna Paulowna, the Russian czar's sister."

"I don't believe you," Pauline says flatly.

"Then I suppose Maman didn't show it to me. Perhaps I was dreaming—"

"He would never marry an Austrian!" Pauline exclaims. "The last Hapsburg queen of France lost her head."

"That was sixteen years ago. Who even remembers Marie-Antoinette now?"

All of Haiti, I think. She is the reason that Toussaint declared an end to slavery on behalf of every *gens de couleur*. If not for her, there would never have been a revolution. And if not for the Revolution, with its Declaration of the Rights of Man and Citizen, Toussaint would never have been inspired to declare Haiti free from slavery and oppression. It took thirteen years and a hundred thousand lives before the French were removed from Haiti, but four times this number were slaughtered after Marie-Antoinette lost her head. *So surely, they will not want another Austrian for their throne?*

"Then again," Caroline adds lightly, "it could be the Russian. Or any number of minor princesses." She is torturing Pauline.

"He will not remarry yet," Pauline counters, but she seems uncertain. She is twenty-nine to Caroline's twenty-seven, but she might as well have been the younger sibling. I study her in the morning light: the graceful curve of her neck, the deep chestnut of her hair, the new lines etched by worry between her brows. I remember the afternoons we shared together in Haiti, the air heavy with orange blossoms and the scent of summer rain. Now that world is gone, lost in the savagery of war that took my family along with my home. But the island remains. My mother's songs remain. And someday Pauline must see that all this is futile, must realize that life was simpler and sweeter when it was the two of us in my country.

"And the announcement?" she asks, bringing me back to the present. "Has Maman said—"

"The fifteenth." Caroline adds meaningfully, "of December. He won't decide on a new wife before then."

Their eyes meet, and they are like a pair of jackals working together for the success of the hunt.

CHAPTER 4

MARIA LUCIA,
ARCHDUCHESS OF AUSTRIA

Schönbrunn Palace, Vienna
December 1809

As soon as the summons comes from my father, I know. In eighteen years, my presence has never been requested in my father's council chamber without my brother. I put on my muff for the walk across the palace, then call Sigi from his cozy bed near the fire. If I am to face the news that the Ogre of France, or *der Menschenfresser* as the Austrians call him, wishes for my hand in marriage, then I will do it with a friend at my side.

I scoop up my little spaniel, and he rides in the crook of my arm as I make my way through the icy halls. Every winter my father spends a fortune to warm the palace, but it is never enough. The guards can see their breath on the air, and the courtiers' wives, despite their vanity, are wearing thick cloaks and wide fur hats. "Your Royal Highness." The men bow to me as I pass, but I don't see the one I am looking for. When I reach the Blue Salon, where my father holds his council, I pause before the doors. I want to glimpse Adam Neipperg's face, to see the conviction in his eyes as he tells me—as he certainly will—that I have nothing to fear from this meeting, that my father will never marry me to an ogre, not for all the money in the world. But he is nowhere to be found. So I stand before my father's council chamber, and the guards wait for my nod. When I give it, the doors are thrown open.

"Archduchess Maria Lucia of Austria," they announce.

I step forward and halt immediately. Everyone is inside, including Adam Neipperg and my stepmother, Maria Ludovika. Maria passes me a warning look as I approach the table, and suddenly the room is silent. My father indicates a chair across from him.

"Maria," he begins, but can't seem to find words to continue. I bury my fingers in Sigi's fur and wait for my father to say it. Clearly, the French emperor has asked for my hand, and now Austria must begin the tricky dance of turning him down without grave offense. He looks to Prince Metternich, who clears his throat.

"Your Highness," the prince says, "there is joyous news."

I make a point of raising my brows, then looking around the table from face to solemn face. If this news is so joyous, why does everyone look as if someone has died?

"The emperor of France," Metternich continues, "has requested your hand in marriage. As you know, this is a great honor for the house of Hapsburg-Lorraine, for there has not been a marriage between Austria and France for thirty-nine years."

"Yes, and that ended well," I reply. But no one smiles. My father shifts in his seat, and when I look at Count Neipperg, his face is grave.

"The emperor is a man of swift decisions, Your Highness. Three days ago he sent his stepson, Eugène de Beauharnais, to our embassy in Paris to ask for your hand. Our ambassador was told he must accept the offer at once or risk displeasing the emperor . . . *greatly*."

My heart begins to race beneath my cloak. "So what are you saying?"

Metternich glances at my father before speaking. "That the offer was accepted, Your Highness."

The room blurs. The Chinese wall hangings fashioned from blue rice paper take on a whitish hue. Sigi nuzzles my arm, and his cold nose against my skin brings it all back into focus.

"Maria," my father begins, and the heartache in his voice is unbearable. "It is still your decision—"

"But understand," Metternich interjects swiftly, "that this decision comes with lasting consequences."

He means that if I refuse, my father will lose his crown. If I refuse, eight hundred years of Hapsburg-Lorraine rule will be ended with the unwillingness of an eighteen-year-old girl. And still my father is asking me to choose.

I have never loved him more than I do now.

I look at the faces assembled around the room, then at the long council table gleaming red and gold beneath the chandeliers. I had not imagined this to be the place where my marriage would be decided. I had imagined it would happen in my late mother's quiet study, or in the eastern terrace with its frescoed ceiling of angels.

"Your Highness, we need your answer," Metternich says. *Because tomorrow there shall either be a wedding or a war.*

My stepmother's face is pale, and next to her, Adam Neipperg looks murderous. But I cannot allow myself the luxury of considering either of them. I know my duty to my father and my kingdom. My eyes burn, and though I feel my stomach rise, I will the word to come. "Yes."

Metternich leans forward. "*Yes* to what, Your Highness?"

"To . . ." I breathe deeply. "To the marriage with the Emperor Napoleon Bonaparte."

There is a moment of silence while everyone comprehends what has just happened. Then they all begin talking at once. Adam Neipperg, who has been so dear to me since his return from our campaign against Napoleon last year, bangs his fist against the table and shouts, "I stand firmly against this!"

"There is nothing to stand against," Metternich retorts, and the two men rise from their seats. But Metternich is no match for Adam, who is the opposite of the prince in every way. At thirty-four, Adam has experienced more war than peace. He was part of the Blockade of Mainz, and at Dolens, after his right eye was taken by bayonet, he was left for dead on the battlefield. Despite these wounds, he recovered, and now he wears a silk patch over his eye. There is no woman in Austria who has not heard of Adam's daring feats, so when he leans across the table, Metternich backs away.

"Enough," my father says, and when no one can hear him he shouts, "*Enough!*"

Both men sit down, and I avoid Adam's gaze.

"This council is dismissed. The answer has been heard, and no one is to speak of it. Count Neipperg, Prince Metternich, please stay." The other men push back their chairs to leave, and when my stepmother rises as well, my father puts a hand on her arm. "You should be here. For Maria," he adds.

I watch the chamber empty, and when there are only the five of us in the room, it suddenly becomes real. I will never be regent for my brother, Ferdinand. Who knows who the task will be left to, but I will not be here to guide him. Instead, I am to marry the man who stripped our kingdom of its wealth and slaughtered more than three hundred thousand Austrian soldiers, a man whose taste for the lavish, crude, and unrefined is known throughout Europe. I look down at Sigi, and my tears dampen her fur.

"Maria," my father begins, and I realize how pale and drawn he looks. He has been struggling with this knowledge for two days. "I want you to know there was nothing any of us could do."

But there is nothing anyone can say to remedy this. "Yes. I understand."

"Whatever you need, whatever you want to take with you to France, you shall have."

I swallow my pain and try to sound grateful. "Thank you."

"The French court will be very different from Austria," he warns. "Prince Metternich can explain—"

"Everything," the prince says eagerly, and I realize that of the five of us assembled, only he is excited. I wonder what his role has been in this marriage, and whether my father might find a handsome payment from the French if the prince's accounts were exposed. "Over these next three months—"

"Is that when the marriage is to take place?" I ask him.

"Yes. But first there will be a ceremony here."

"Then Prince Metternich and Count Neipperg shall be escorting you to the border," my father explains, "and a second ceremony will be held in Paris."

My heart races. "But his divorce—"

"Is to be announced tomorrow. This contract will not be public knowledge until the new year."

Then there's hope! Perhaps in three months the French emperor will change his mind. Perhaps he will find a Russian who is more to his liking. But my father sees the look on my face and shakes his head.

"Maria, this emperor is not like your mother." Who could change her mind three times in a day. "He looks to marry the great-niece of Marie-Antoinette."

I had thought myself fortunate to be a Hapsburg princess. I was wrong.

"He will wish to change your name," Prince Metternich warns. "The Empress Joséphine was once Rose de Beauharnais. And he will want to choose your outfits," the prince continues. "He is very particular about what his women—"

"This is ridiculous!" Adam Neipperg shouts, and the longing I feel for him is unbearable. I will never hold him again, never touch his face or run my fingers through his hair. "What does it matter what she wears?"

"Perhaps it doesn't," Metternich says hotly. "But these are not my rules. If you don't like them, I suggest you speak with the French emperor."

"Am I allowed to bathe myself, at least?"

Metternich sighs, and this is the first time I have seen him appear at all sympathetic. "He will be a difficult man to please, Your Highness. He is stubborn and jealous and filled with ambition. But he is also a visionary. That should be something."

But it isn't.

In the hall outside the council chamber, Adam remains after the others have gone. "You can refuse this," he tells me, leaning close to my ear, and I am touched that he thinks I am worth fighting a war over.

"I am no Helen of Troy," I say. "This is my father's crown. The Empire of Austria is everything to him."

"And there's no reason to believe he wouldn't keep it."

"Except the Treaty of Pressburg and the Treaty of Schönbrunn," I answer, naming our two previous defeats against the "Modern Alexander."

"Trust me, Maria." He reaches out to take my hand and I blush to hear him use my Christian name. "Your father and I will come for you."

But I must not believe such promises. Next week I will be nineteen, and more likely than not, I shall pass every future birthday in France. I swallow against the tightness in my throat. "Thank you, Adam."

"This is not an idle promise," he swears. "We *will* come for you." He squeezes my hand. "That is a vow."

CHAPTER 5

PAULINE BONAPARTE, PRINCESS BORGHESE

Tuileries Palace, Paris

"Pauline Bonaparte was as beautiful as it was possible to be. . . . She was in love with herself alone, and her sole occupation was with pleasure."

—Prince Metternich, Austrian statesman

I lean toward my mirror and marvel that none of the pain shows in my face. My stomach has been cramping since dawn, and though the doctors insist that an "excess of nightly passion" is to blame, I know it isn't true. This is something more. But ill or not, I will look my best tonight.

I arrange my hair around my face, and try to imagine how I shall look in Joséphine's crown once my brother acknowledges that I should be queen. Of course, the design will have to be altered. Or perhaps I will use the Egyptian crown he gave me. I would never want to be seen in anything she wore, although diamonds and sapphires have always suited me.

"What do you think?" I turn to face Paul and hold up two gowns, one in cerulean blue, the other in bright cerise.

"The blue," he says. "This isn't a ball."

I toss the blue back into my commode and put on the deep red; it's more festive. "You're wrong, you know. There'll be dancing tonight. He sent out invitations." My chamberlain thinks Joséphine walks on water. *Sweet* Joséphine, *charming* Joséphine. Was she sweet when she cuckolded my brother the first week they married, sleeping with that lieutenant, Hippolyte Charles? And was she charming when he discovered that she had lied about her debts, year after year? She ruined my relationship with Fréron, and he still has sympathy for her. "What time is it?"

Paul watches me slip on my gloves. My mother taught me the proper way to do it when I was eight. "You begin with your bare arm outstretched," she said, then showed me how to slowly, *very slowly*, tease them on and off. *And if every man in the room isn't watching*, she added, *you've done it wrong.* He leaves his book—Machiavelli's *The Prince*, my very first gift to him—to look at the clock in the salon.

"Twenty till eight," he calls to me.

My God, it's all going to happen in twenty minutes. My heart is beating so swiftly that I can see its rise and fall through the light fabric of my dress. Then a spasm in my stomach nearly makes me bend double. I sit on my chaise and look around my chamber. From the pillars of gilded bronze to the statues of Isis, my brother has recreated the Palace of Thebes for me in here. We belong together. And tonight, when he is free of Beauharnaille, I will convince him to return to Egypt.

When the clock strikes eight, Paul offers me his arm, and we cross the palace toward my brother's Throne Room. The halls are filled with dignitaries, all hurrying to get the best spot in the chamber, like a rushing stream of white diamonds and feathers. Nearly a thousand courtiers have arrived, including Eugène de Beauharnais and his sister, Hortense, looking sorry for themselves. It was my brother who insisted that Joséphine's children be here tonight. Many years ago he made Eugène the prince of Naples, and Hortense the queen of Holland. I doubt he will take their titles away, so they could at least try and look grateful.

"Your Highness." The ambassador of Russia bows deeply to me, and I acknowledge the governor of Paris.

As we ascend the marble staircase, Paul whispers in my ear, "Look at your sister, Queen Caroline."

I follow his gaze to my younger sister. She is talking eagerly to a man I don't recognize, and the pair of them are ascending the stairs together. "Who is he?"

"The ambassador from Austria," Paul says.

"What's she doing with him?"

But he can no longer answer. We have entered the Throne Room, with its red velvet hangings and elaborate gold paneling. This was once the bedroom of King Louis XVI, but my brother has turned it into his Salle du Trône. After the barbarism of the Revolution, there wasn't a single item of value left in the Tuileries. Since everything had either been stolen or sold, one room was the same as any other. I wonder how many of these courtiers realize how empty these halls were when my family first arrived. It was my brother who turned this ruin back into a palace; my brother who restored this country's greatest treasures to their former glory. I step forward, and when I am the only figure in the door, I nod.

"Her Royal Highness the Princess Borghese," the usher announces grandly.

The entire chamber turns, and the women gasp as I pass through the chamber, snapping open their fans to gossip behind them. *Yes, keep up your nattering,* mes chéries. *I know what I'm wearing, and that you're all dressed in black, as if we're here for a funeral and not an act of separation.* A second usher appears to guide me toward the dais, and Paul follows behind. I can feel his presence like a steady shadow, and when we've taken our places before my brother's throne, I lean over and whisper, "Did you see their faces? Those women nearly expired!"

"You never tire of creating a scandal, Your Highness."

I look toward the dais, where a single gilded throne remains: Joséphine's has been removed. I remember the night the carpenter, Jacob-Desmalter, was summoned to the palace and told he must create something entirely unique. "Blue silk and blue velvet," Napoleon said. "And it should be embroidered with a single 'N.'"

"You must also include your three insignias," I urged him. So the giant eagle, the Legion of Honor star, and golden bees were all embroidered into the fabric.

The chamber grows silent as liveried trumpeters herald my brother and Joséphine's approach. I clutch my *réticule* so tightly that I can feel my knuckles turning white on the clasp. "Remember to breathe," Paul advises.

It's true. I don't want my brother to see me red-faced when he looks down from the dais. I have prepared fourteen years for this moment, and my complexion is not going to ruin it for me. And then: there they are. *My God, look at Joséphine's pallor.* It couldn't be more unattractive. As she takes her place next to my brother, she looks as if she might faint. For a moment, I almost feel sorry for her, standing in front of a thousand people to surrender her crown. It must be mortifying. And then I study her more closely: she has actually purchased a new gown for the event! And those diamonds in her hair did not come cheap. No doubt he will let her keep them.

"To my devoted stepchildren," my brother is saying, "I am immensely grateful. Eugène and Hortense are like my own . . ."

Please. If that were the case, there would be no divorce.

"God alone knows what this resolve has cost my heart," my brother continues.

He can really lay it on thick when he wants to. "I have found courage for this act only through the knowledge that it serves the very best interests of France." There is some murmuring among the assembled. "I have only gratitude to express for the devotion and tenderness of my well-beloved wife. She has adorned fourteen years of my life, and the memory of those years will remain forever in my heart."

I think to clap, but everyone else is still, so I refrain.

Then my brother steps back, and Joséphine takes his place in the center of the dais. Now the room has gone utterly silent. You can hear the rustling of women's gowns, and the heavy, labored breathing of the old men behind me.

"With the permission of my dear and august husband," she begins, "I offer him the greatest proof of devotion ever given to a husband on this earth . . ."

The room waits for her to continue, to say the lines she must have rehearsed a dozen times for this performance, but she begins trembling violently. The silence is excruciating until she reaches into her *réticule* and pulls out a folded paper.

"Monsieur Moreau." Incredibly, Napoleon crooks a finger at my chamberlain. He wants Paul to read the rest of Joséphine's speech!

I know my brother has great esteem for Paul, but this is unprecedented. I glance at the men standing in my immediate vicinity and spy the actor, Talma, dressed in a red velvet coat with white cashmere breeches. For Christ's sake, why not ask him to perform for her?

I will Joséphine to get a hold of herself, but Paul begins speaking in her stead. "I respond to all the sentiments of the emperor in consenting to the dissolution of a marriage which henceforth is an obstacle to the happiness of France by depriving it of the blessing of being one day governed by the descendants of that great man, evidently raised up by Providence, to efface the evils of a terrible revolution and restore the altar, the throne, and social order."

I stare directly at Joséphine. This is her moment to deliver a performance the court will never forget, and what does she do? Hand her part to someone else.

"But his marriage will in no respect change the sentiments of my heart; the emperor will ever find me his best friend. I know what this act, commanded by policy and exalted interests, has cost his heart, but we both glory in the sacrifices that we make to the good of our country. I feel elevated by giving the greatest proof of attachment and devotion that was ever given upon earth."

She is an imbecile.

As the divorce papers are being signed, no one knows what to do. Should they talk? Remain in dignified silence? In the middle of writing his name, my brother breaks his quill, and a nervous murmur spreads until a new one is brought. From somewhere behind me, I hear a woman click her tongue and whisper, "Obviously a sign." But when my brother dips the new nib into the ink and finishes his signature, no one dares to speak. A sharp crack of thunder echoes from outside, and the courtiers look to my brother for their next cue.

"For the good of France," Napoleon announces loudly, and everyone repeats his sentiment.

As people begin to move toward the doors, Talma shakes his head. "Unbelievable."

"Isn't it?" I can't keep myself from smiling. My God, anything might happen now. And from this day forward, Napoleon will look to his real family for support. He already knows what an ideal queen I would make. . . . But when I see Napoleon take Joséphine's hand, my heart stops beating. "He's not really going to walk her to her apartments?" I exclaim.

Talma stares at me. "Why not?"

"Because it's a divorce, not a waltz!"

He makes a noise in his throat. "Hard to tell the difference."

"I hope you're not implying that this is somehow inappropriate," I say, searching for Paul in this insane melee.

"Of course not. If I ever divorce, I want it to be a grand affair, with dancing and feasting and at least a thousand guests."

"I'm not finding you humorous." *Where the hell is Paul?*

"No?" He smiles, and it's impossible to resist him when he does this. "If you're looking for your chamberlain, he's over there—with the Austrian ambassador."

"And why is *he* so popular today?"

Talma looks incredulous. "It's the loudest secret in Paris," he says. "Your brother is to marry an Austrian princess. It was finalized this morning."

CHAPTER 6

PAUL MOREAU

Tuileries Palace, Paris

"A thousand idle stories have been related concerning the Emperor's motives for breaking the bonds which he had contracted upward of fifteen years.... It was ascribed to his ambition to connect himself with royal blood; and malevolence has delighted in spreading the report, that to this consideration he had sacrificed every other."

—Duke of Rovigo

I try humming a tune to lighten the mood, but even the weather feels like a conspirator. Sheets of rain have been bearing down against the windows all day, and the thunder has sent Aubree whimpering beneath the bed, so that even if Pauline had been cheerful to start with, she would have flown into a temper anyway.

"I will never recover from this, Paul. *Never.*" The princess is lying on her favorite chaise in a gown more suitable for a gala than a day of lying-in.

"Would you like me to order up some more granadilla?"

This was her favorite drink in Haiti, and the emperor has it shipped here each month for her pleasure.

"Of course not. Does it look like I can drink?"

"Your Highness had tea this morning."

She ignores my response. "Have you sent for Dr. Corvisart?"

"An hour ago."

"So where the hell is he?"

I stare at her from behind my book. I won't answer if she yells. This is the mistake her lovers make, trying to reason with her when she is being unreasonable. But the Princess Borghese is a woman of great passions. When she loves, it's with her entire heart. And when she hates . . .

"He did it on purpose," she says, resting her head against a satin pillow. I catch her wincing and wonder if it's real or imagined. "He wanted me to be the last to know."

"Do you really believe the emperor thinks this way?"

"He doesn't think at all!" she cries. "That's why he's chosen a fat-lipped Austrian for the future empress of France. And *I* am the last to know. I suppose you've already heard where he's been these past three days?" She doesn't wait for me to answer. "Versailles. Caroline said he returned this morning and didn't want to see anyone but *you.*"

Pauline watches me from her chaise, and the accusation is clear. "He told you he wanted the Austrian, didn't he?"

"Yes."

"And you hid it from me?"

"He asked that I keep my silence."

"I'm his *sister!*" she cries. "And your loyalty is to *me.*"

"Over the emperor of France?"

She puts her hand on her stomach, but I can see that, this time, it's her pride that's been hurt.

"Let me read you some Ossian," I suggest. When she doesn't object, I go to the bookcase and take out the works of the blind Scottish bard. The leather cover is worn, and even the pages are faded. "*Cath-loda*," I begin, and when I come to her favorite line, "Fair rose the beam of the east," Pauline begins to recite the words with me.

"'It shone on the spoils of Lochlin in the hand of the king. From her cave came forth the beautiful daughter of Torcul-torno. She gathered her hair from wind, and wildly raised her song.'" Then she stops, and says the king's name again. "Torcul-torno."

"'Of aged-locks,'" I reply, using the poet's best description.

"It's a funny name, isn't it?" she asks.

I can see her thoughts straying and put down the book.

"Almost as ridiculous as Maria-Lucia."

I sigh.

"What? You do realize he'll have to change it to something French."

Already I feel pity for the new empress.

"And do you know what else Caroline told me?" she whispers, though no one is in her salon but us. "He's giving Joséphine the Élysée Palace. That's in addition to Château de Malmaison. *And* she's to keep the title of Empress! I want to see this harlot from Vienna's face when she learns about *that*." She lays back on her pillow. "Go," she says, the most tragic figure in the empire, twisting herself as if her pain were real. "My brother called you to his study for twelve. But

I want to know everything he says about her." She sits up. "*Everything!*"

I leave the princess's apartments, and immediately I notice the change. There is no laughter in the halls, and the faces of the courtiers look worried and drawn. Although Pauline has an endless list of grievances with her brother's former wife, the people of France have always believed that Joséphine is his talisman, his good luck charm in times of peace and war. It is widely known that she made donations to the poor and funded hospitals for the sick, and before every battle she could be seen on her knees in Notre Dame, offering prayers for the soldiers. Even Parisians, who are cheap with their praise, call her Madame Victoire.

"It's an ill omen," I hear a woman say. "She left in a thunderstorm, and it hasn't stopped raining since."

"Did you see how Monsieur Eugène and Madame Hortense were crying? Bonaparte's the only father they've ever known."

"A nineteen-year-old wife *and* a Hapsburg!"

Outside the emperor's study, two soldiers are having a similar conversation. I recognize them both. Dacian, who is tall and well liked by women, was a good friend to me when I arrived in Paris, instructing me on court etiquette. It was François taught me how to fence. As soon as they see me, they smile.

"Paul." Dacian claps me jovially on the back.

"Is the emperor inside?"

"He's with his secretary and the Comte de Montholon." Dacian glances around. When he's sure the hall is empty, he whispers in my ear, "Is it true then, that he's to marry an Austrian?"

"Marie-Antoinette's great-niece?" François puts in.

I nod.

"I heard the emperor sent his stepson, Eugène, to the Austrian ambassador to broker the deal. Can you imagine sending your ex-wife's son to ask for a new woman's hand in marriage?"

No. But then that would never happen in Haiti. For all of our supposedly backward ways, we do not marry and divorce our wives for sport.

"It isn't right," François continues. "She was Madame Victoire. He's aiming too high, wedding some Hapsburg princess."

"Come. We should announce you," Dacian interrupts. Or perhaps he realizes this conversation is better suited to the gardens or the stables. He swings open the double doors, and my name echoes through the emperor's study.

I catch my reflection in the silver mirrors as I enter, and a tall man in black riding boots and gilded epaulettes stares back, part French, part Haitian, with green eyes and dark skin that no one can place. I have no fortune to speak of, no family name to commend me to any post, but none of that matters in this court.

"Paul!" the emperor shouts from across the room, and I can see the disappointment on the Comte de Montholon's face, since this is Napoleon's favorite trick. "My sincerest apologies," Napoleon tells the *comte*. "My favorite chamberlain has arrived. We shall have to continue this discussion some other time."

The *comte* stands from his chair and passes me a withering look. But this is Napoleon's joke, not mine. He enjoys dismissing members of the ancien régime for an audience with a commoner.

"Your Majesty." I bow before the emperor, and he stops pacing only long enough to smile at me. He does not look like a man who has divorced his wife and sent an empire into a panic. His dark hair has been neatly combed, and he is wearing his favorite red velvet coat embroidered with gold.

"Have you heard?"

I am certain he is speaking about the archduchess Maria Lucia, but I am cautious. "Your Majesty?"

His gray eyes fix on mine. "No one is talking about it?"

I glance at his harassed young secretary, Méneval, who has been at Napoleon's side for years. He is a handsome man, tall and lean, with thick dark hair and brown eyes. Every major decision the emperor has made, he has dictated first to Méneval. Somewhere in the palace, there are thousands of pages filled with his lists—detailed instructions the emperor needs written at two, sometimes three in the morning. Méneval has put down his quill and is closing his eyes behind his desk. It's likely the first break he has had since the emperor arrived at six this morning.

"Is Your Majesty referring to the possibility of an Austrian marriage?" I ask cautiously.

Napoleon laughs triumphantly. "So they *are* talking!" This is what he wants. More than wealth or women or even power, the Bonapartes crave fame. "Tell me." He steps closer. "What are they saying?"

I watch him carefully, but there is no telling what his intentions are with these questions. "The talk is that a wedding will happen in the new year," I say honestly. "Possibly as early as March."

For several seconds he is silent, purposefully leaving me in suspense. Then he reaches out and clasps my arm. "You're the first person to tell me this. I *knew* there must be whispers. But do you think my chamberlains tell me about it?" he asks angrily. "My own soldiers keep the truth hidden from me!"

I keep my face neutral. There was a time when none of his soldiers wanted to be the one to tell him that Joséphine had been fornicating with one of his underlings. He still thinks about this betrayal.

"Even Méneval," he shouts, and his secretary's eyes are suddenly open, "played the ignorant ass. But I knew the court was talking. What are they saying about her?"

That she is a bad luck wife, just like her great-aunt. That she is a Hapsburg, who knows nothing about the French. And that she is nineteen this month, and what do you know at nineteen about running an empire? But I say none of these things. Not a lie—an omission. "There is talk that she is musically inclined. She plays the piano—"

"And the harp," he adds. "What else?"

I think back on my conversation with the Austrian ambassador, Prince Metternich. "She is talented at languages. Aside from her native German, she has French, Italian, English, Latin, and Spanish. Plus, she can paint."

"In watercolor and oil." He nods. He has done his research, planning this marriage like a new campaign. "But," he adds forcefully, "there is something more important than all of this."

I can't think of anything I've missed. Her beauty? She is said to be tall and plump.

"Her great-grandmother had twenty-six children," he says crassly, "and her mother thirteen."

"So she is fertile."

"Like a walking womb! I'll have a child on her by the end of the year. And for that, I'll make her the most pampered wife in Europe." He takes me to the far side of his study where fifteen chests have been arranged, each half-packed with its lid thrown open. "Méneval, come!" the emperor shouts. "Give me the list!"

Méneval produces a long paper, and the emperor scrutinizes it for a moment. A deep frown appears between his brows. "I asked you to write larger. The last time we looked at this, I told you it should be bigger."

"It is, Your Majesty. I'm not sure—"

"Whenever you're *not sure*," the emperor roars, "you should ask me! *Leave.*"

Méneval is standing in stunned silence. Then in a single movement—and it happens so fast that even I'm unprepared for it—the emperor removes his hat and cuffs his secretary across the face. "*Leave!* You can sleep just as well in your apartments as on my desk. I will see you tonight."

Méneval bows quickly, and his voice shaking when he replies, "As you wish."

I watch him go and wonder what I would do if the emperor dared to strike me.

"All that man can think about," the emperor says as soon as the doors swing shut, "is that slut of wife he's just married."

He means the woman who wouldn't bed him even after he plied her with a ruby pin and diamond earrings. It's well known at court that the emperor likes married women. They are more of a challenge, in his opinion, and rarely a liability. "With a married woman there are never awkward scenes," he once told me. "There's no having to convince her to leave in the morning or disappear once you're finished with her at night." And this is how Napoleon likes his conquests: expedient, convenient, but most of all, humiliating for the men who lose.

"So what do you think?" he asks, indicating the chests filled with muslin and silks. "Shall I read you the contents?"

He begins with the clothing he's ordered. Gowns trimmed in mink, shoes lined with ermine, swan's down fans whose handles have been inlaid with diamonds, and court dresses so lavish that—had she still been able to—Queen Marie-Antoinette would have blushed to see them. There are innumerable riding habits and cashmere shawls. Even the princess's bed slippers and underwear have been chosen. And then there is the wedding dress, a satin and ermine creation so elaborate, it must have taken his seamstresses an entire month.

"But that isn't it," he crows, saving the best for last. "Look at this." He walks me to the heaviest wooden chest, filled nearly to bursting with small wooden boxes. "Jewels fit for an empress," he says, opening each box so I may marvel at their beauty.

There is a ring with more than ten carats of diamonds set in gold, and earrings so heavy with rubies that they will tear at her ears. Then he comes to the *parure,* a set of matching earrings, necklace, and tiara that our future empress will wear for every portrait and national occasion. He holds the tiara up to the window so that the diamonds and emeralds catch the low winter's light.

"Three million francs," he says proudly.

I am breathless at the extravagance. It is a sum grand enough to rebuild Haiti into the country it was before the emperor destroyed it. Enough to pay reparations to every family that suffered the death of a son or daughter in the emperor's war to keep Haiti enslaved to France. I swallow my bitterness. "There has never been a bridal trousseau like it," I say.

"Do you think she'll be impressed? They are Hapsburgs," he reminds me, and it's the first time I've seen Napoleon uncertain. This man, who has conquered a dozen nations, is made nervous at the idea of a girl with royal blood. "She comes from eight hundred years of tradition."

"Then she will be proud to link her fortune to the emperor of France."

"Yes." Napoleon stands a little taller. "Yes. And Pauline? How is she taking the news?"

So this is why he has called me here today. Not for an opinion on Maria-Lucia's new clothing, but to gauge his younger sister's reaction to his second wife. "She isn't happy."

"She wants to marry me," he remarks, as if he's talking about one of his half-dozen mistresses. "She thinks to become queen of Egypt while I crown myself pharaoh. Can you imagine?" His gray eyes meet mine, and instead of anger, there's amusement in them. "You're a clever man, Paul. Would you care to guess what the courts of Europe would say?"

"No."

He laughs. "Neither would I. Yet . . ."

I wait for him to finish his statement, but his words trail off, and I watch him closely to see if his "yet" could really mean that he would marry his own sister if not for the furor it would create.

"I don't want her to be jealous," he says at last. But I suspect this is a lie. Why else would he show me the emerald *parure,* the gowns dripping with diamonds, the fans encrusted with gems, when he knows it will all be reported back to her? "She values your opinion greatly," he continues. "So I need you to explain to her the necessity of appearing in this wedding."

I am confused. "Your Majesty?"

"She is to carry the bride's train," he explains, "along with Caroline and Elisa."

For a moment, I am entirely without words. He made this same request when he and Joséphine were crowned at Notre Dame, and the fiasco that ensued was the stuff of legend—people still laugh about it behind closed doors. The Bonaparte sisters swore they did nothing untoward, but there wasn't a person in that cathedral who couldn't see plainly that as Joséphine advanced toward the altar, all three sisters pulled back on her train, immobilizing the empress.

They pinned her so tightly and for so long that Napoleon was forced to turn around and see what was causing Joséphine's delay.

"I know what you're thinking," he says darkly. "But there will not be an encore performance. The world will see the Bonapartes as one. Not just the Bonapartes—the Beauharnais."

"Your stepchildren will attend?"

The emperor nods curtly. "Eugène is coming from Italy, and I have told Hortense she is to be my new wife's Mistress of the Robes."

I hope my eyes don't reveal what I think about a man who would command his twenty-six-year-old stepdaughter to serve his teenage wife immediately after she has been forced to see her own mother tossed aside. I picture Hortense with her mousy brown hair and pale, innocent eyes. *Yes, Your Majesty. No, Your Majesty. Of course, Your Majesty.* An entire life of subservience, first to her dramatic mother, then to her husband, Louis Bonaparte—the ill-tempered king of Holland—and now to the second empress of France.

"Everything will be perfect this time," he tells me. "I'm sending Caroline to collect the princess from Austria, and you will be there to report what happens."

"Your Majesty?" This is the first I've heard of it.

"Is there anyone else who will tell me the truth in this court?"

I stop to think. "No."

"Which is why I need you. I will surprise your entourage

in Compiègne. I'm traveling there tomorrow to see that her apartments have been suitably redecorated."

"Your Majesty is going to great expense." It is a neutral statement, something that can be taken either way. But Napoleon smiles.

"This is the marriage I was destined to have. A Hapsburg princess as fertile as a sow. And I have hired the same Master of Ceremonies used by King Louis XVI and Marie-Antoinette."

"Won't the people say that's bad luck?"

"If they are fools!" he thunders, and his gray eyes are wide, like those of a man possessed. "Why? Is that what they're saying?"

"I don't know," I admit. "But when they hear about King Louis's—"

"Then they will know that this is a wedding of immense significance. I have planned it all," he confesses. "There will be fireworks and fêtes, and two thousand prison sentences will be commuted. I am renovating the entire Château de Compiègne in under two months. They are working on it night and day."

"And she expects this?"

"*I* expect it. I am the emperor of France."

Yes, despite a revolution fought to bring an end to such titles. He notices my hesitation and his neck grows red.

"*What?*"

"Nothing, sire."

"The thoughts that are going through your head," he commands. "Word for word."

"'It is not titles that honor men,'" I reply, "'but men that honor titles.'" A quote from Machiavelli.

He stops to think how this applies to him and realizes what I'm saying. There is nothing inherently great about his title of emperor. But because the people believe in it, they will break their backs building, and decorating, and renovating. Parisians will live in thrall to their new empress until the shining title becomes tarnished in their eyes. It happened twenty years ago, and there's no reason to think it won't happen again. "'The governments of the people are better than those of princes,'" he quotes back at me. "Is that what you believe?"

"I am too young and inexperienced to say, Your Majesty. But I believe in freedom."

He smirks. "Of course. For the people of Haiti and all of our colonies."

"Yes," I say boldly. "And it's an accident of birth that your mother wasn't born a slave in Martinique."

There is a moment of silence between us, and as he watches me intently, my stomach tightens. "I once believed that General L'Ouverture was the most dangerous threat in Haiti," he says. "But perhaps I was wrong." He continues to watch me, and I think of what the French did to L'Ouverture when they captured him. Then suddenly Napoleon laughs. "*Martinique?*" he repeats, slapping me on the back. "You never give up, Paul, do you?"

"Your Majesty."

"You truly think that someday I'll change my mind. But believe me"—he sobers—"as long as there are men on this earth, there will be other men who enslave them."

"That it exists doesn't make it right." I am pushing him, but he has a marriage before him and his mood is good. If he can't listen to debate now, then when?

He considers this argument briefly and shrugs. "It's the way of the world, Paul. Be thankful your island is free—for now." He turns my attention to the last wooden chest, and our conversation is over. "For Joséphine," he says. Inside is an expensive china set, Sèvres porcelain. "Do you think she'll like it?"

Not as much as her wedding ring, I want to reply, but the amount of honesty a king is willing to tolerate is not as great as a commoner. "Yes. She will entertain well with it."

He glances down at a letter on Méneval's desk. I can't read who it's addressed to, but I can see the date. *July 17, 1796.* "She kept them all, you know."

"Who, Your Majesty?"

"Joséphine. She gave this one back to me last night. I was wildly passionate about her once." He picks up the letter, and even after thirteen years, the ink is still crisp. The emperor hands it to me and says quietly, "See for yourself."

It's not addressed to Joséphine, but the intended recipient is clear.

I have received your letter, my adorable friend. It has filled my heart with joy. I am grateful to you for the trouble you have taken to send me the news. I hope that you are better today. I am sure that you have recovered. I earnestly desire that you should ride on horseback: it cannot fail to benefit you.

Since I left you, I have been constantly depressed. My happiness is to be near you. Incessantly I live over in my memory your caresses, your tears, your affectionate solicitude. The charms of the incomparable Joséphine kindle continually a burning and a glowing flame in my heart. When, free from all solicitude, all harassing care, shall I be able to pass all my time with you, having only to love you, and to think only of the happiness of so saying, and of proving it to you? I will send you your horse, but I hope you will soon join me. I thought that I loved you months ago, but since my separation from you I feel that I love you a thousand fold more. Each day since I knew you, have I adored you yet more and more. This proved the maxim of Bruyère, that "love comes all of a sudden," to be false. Everything in nature has its own course, and different degrees of growth.

Ah! I entreat you to permit me to see some of your faults. Be less beautiful, less gracious, less affectionate, less good, especially be not overanxious, and never weep. Your tears rob me of reason and inflame my blood. Believe me, it is not in my power to have a single thought that is not of thee, or a wish I could not reveal to thee.

Seek repose. Quickly reestablish your health. Come and join me, that at least, before death, we may be able to say, "We were many days happy." A thousand kisses, and one even to Fortuna, notwithstanding his spitefulness.

—BONAPARTE

For a moment, I don't know what to say. The letter is incredibly intimate, and not something he should be showing his sister's chamberlain. "Who—who is Fortuna?" I finally ask.

"Her dog. She was insanely fond of him. The children used

to bring him to visit her in prison during the Revolution," he remembers. "So much history . . ." He shakes his head. "I've instructed the entire court to visit her at Malmaison. She'll never be lonely," he swears. For a moment, I am moved by this compassion. Then he slips his hand beneath his jacket and adds, "She adores me, Paul. I could marry seven more times, to any woman I wanted, and she will still need me. That's what's important."

To the empress at Malmaison.

December 1809; 8 o'clock in the evening.

My love—I found you more feeble today than you ought to be. You have exhibited much fortitude, and it is necessary that you should still continue to sustain yourself. You must not yield to funereal melancholy. Strive to be tranquil and above all to preserve your health, which is so precious to me. If you are attached to me, if you love me, you must maintain your energy, and strive to be cheerful. You cannot doubt my constancy, and my tender affection. You know too well all the sentiments with which I regard you, to suppose that I can be happy if you are unhappy, that I can be serene if you are agitated. Adieu, my love. May you have peaceful sleep. Believe that I wish it.

Napoleon

To the empress at Malmaison.

Tuesday, six o'clock.

The queen of Naples, whom I have just seen at the chase in the woods of Boulogne, where I ran down a stag, informed me that she saw you yesterday at one o'clock in the afternoon, and that you were very well. I pray you to tell me what you are doing today. As for me, I am very well. Yesterday, when I saw you, I was sick. I think that you have been out to walk. Adieu, my love.

Napoleon

To the empress at Malmaison.

Tuesday, seven o'clock in the evening.

I have received your letter, my love. Savary tells me that you weep continually. That is not right. I hope that you will be able to go out to walk today. I sent you a line from the chase. I shall go to see you, as soon as you inform me that you are reasonable and that your fortitude resumes its ascendancy. Tomorrow, all the day, I shall be occupied with the ministers.

Adieu, my love. I am as sad as the weather is gloomy. I have need to know that you are tranquil, and to learn that you have regained your self-control. May you have peaceful sleep.

Napoleon

To the empress at Malmaison.

Thursday, at noon, December 1809.

I have wished to go to see you today, my love, but I am very much occupied and a little unwell. Nevertheless, I am going to the cabinet council. I beg you to inform me how you are. The weather is very damp and not at all healthy.

Napoleon

1810

CHAPTER 7

MARIE-LOUISE, EMPRESS OF FRANCE

March 11, 1810

I have a new name. From now until the end of my days, I am to be the Empress Marie-Louise. I say it a few times in front of the mirror, trying to match this new title to the same plain face that has always stared back at me. But each time I say it, the reality seems further and further away. In a few minutes, my father will send a courtier to fetch me from my rooms, and my family will ride to Hofburg Palace, where I'll be married by proxy to the Emperor Napoleon. I want to reconcile myself to this—to be impressed with my new fortune and rank—but I am sick with dread.

I try not to meet Maria's eyes in the mirror. She has been sitting on my bed since dawn, cradling Sigi. She has not stopped crying since she arrived. Tomorrow morning, when I set out for Compiègne, I suspect the scene will be the same. It will take all my reserve not to become hysterical when I leave. This palace, these rooms, these people with their familiar hatreds and desires, have all been mine since birth.

And now, when my brother Ferdinand is made emperor of Austria, I will not be his regent. Someone else will have to guide his hand, and who knows if they're prepared for his outbursts and seizures. At least Maria-Carolina will have it easier. She will be kept from the public eye and quietly married. I look up at the family portraits on my wall. Ferdinand, Maria-Carolina, Maria, my father . . .

In twenty-four hours, I will never see any of them again.

There is a knock at my door, and Sigi whines. Maria rushes from the bed and wraps her arms around my shoulders. "Change your mind," she says. "You don't have to go."

For the first time, my resolve begins to crumble. "And lose my father his crown? What would happen to Austria? What would happen to you?"

"I don't know." Maria weeps.

I bite my lower lip. I will not cry. There is nothing anyone can do, and I will not destroy my father by letting him see me in such misery. None of us wanted this marriage, but Napoleon has made his choice, and only an act of God will see it undone.

There is a second knock, and this time I answer. A man in my father's red and gold livery makes a deep bow. "Your Majesty," he addresses Maria. "Your Highness." He looks sadly at me. Even the pages are loath to see this happen. "The carriages are ready," he says quietly.

"I would like to see my brother first."

"He is waiting in the courtyard—"

"Please bring him here. I would like to see him before I leave. In private."

The page bows at the waist and is gone.

"He won't know what to do without you," Maria worries. "How will they control him?"

I don't know. I sit on the bed and take Maria's hand. "Be patient with him," I beg her. "Don't let him have his own way. He can't eat sweets for breakfast and then again for dinner."

"Your father and I will both see to that."

The door opens slowly and I rise from the bed. "Ferdinand."

His eyes are red. He's clearly been told that I'll be going away and not returning. It breaks my heart to see him weep. He takes my hands in his. "I don't understand. I—I don't understand."

"I'm getting married, Ferdinand. My husband is the emperor of France. Do you know what that means?"

"That you want to love him and not me."

I inhale deeply. I will not cry. But Maria stifles a sob, and now it's impossible not to weep. "Ferdinand, I will *always* love you—if I'm in Austria or France."

"But when will you return?"

I look into his eyes. He is such a handsome boy. If only God had also blessed him with good sense. As it is, someone will always have to be there to guide him. If I had married Adam and lived my life in Schönbrunn, it would have been me. But now someone else will fill this role. I reach out to caress his hair, and his tears wet the palm of my hand. "I don't know when I will be back," I admit. "But you can write to me anytime you wish."

"Can I visit?"

I swallow the pain in my throat. "If you behave." But this is a terrible lie. Although there may be talk of his dull-wittedness and ill health, no one knows just how devastating the seizures are. Our family has been diligent in hiding them. It was cruel enough for my father to see one child suffer, but when Maria-Carolina's fits started too . . . It isn't fair. But then, Christ never preached about fairness. Only forgiveness and faith.

I exchange a look with Maria, who is too upset to speak. "I want you to keep studying while I'm gone, Ferdinand. Father is depending on you. I want you to memorize your letters, and every new thing you learn, you must write to me about it. Will you do that?"

"I will," he swears.

"And be kind to the cooks. They can't bring you apricot dumplings every morning."

He makes his sad face, and even through my tears, I laugh. Then there's a sharp knock, and the three of us freeze. My father's page has returned. And this time Adam is with him.

"They are all assembled and waiting, Your Highness."

Adam crosses the room and takes my hands. "I'll look after him," he swears.

"He needs so much help, and father isn't patient—"

"I am." Of all the soldiers in Schönbrunn, only Adam took the time to teach Ferdinand how to ride. And it was Adam who bought him his first set of brushes so that he could be like me and paint.

I look into Adam's face and wonder how I will ever manage to live without him. "I will miss you so much," I whisper.

At the door, my father's page is waiting with his eyes averted. Adam's love for me is no secret, and when I greet Napoleon, it will not be as a blushing bride. The man clears his throat, and I cling to Adam tightly.

"It's time," Adam replies, and his voice is thick.

Maria takes my arm, and suddenly it is real. We pass through Schönbrunn, and the courtiers step back as if we were a funeral, not a bridal procession. A few bow deeply as I go by. They know the sacrifice I am about to make, and how a commandment from Napoleon is second only to a commandment from God. He rules the Western world, from Rome to the Netherlands, and not even the Church has power over him. I am marrying a man who has been excommunicated, an emperor who has divorced his first wife without the pope's consent. Since the Church has not granted him a divorce, what am I to be? My father says he has allowed Joséphine to keep her title. So we are both to be called Empress.

When we reach the courtyard, a small, silent group is waiting for me. In addition to my father and Prince Metternich, there is my sister Maria-Carolina, who never speaks, and my youngest sister, Anna, who is holding her stuffed bear and weeping into its fur. Even my youngest brothers are here. Every face is solemn except Metternich's. If he is to come with me to France, I will never put my faith in him. Never. Perhaps he did not arrange this marriage himself, but someday, when I have gained Napoleon's trust, I will mention Metternich's name, and he will tell me that my father's adviser was the one who first suggested me to him. I am confident in this.

"Metternich is to ride with us," my father says. He looks old, his face marked by the heaviness of loss. "The prince has advice he would like to give you."

I follow Maria into the royal carriage, and Metternich begins by complimenting us both. "On such difficult days, the Hapsburg women are examples of resilience."

I do not return his smile. As the carriage lurches forward, I say flatly, "I hear you have advice. Please give it."

My father doesn't chastise me for my rudeness.

"I know you are unhappy," Metternich begins. "There is no one in this carriage, possibly in all of Austria, who would have wished to see this marriage come to pass. But for all of the pain he has inflicted on this kingdom, the Emperor Bonaparte has also done some good."

I raise my brows, and when I don't say anything, he continues.

"The Code Napoleon, for instance. The emperor has created a set of civil laws for his empire to follow. Under the ancien régime, what was legal in one town might be illegal in the next. Now, a strict set of laws governs all of France. It is based on the Corpus Juris Civilis, written in the sixth century by the Emperor Justinian."

My father grunts and looks out the window.

"But you haven't told her the best part," Maria says, her voice icy and out of character. "Come, you know. How 'women these days require restraint. They go where they like, do what they like.' How 'it is not French to give women the upper hand.' That's part of the Code Napoleon too, isn't it?"

"That has nothing to do with Her Highness—"

"No?" Maria looks at my father. The muscles in his jaw are working fast.

"You'll be an *empress*," Metternich tells me.

A second empress.

When he sees he is not winning my enthusiasm, he tries something else. "I know how Your Highness feels about the Jews, given that your nurse was a Jewess. Perhaps you will be interested to know that the emperor has not only emancipated the Jews in France, he has also called for a Jewish state."

I lean forward, despite myself. "Where?"

"In Palestine."

"And he can do this?"

"He conquered Egypt," he replies, as if this small and fleeting victory meant that now anything might happen. "Look," he says, and he takes from his pocket a small gold locket, handing it to me. "From the emperor to you."

I open it and study the picture inside. If this is a real likeness—and it probably isn't— then he looks far younger than his forty years. The artist has painted him in an embroidered coat, with his dark hair parted to one side and his gray eyes looking off into the distance. He appears cold, emotionless, a man with foreign lands on his mind, not family or love. I think of Adam, whose dark eyes always look warm, even in charcoal drawings, and suddenly I can't stop the tears from coming.

"Maria!" my father exclaims, but I raise a gloved hand.

"I'm fine."

He passes a threatening look at Metternich, but the prince

is unaffected. I am a warhorse going into battle, to him. I was born for this duty, and now I am fulfilling it. No matter that I love another man or that Napoleon is old enough to be my father. The Hapsburg Empire must be preserved.

"The emperor sent this locket to you from Paris," Metternich explains. "I would suggest that when Bonaparte asks about it, you tell him that his picture did not do him justice."

My eyes go wide. "Is that true?"

"Of course not."

"Then why would I say it?"

"Because his ego is delicate," Maria puts in, and when I look from my father to Metternich, neither contradicts her.

"What, is Napoleon a child?"

"He is an emperor with a new throne," my father says wearily. "Old crowns never have to be polished in this way."

"But that also means you will be treated to more furs and jewels than any empress in Europe," Metternich adds. That he thinks this is appealing shows how little he has learned about me these past nineteen years.

"Does he paint?"

Metternich frowns. "He is an emperor, Your Highness."

"Does he at least have an appreciation for the arts?" I demand.

Metternich shifts on his seat, and I can see that he is becoming frustrated. If only I could be an empty-headed girl content with new gowns. "I do not know these answers," he replies curtly. "But the emperor has prepared extensively for this wedding, and no expense has been spared. There are new apartments ready for your stop in Compiègne—"

"I'm to visit the same city where King Louis first greeted Marie-Antoinette?" No one has told me this, and now even Maria looks away.

"I shall hope you are not superstitious as well as romantic," he says dryly.

I stare at him to see if he is joking, but he is my father's foreign minister, a diplomat through and through. I spend the rest of the ride in silence, listening while he tells me about Napoleon's daily regimen. He is up at six and has a cup of orange-flower water at seven. By eight, he has read through all his letters, and the valet has finished drawing his bath. By nine he is dressed and in his study, where no one is allowed to disturb him until noon.

"And what does he do in there?" Maria asks.

Metternich glances at my father. "The same thing your husband does, Your Majesty."

I laugh sharply, for I very much doubt this. My father has never locked himself in his rooms plotting the overthrow of the Western world. Nor has he journeyed to another continent to subdue its people and pillage its wonders.

"He answers letters," Metternich continues, ignoring my outburst, "and dictates instructions to his secretary, Méneval."

"What sort of instructions?" my father asks. I know he is intrigued by this man, in spite of himself; a commoner who at twenty was made Lieutenant Colonel and by thirty-six had crowned himself Emperor of France.

"If a new chair is needed for the Tuileries Palace, he is the one to choose its color. He wrote fifteen thousand letters from his tent in Poland—"

"He was only there for six months!" my father exclaims.

"Nothing escapes his notice. There are also eccentricities Your Highness may wish to note . . ."

Maria meets my gaze. But Hapsburg women have faced far worse than this.

"At his desk, the emperor keeps figurines," he explains. "No one is to touch them. They are arranged in a very specific way. While he is working, or thinking in his study, his papers will be strewn all about the floor. They are garbage, but no one is allowed to clean them until night. And every book that is published in Italian or French is brought to him immediately."

"He reads them all?" my father asks.

"Not exactly." Metternich uncrosses his legs. "The nonfiction he keeps. The fiction he often burns."

"*What?*"

Metternich shrugs, as if we all burn unwanted literature in our fireplaces.

I sit back against the seat and close my eyes. I don't want to hear any more.

"But he likes to read," Maria says hopefully. "His conversation—"

"Is not about books," Metternich warns. "He will not discuss literature with anyone but a Haitian servant named Paul."

My father is astounded. "He keeps *a slave?*"

"The man is the Princess Borghese's chamberlain."

Metternich prattles on about the emperor's schedule—his Spartan lunch at noon, his twenty-minute dinner at eleven—but my head is throbbing and I'm only half listening. "And there is one last thing," Metternich adds, as the carriages roll through the gates of the palace. "It is the emperor's younger sister, Queen Caroline of Naples, who is arriving to meet Your Highness in Braunau."

My father's reaction is so violent that the coachmen stop the carriage to see that he is well. "Is this an insult?" he rages, and suddenly I am fully awake. "*That* crown belonged to her grandmother," he shouts, "not some Corsican commoner! Queen Caroline *of Naples*?"

I have never seen him so angry, but it was my grandmother, Queen Maria Carolina, who once sat on that throne.

"If this is intentional—"

"Your Majesty," Metternich interjects, and his voice is smooth, "this was not intended as a slight. He only wished to send an equal to greet his wife. It was either Queen Caroline or the Princess Pauline."

But my father is not convinced. He calls out the window for the carriage to continue, and we come to a stop before the Innenhof, where my uncle is waiting to stand as a proxy for Napoleon Bonaparte. I am normally glad to see the soaring white marble of my father's favorite residence, but today the Hofburg looks imposing and cold.

"Your Highness," Metternich begins solemnly, "Austrians from Prague to Carinthia understand the sacrifice you are about to make. If I may give one last word of advice?" he asks.

I nod shortly, and Metternich clears his throat.

"When Queen Caroline meets you in Braunau, obey her in everything. She will bring with her French perfume, French clothes, French food. She will instruct you in all the ways of the French. You are French now. The Empress Marie-Louise."

I fix the prince with my gaze. "No, I am not. And this masquerade," I tell him, looking down at my red velvet gown with its gold embroidery and ermine trim, "is for the emperor's benefit. He may dress me in white silk and put a crown on my head, but I will always be the daughter of Francis I. And I shall never stop being an Austrian."

It is a brief ceremony.

My uncle stands in for Napoleon, and a French official is there to record that it is done. When the ceremony is finished, there is no celebration. If I had married anyone else—a lowly deputy even—the streets would be filled with singing and dancing. Flowers would be tied to every wagon, and the public squares would be flowing with wine. But no one is in a celebratory mood. Austria has been beaten, her royal house humiliated, and the Hapsburg emperor has been forced to give his daughter to the son of a petty Corsican nobleman.

Outside, a light snow has begun to fall, and I wonder if it ever snows in France. Surely, it must. But truthfully, I don't know.

Our carriage ride back to Schönbrunn is solemn. Even Metternich keeps his silence. But before we part company on the icy steps of the palace, the prince holds out a hand to stop me. I step back, and he leans in to my ear to whisper, "Pride is not a trait the French value in their rulers. They killed a queen for less."

I study him in the cold light of the afternoon. His nose is

red and his cheeks are flushed, but his eyes are bright and alert. "Are you saying I'm in danger?"

"Your great-aunt was beheaded seventeen years ago." He pauses for a moment before adding, "The people haven't changed."

I watch him disappear into the palace behind my father and stepmother. I cannot bear the thought of them ever receiving the news that I have been killed, that the French mobs have torn me apart, limb from limb, like the Princesse de Lamballe, or sentenced me to the guillotine. I will behave. I will do my duty as a daughter and a queen and be a credit to my Hapsburg ancestry. But when I pray, it will be as Maria Lucia.

God, at least, will know my name.

Inside Schönbrunn, I walk the halls of my childhood home and try to commit it all to memory: the candlelit chambers, the painted ceilings, the marble fireplaces where my sisters and I played dolls and painted pictures of snow-capped roofs. I avoid the curious gazes of the courtiers, who all want one last word with me, and hurry instead to my studio. The door is open, and I let myself in. Immediately, I shiver. Without a fire, the chamber is cold. I hug my cloak closer to my body and cross the room. All along the walls are framed images of my family: sisters, brothers, uncles, cousins—generations of faces I will never see again. And on an easel at the far side of the room is the painting of my youngest sister, Anna. There will never be time to finish it now. I look at her sweet face and wonder what she will be like when she's nine, twelve, fifteen even.

"I thought I'd find you here."

My stepmother, Maria, is standing in the doorway, framed like an angel by the hall's chandelier. "My father told me to make my farewells," I say, and I squeeze my eyes shut. "I'll miss you so much. And father. And Schönbrunn."

"It's not impossible to think you'll return," she says desperately, crossing the room. "He might let you visit." She takes my hand. "Be kind to him," she advises. "Let him think you're in love. When he takes you for the first time—"

I gasp.

"You're a married woman now. It'll happen."

Yes, but I have tried not to think on it.

"When he takes you, ask him to do it again."

I stare at her, but she nods. "They want to believe they're irresistible. If you please him in bed, he'll please you in other ways." I try not to imagine her doing these things with my father, but she is my stepmother as well as my friend. It is her duty. "And *never* compete."

I frown. "Have you ever seen me at games?"

"All the time! Chess. If he asks to play, you should refuse. Or lose."

"Never." I could never do that.

"You should not have so much pride," she warns.

I think of Metternich's warning and hesitate. She rests her head on my shoulder, and I can smell the scent of lavender from her hair. "You're the closest friend I've ever had," she whispers.

She comes with me as I make my goodbyes.

I go first to Nurse Judith, who had the job of raising

me until I was grown. She caresses my hair and tells me not to weep. "He has shown great kindness to the Jews. Perhaps God has a plan."

"I hope so," I whisper. But what if He doesn't? What if He's forgotten the Hapsburg-Lorraines?

Then I go to visit my ladies-in-waiting. And finally I see my youngest siblings in their nursery. There is much confusion. At eight years old, my brother Karl does not understand the concept of marriage. When my father appears to say goodnight, he is the one who explains what it is to be married.

"Then I will leave as well?" my brother asks.

"No, you are a boy," my father says.

"Then Anna will leave?" Karl asks, and now there is no consoling Anna at all. The sobs that wrack her body are pitiful to see. I take her in my arms.

"Shhh," I stroke her hair. We share the same golden color.

"I don't want to go."

"You're not going anywhere," I promise.

"But I don't want *you* to leave."

"Why don't you kiss Maria goodnight," my father offers. "Then we can walk her to her room," he suggests comfortingly.

Anna nods. Then we walk the halls together one last time as a family.

CHAPTER 8

PAULINE BORGHESE

Tuileries Palace, Paris
March 1810

"I want you to teach me how to waltz."

I stare at my brother in his military coat and black riding boots, and I'm sure I've heard wrong. "Since when have you wanted to waltz?" I ask. It's ludicrous. No, it's laughable. In forty years he has never danced, not even with me.

"My wife will expect it," Napoleon says, and immediately I feel my temperature rise. So *that's* why I was called to his study! Not for any great purpose, but to help him impress an Austrian whore.

"Absolutely not."

"What do you mean?" He rises from his desk, but I'm not intimidated.

"I can't teach you to dance. I'm not an instructor."

"You're the finest dancer in Paris."

"And that comes naturally." I smile. "I wouldn't know the first thing about teaching someone else."

"You're lying."

Yes. But he doesn't know that. "Ask Hortense," I suggest. Hortense is fool enough to do whatever she's told. After all, she's Joséphine's daughter.

He studies me for a moment, hoping that I'll blush or that my lie will come out in some other small way. But Talma always says I was destined for the stage, and my face betrays nothing. "Then I want you to see this," he says instead. "Everything must be perfect for her arrival, Pauline. *Everything.*"

I see the fifteen chests Paul told me about three months ago and I realize he is truly concerned about this. A nineteen-year-old girl intimidates him because of her name. It is as if he has forgotten that God protects the Bonaparte clan. Look how far we've risen! God *chose* us for greatness, and there's no reason to suspect He will disappoint us now. But my brother's eyes are full of worry, and I wish I could make him understand that even without this palace and his crown, he is a king.

"Look closely," he instructs. "If there's anything I've missed, Méneval will get it."

"Is there a list?" I ask. For all his talk about equality and common blood, I know the truth. He wishes he were royal, too.

He hands me two pages filled from top to bottom with Méneval's writing. There are a hundred and fifty pairs of stockings, thirty-six petticoats, a hundred and forty-four embroidered chemises, eleven silk dressing gowns, eighty lace nightcaps, countless handkerchiefs, and sixty-four—sixty-four!—dresses tailored by Leroy.

"There's a third page as well," he says anxiously. "On the back."

"You have ordered her *underwear*?" I imagine my imbecilic husband Camillo Borghese daring to purchase my undergarments for me, and I am horrified.

"You don't think she can choose these things herself," he says. "She's a child."

"She's nineteen."

"Exactly. Old enough for motherhood, young enough for obedience." My brother slips his hand beneath his coat in a gesture that's become so familiar that artists have begun painting his portraits this way. But I wonder suddenly if his stomach ails him, too. He has never mentioned it, but then he has never mentioned the medicines he takes for his seizures.

I sit on the edge of his desk and ask quietly, "Are you well?"

"What makes you think otherwise?" he asks. Then he follows the direction of my gaze, and withdraws his hand from his coat. "Of course."

"You would tell me if you were sick—"

"Why?" He sits next to me. "Are you a doctor?"

"No, but I would find the best for you."

He takes my hand tenderly in his and squeezes softly. "You are a good sister, Paoletta."

I look back at the chests filled with swan's down cloaks and lilac chemises, and my envy is unbearable. I would look far better in these clothes than any Hapsburg ever will. *What's the point of wearing a russet silk gown when you are a waddling sausage?* "I hear she's fat," I say, knowing he hates fat women as passionately as he does tall ones.

"Who said that of her?" he demands. There is an edge in his voice, and I counter it with indifference.

"No one." I give a little shrug. "It's evident from her picture."

And we have all seen that. Sitting like a shrine in the middle of the Throne Room, elevated on steps like an image of the Virgin Mother.

"I suppose we'll know soon enough." I stand. "At least Caroline will. Paul says you're sending her to Compiègne because she's a queen?"

"It's a matter of rank. And when she arrives, you will not insult her." He rises. "She's a Hapsburg princess."

"Or what? You'll banish me?"

He grabs my arm. Suddenly he's so close, I can feel the desire in his breeches. "You will behave yourself," he warns through clenched teeth. "At the church, at every *fête*, even in the birthing room when she gives me a son. This is not a game."

I pull my arm away. But his eyes are dark, and I wonder if I have pushed him too far. He has ordered men killed for less. He does not do it himself. He sends them to the fronts, to the most dangerous fighting, and when they fail to return, he is all polished speeches and feigned regret. I've had lovers die this way. "What is that?" I ask quickly, turning his attention to the miniature city recreated with clay models on his desk.

"The streets of Paris," he says irritably. "I instructed Méneval to prepare it."

Just as he had Méneval prepare half a dozen models, each

the height of my hand, for his coronation. My brother leaves nothing to chance. He is dangerous to cross, but anyone must admire a man who can plan a wedding like a military campaign. I move closer to the model of our city. The route to the Louvre has been traced with string, and next week, on the first of April, the wedding procession will pass through my brother's unfinished Arc de Triomphe, down the Champs-Élysées and through the Tuileries Gardens. I have already picked out my dress for the ride. Yellow satin and tulle with a rabbit's fur muff.

"What do you think of the Louvre chapel?" my brother asks. "I had it renovated."

Yes, and even looking at it in miniature, it's possible to see just how beautiful it is. I think of how young I'll look in the soft light of the nave, with the silvery light of the stained glass on all sides of me. "Pretty." Then I notice that Méneval has found some entertaining figures to represent those who will be in attendance. There is Napoleon, painted in red and black, with a bicorne hat and black knee-high boots. And Marie-Louise, with hair made of old straw. My figure is dressed in the purest white, and someone has even remembered my cameo necklace. I am standing behind the bride, and though I have the urge to point out that she will be taller and more ungainly in real life, I do not.

My brother's shoulders grow tense. "I want an heir, Pauline."

Paul told me he called her a *walking womb*. "What happens if she isn't fertile?"

He turns to me and his eyes are wild. "Why would you say that?"

"Because it happens—sometimes."

"It will not happen to me."

"If she fails to give you a son, you could always dismiss her," I say. "Then you could find someone else." Only, it wouldn't be me. My childbearing days are finished. The doctors told me this after the birth of my son. So if it's not Marie-Louise, it will only be someone else.

"She will give me an heir," my brother says firmly.

I nod, suspecting he's right. Then perhaps he will grow tired of her, the way he grew tired of Joséphine, who, delightfully, has been told to leave Paris for the Château de Navarre when Marie-Louise arrives. The press has been forbidden to mention Joséphine's name. Imagine having to move to Normandy. That far north, you had might as well be dead.

"I want you and my new wife to become good friends," my brother says.

"Oh, we'll be very close, I'm sure."

He gives me a sideways glance. "You will not bait her, Pauline. You will not treat her the way you treated Joséphine."

"Beauharnaille was a liar."

"And Marie-Louise is a princess. A *real* princess, with eight centuries of Hapsburg blood in her veins. And if it's a choice between her and you," he warns, "then I will choose her."

CHAPTER 9

PAUL MOREAU
BRAUNAU, AUSTRIA

"[With Caroline] I have always had to fight a pitched battle."
—*Napoleon on his sister*

The *cocher* says we are to reach the Austrian border in an hour. If he's lying, I will take my chances in the driving rain and walk to Braunau rather than listen to Queen Caroline complain any longer. Yes, the ride has been unbearable. Yes, it has been rough. But at least we are not horses. They have had to swim most of the way from Paris in all this melting snow and mud.

The emperor gave instructions that we are to bring the princess back by the twenty-eighth of March. But like most things the emperor wants, it's a near-impossible task. It's meant driving for eight days through the rain and sleet with just a single break, then riding again until well after night-fall. Everyone is in a foul mood, especially the women who aren't used to such journeys. But only Queen Caroline feels the need to express her discontent.

"I can't understand how these Austrians can eat *Spätzle*," she complains. "Can you imagine eating that dish, day in, day out? It's no wonder they're all so fat."

"That's what my father says," Collette replies. Of the seven ladies-in-waiting who have come on this trip, she's the queen's favorite, a seventeen-year-old raised in a country château and brought to court for an education. And it is some education she's getting. I have not seen a dress anywhere in Paris as low-cut as hers, or shoes so high. "That our new empress will be as large and stupid as an ox."

"Well, I'm not bringing home some farm animal to my brother. If we have to starve her from here to Compiègne, then that's what we'll do."

The talk in the carriage continues like this until we arrive in Braunau an hour before sunset, and I begin to regret accepting the emperor's request to act as his ears and eyes on this trip. Nothing is good enough for Her Highness. The beer served to us at dinner is too strong, the food is too bland, the people have no sense of fashion. But as soon as the horses slow to a trot, the mood in the carriage lifts. For days it's been nothing but rolling hills and mist. The scent of fire has lingered with us everywhere, yet now, as a castle's towers appear in the distance, there's the smell of a bustling city as well—of cooking, and horses, and brewers making ale. I look out across the lake to the palace beyond, where the new empress will be waiting for us with her Austrian escort. I wonder if her portraits are accurate, or whether the painter has flattered her, as artists often do.

"The second empress of France," Queen Caroline says as

the carriages roll to a stop before Schloss Hagenau. "I'll bet her French isn't half as good as Metternich promised." From the fur trimming on her cloak to the silk lining of her boots, the queen is dressed almost entirely in black. It is an outfit suited to a funeral.

"What if she can't speak any French at all?"

The queen cuts her eyes at Collette. "Then life will be very boring for her in Paris, won't it?"

As we descend from the carriage, a pair of liveried guards open the wooden doors of Schloss Hagenau, and a man in an eye patch emerges from the castle. His black hair is tied back with a golden cord, and his embroidered cloak is exceedingly fine.

Queen Caroline turns to me. "My God, he's even taller than you."

And like me, his shoulders are broad. He has either worked on a farm or spent a great deal of time preparing for war. Perhaps Germans aren't so fat and lazy after all.

"*Really*," Caroline adds as the man comes closer, "he must be a giant." She looks from one of us to the other, as if she's expecting some kind of trouble. "You remember what my brother said?" she asks nervously. "Nothing can go wrong tonight. He's desperate for this match."

"The ceremony has already happened," I reply.

"That doesn't mean anything until he's had her."

The man stops in front of us, and he looks furious. Clearly, his French is good. "Count Adam von Neipperg," he says shortly. The bow he gives us is as brief as decorum can allow. "I expect you are Caroline, queen of Naples."

"I am." She brings her black sable muff up to her cheek and shivers for effect.

He takes in the velvet seats and plush satin pillows of the coach behind us. "It must have been a very difficult journey," he says, then adds dryly, "Terribly unpleasant."

"We have been on the road for eleven hours today," Caroline replies, caught off guard by his remark. "I hope you are not mocking me."

"Not at all, Your Highness. It is a pleasure to have the emperor's sister in Austria."

As soon as Count Neipperg says this, an army of servants appears from the castle to take our belongings. "And you must be Paul," he says to me, "the Haitian chamberlain." I bow, and this time his smile is genuine. "We've heard of you even in Vienna," he says.

I can't imagine what it is the Viennese have heard, but there is no time to find out. Collette's teeth are chattering, and the count ushers us quickly through the icy courtyard. The scent in the air tells me it will snow tonight, making the roads slick and dangerous for travel. Still, we must leave early in the morning if we are to achieve the emperor's schedule.

We follow Count Neipperg through the paneled halls. I inhale the rich scents of cedar wood and coffee. In Paris, the emperor spends a king's ransom on heating; these halls retain a chill the emperor would never allow. We walk through a passage lined entirely with mirrors, and the queen can't keep her eyes from her own reflection. She is an imposing figure, a twenty-eight-year-old woman who appears forty-five. She tries a brief smile, but the act looks painful. I wonder how she behaves toward her four children in Naples, and whether she sees the same old woman I do in the glass.

We pass through a series of chambers decorated by someone with a love for thick carpeting, and when we reach a cozy salon, I recognize the empress at once. She's sitting calmly in the middle of the room with a dog in her lap, surrounded by women the same age as she— eighteen, nineteen, twenty perhaps. She nods formally when she sees that we have arrived, but it's only when she recognizes Queen Caroline that she rises. The artists have been faithful to her appearance. She is plump, with large lips and a slightly hooked nose. But her hair is thick, and her eyes are an extraordinary shade of blue.

Queen Caroline whispers, "She's as tall as the count!"

It's an exaggeration, but as Marie-Louise makes her way toward us, it's clear that she will tower over the emperor. Napoleon doesn't like his women tall. Or plump.

"Your Majesty." Queen Caroline curtsies low, and behind her, the seven ladies she's brought with her do the same. "It is an honor to greet the new empress of France."

"Welcome to Austria," the new empress says. A flush comes over her cheeks, and I wonder what it must be to have skin so translucent that every emotion shows on your face. "I imagine your journey has been difficult so far. Would you like to stay here and speak with my ladies," she asks, "or retire to your rooms upstairs and rest for the night? We have some lovely excursions planned for tomorrow."

Queen Caroline exchanges a look with Collette. The empress's French is absolutely flawless.

"That is gracious of you," the queen replies, and I am reminded anew that the Bonapartes speak French with an Italian accent. "But this is the only time we'll have together."

The empress frowns. "What do you mean?"

"We leave for Compiègne in the morning."

The empress turns swiftly to Count Neipperg, and a heated conversation is exchanged in German.

The count clears his throat. "I'm not sure we understand, Your Highness. Your party has just arrived. Surely, the emperor would want—"

"What the emperor wants," Caroline interrupts, "is his bride. The ceremony has been performed, so why wait?"

The empress touches Count Neipperg's arm, and a tender look passes between them. Francis has sent his daughter's lover with her as an escort, I realize. I glance at the queen to see if she has noticed, but she has eyes only for the spaniel in the empress's arms. Unlike Pauline, the queen has no affinity for dogs. A coolness descends over the salon. Finally, it is the empress who says, "Tomorrow, then. Shall we talk in here, or somewhere more private?"

"This will be fine." Caroline moves across the room, and the empress's ladies step back to make way. She takes a grand chair with padded arms and heavily embroidered cushions. When she has arranged herself, she surveys her domain, and the rest of the women hurry to take their places.

The empress, by contrast, joins Count Neipperg on a small settee near the fire. He briefly touches her knee, and I gasp.

He had might as well be openly courting her! But there is only the thrill of the hunt on Queen Caroline's face. She has been waiting for this moment, and as she sits forward in her chair, I have a good idea what she's going to say.

"So tell me, Your Majesty, how does it feel to be the empress of France?" Caroline, a queen with riches beyond imagining, is envious of this nineteen-year-old girl.

Marie-Louise hesitates. She has no idea how competition runs in the Bonaparte blood. "It—it is a tremendous honor," she replies.

"Not yet twenty, and the entire world before you. What do you want to do, now that you're married? What goals do you hope to accomplish?" Caroline wants to know how her life will change on Marie-Louise's arrival.

The room waits tensely for her answer. Perhaps it's the firelight on her golden hair, or the earnestness in her gaze, but there is something appealing in this second empress. "I can think of nothing I wish to accomplish," she says, "but to be a good wife to my husband and serve the nation."

Caroline turns to Collette and laughs. She thinks Marie-Louise is toying with her. "A good and obedient wife," she repeats. "How charming."

"You asked what I hoped for," the empress replies, "and those are my desires."

Queen Caroline stiffens. "Well, the first empress was loved in Paris," she says. "*No one* in France had more class or style. So if you wish to be a good wife, I suggest you pay attention. Tomorrow I will give you appropriate clothing. And that dog"—she wrinkles her nose in distaste—"will have to stay here."

"No one is taking Sigi!" The empress rises, and Count Neipperg stands as well. "He goes with me or I do not go at all."

"Your husband does not like animals, Your Highness. I suggest you make your farewells tonight. And not just to Sigi," she adds cruelly, "but to all things Austrian. Including your ladies. These are instructions from the emperor himself."

"That she leave her *spaniel*?" Neipperg challenges.

"It's an *animal*," the queen replies, as if no one could ever grow attached to such a thing. "It will find a new owner."

Marie-Louise buries her face in the dog's fur, and the only sound in the room is the crackling of the fire. When my father taught me history as a boy in Haiti, he spoke of just such a scene when Marie-Antoinette was sent from Vienna. "I won't leave Sigi behind," she swears.

But Caroline is unmoved. "You do not have a choice."

Marie-Louise looks at Neipperg, as if the final decision rests with him. "We are done here," he announces, and takes her arm.

The Austrian women hurry to rise, and Queen Caroline calls after them, "We leave at eight." But no one is paying her any attention. "Tell them, Paul! Make sure they understand—"

Marie-Louise spins around. "We understand *perfectly*. My hearing," she explains, "is as good as my French."

Collette covers her mouth in shock as the new empress turns on her heel and walks away.

As soon as the Austrians are gone, the queen whispers, "He will lock her in his rooms and throw away the key. Paul,

I want you to be sure that girl is ready for eight. That means up at five and dressing by six. She will look French whether she wishes it or no."

"And the count?" I search Caroline's face, to determine whether she can really be so ignorant. "Shall I wake him as well? He will want to come."

"He may want all sorts of things," she says viciously. "Unless his name is Metternich, he stays here. In Austria. Our little swan is a married woman now. If she was foolish enough to take the count as her lover, that is no concern of mine."

So she did see the way he touched the empress's knee, and how she watched him when he rose angrily to defend her.

Half a dozen servants arrive to show us to our chambers, but when I reach my room, sleep does not come. It's bitterly, bone-chillingly, impossibly cold. But that is not what is keeping me awake. Tomorrow a young woman's life will be altered. Whether or not she has bedded the count, the empress's childhood will come to its real end when she crosses the border from Austria into France. Braunau will be the last Austrian city she ever sees, and the food she's had tonight she will never taste again. Tomorrow she will ride toward Compiègne to meet her husband. *Like a lamb to a pack of wolves,* I think, and close my eyes, remembering what I had hoped for on my first voyage to Paris.

I was almost eighteen—nearly the same age as the empress—when Pauline convinced me to leave Haiti. But unlike this girl, the choice had been my own. The war was tearing apart my family, and my mother refused to speak with my half-brother when she saw how he supported Napoleon's invasion. She had been like a parent to him. Luc's own mother had died when he was seven years old. Yet here he was, offering the French soldiers free food and wine, knowing they wanted to enslave the woman who had raised him. I was tired of the anger poisoning our house, and with Pauline, there was the promise of a future—and calm.

My mother cried tears of relief that I was leaving and would no longer be caught up in France's war. But by leaving my father's plantation, I abandoned my family to a fate far worse than discord. The message that arrived telling me of their deaths was written by our neighbor.

"*They are gone,*" he wrote a year after I arrived in Paris, "*and I am returning to France and civilization.*" But it was the *French* who killed my family, the *French* who enslaved my Haitian mother, and the *French* who started the war.

Yet if not for the French, I wouldn't exist.

I think of my father and how happy he would be to know that of all the learned men in Paris, I am the one the emperor seeks out when he wants to discuss Voltaire. If he were alive, he would be writing me letters about the winter's harvest, telling me how tall the beans have grown and how lazy Luc is still. We would joke about Maman's weariness of the rain and avoid the subject of war at all costs.

No one should lose their family. But tomorrow, when we set out for Paris, this is how the new empress of France will feel. I think of the sacrifice she is making for her father as the cold hours pass. Then a cock crows on the grounds of this palace of ice and snow, and I rise to dress. When I open the door to peer outside, the halls are still dark. There are guards positioned at every stairwell, and I ask the nearest man how to find the empress's chamber.

"Up there. Largest door on the right."

I climb the stairs and imagine how warm it must be right now in the Tuileries Palace. A careless servant has forgotten to shut a window, and outside a heavy mist has enshrouded the trees. There is no understanding how these people can survive like this, in cold so intense it can take away your breath.

When I reach the empress's door, a pair of Austrian guards step forward.

"What is your business here?"

"I've come to wake the empress."

"Her Majesty has ladies for that."

I look at the young man and can see him fighting to keep awake. "This is by order of the queen, who has been given her orders by the emperor of France. The empress must be woken at six o'clock."

The boy glances at his fellow guard, and the other man shrugs.

The men move aside and allow me to knock softly. I am expecting a sullen maid instructing me to come back later, so when the empress herself answers, I step back. "Your Majesty." I bow quickly, and behind me, the guards immediately do the same. It is obvious she has not had any sleep. Her eyes are red and swollen. I peer over her shoulder into the dimly lit chamber, but there is no sign of Count Neipperg. If he has been here, she has hidden any traces of him.

"You've been told to bring me to Caroline," she guesses.

I nod. "The queen's desire is to leave by eight."

"Her desire, or her instructions?" she asks.

We stare at each other in the flickering light, and I can see the cleverness in her gaze. She knows this is not a woman's decision. This is the whim of a man who is accustomed to getting everything he wants, a man who doesn't like having to wait.

"Her instructions," I say honestly. When her eyes well with tears, I add quietly, so that not even the lady-in-waiting behind her can hear, "He will be surprising you in a week at Compiègne."

CHAPTER 10

MARIE-LOUISE, EMPRESS OF FRANCE

Compiègne, France

"I think of you always, and I always shall. God has given me power to endure this final shock, and in Him alone I have put all my trust. He will help me and give me courage, and I shall find support in doing my duty toward you, since it is all for you that I have sacrificed myself."

—Letter from Marie-Louise to her father, Emperor Francis I

If my father were to see me today, with my gown cut so low a seasoned *Strichmädchen* would blush to wear it, he would never recognize me. From my narrow leather shoes lined in pale green silk, to the cameo of Napoleon around my neck, I am all but French. I think of Joseph Wright's *The Portrait of a Lady* with her ridiculous hat and impertinent gaze and wonder if this is what Napoleon hopes I'll become. A tear escapes and lands on my necklace.

"What theatrics," Caroline snaps. "It's a change of clothes."

I do not reply. If she can't see that this is nothing to do with fashion, then there is no reasoning with this hateful woman. And while she may be ten years older than I am, she would do well to remember that I am an empress.

Caroline claps her hands for Collette. "Fix her hair," she instructs.

I sit patiently while Collette gathers my hair into a bun, and listen as both women discuss the weeklong journey ahead. We are to reach Compiègne by way of Munich and Strasbourg. Between those cities are to be a dozen stops, so the important men of Europe can say that they've met me.

"Of course, there's nothing to do in Stuttgart," Caroline says, as Collette places tortoiseshell combs in my hair. "But in Compiègne . . ."

The women exchange glances. They don't know that the servant from Haiti has already told me that my new husband will be waiting in this city.

"Well, Prince Metternich will be joining us there," Queen Caroline says.

"*Prince Metternich* will be joining us?" I ask. "I thought he would meet us in Paris."

Both women look down at me, as if they've forgotten I understand French. Caroline shrugs cryptically, and I immediately wonder how well she knows the prince.

Collette steps back to admire her work, and the queen's spacious room suddenly feels oppressive. The fire is too hot, the bed is too near. And what is that in my hair? I lean closer to the mirror and see that the tortoiseshell cameo depicts Alexander the Great. They're all obsessed! With conquest and ambition.

"What do you think?" she questions Caroline, and my sister-in-law appraises me with a look.

"It will do." The queen turns to me, then scowls at Sigi. "Are you ready?"

"You said we would depart at eight o'clock. It's seven-thirty." These were her words, not mine.

"Then make your farewells. And find someone to take care of that dog."

When the two of them leave, I run to my little spaniel. "Maria will take good care of you," I swear. He hangs his head low to the ground, and I'm certain he can understand what I'm saying. "I'll have Adam take you back to Vienna," I say, in a voice full of false enthusiasm. But Sigi whines plaintively, and I think of how my carriage will ride away without him. My hands begin to tremble. We are together every day. I know the sound he makes when he's hungry, and the bark he uses for getting attention. I know when he's tired or just lazy. I can tell when he's anxious because the soldiers in the courtyard have been too loud. I have written Maria a letter instructing as to his precise care.

We lie on the bed together, on the side Adam occupied until early this morning, and he licks my hand while I cry. By eight o'clock I have not made my farewells to anyone.

When Adam knocks on my door, my eyes are nearly swollen shut.

"*Maria*."

"Marie," I correct him, and I can feel his devastation. He wraps me in his arms, and I don't care if the foreign servants in the hall can see. "You'll take care of Sigi on the ride back, won't you?" I whisper.

"I'll take care of him until the day we reunite."

I look up sharply. "I'm a married woman," I reply, though the sentence fills me with disgust.

"Not in my eyes. And not in the eyes of God."

I flinch at the truth in his words. The pope still has not condoned Napoleon's divorce; his marriage to me is without the Church's blessing.

Adam takes my hand and caresses my fingers. "At Dolens I was left for dead," he begins. "The French didn't believe my life was worth saving, and their captain wanted to leave me for the thieves and crows."

My stomach tightens, but I wipe away my tears so I can look into his face.

"No one was with me in those hours before dawn. Just the bodies of rotting men. But I remember a soldier leaning over me the next day. He was French, and when he saw that I was breathing, he knew just enough German to ask, 'How big is your faith?'"

I nod, understanding the point he is trying to make.

"He wanted to know if I believed I'd get better. He didn't want to convince the captain to take me if I would just be a burden to them and die. I said I believed in Saint Augustine's dictum. That faith is to believe what we do not see, and the reward of that faith is to see what we believe. I knew, even as I was lying there in the rain, that my life was not finished. I would be healed. I didn't know when or how. I didn't anticipate the French returning for the dead, or that they'd take me to Paris and nurse me back to health. But it happened. And I want you to have that kind of faith, Maria."

"I will try, Adam. I want to try."

Outside Schloss Hagenau, a long line of fifteen carriages are waiting to begin our journey to France. The horses seem anxious, whinnying and pawing at the ground, but the French women don't pay them any attention. They're too busy shivering in the cold. I join them in my new muslin gown, as ill equipped as they are for this weather.

"How do they expect you to travel through Munich and Strasbourg like this?" Adam brushes his hand against my cloak. Caroline sees, and her lips thin into a line. Several of the French women giggle behind their hands.

"*Auf Wiedersehen*, Adam," I say, with dignity and a strength I don't feel. I want to burn his image into my memory. The way his hair is slicked back behind his ears, and his mustache is thin enough to have been drawn. I want to remember how square his jaw is, and how his black eyes can be brown—or even chestnut—in the light.

He bows formally. "*Bis wir uns wiedersehen, meine Liebe.*"

Standing next to a group French courtiers, he is the only one who looks like a man. He is taller and broader than any of them, with bigger hands and a wider chest. Yet he is cradling a tiny dog in his arms. *Sigi.*

I climb into the carriage I will share with Queen Caroline and Collette, her lady-in-waiting, then push back the curtains to look at Adam and Sigi for as long as I can.

"Enough," Caroline snaps as she enters the carriage. She

shouts through the window at the *cocher*, "Move!" before Collette has fully seated herself.

"What about Paul?" Collette exclaims.

"He is riding behind us."

The sound of a whip cracks the air, and I inhale the scent of Austria one last time; the cedar wood from the chimneys, the *Leberkäs* baking somewhere in the château. I watch from my window until Adam and Sigi are small on the horizon.

"Well, that wasn't so terrible," Caroline says to Collette. Her lady-in-waiting is nearly the same age as I am and a great deal prettier. "At least the beds were good."

Collette stifles a yawn. "How long until we get there?"

"Munich?" Caroline laughs. "You had might as well sleep."

Collette rolls her eyes. Someone has twisted her blond hair into a bun, so that her large pearl earrings can be shown to good effect. And though we both have fair coloring, if I were to wear her puce gown, it would wash out my complexion. She should always be painted in purples and reds.

Both women go to sleep. No one asks if I would like a small pillow or one of the four blankets Collette has hogged for herself. I'm a parcel to be collected and delivered to Compiègne.

So as not to think of what I've left behind, I stare out the window at the passing villages. *What will France be like?* Warmer, for certain. And busier. My father told me that the Tuileries Palace has so many courtiers, they can't all dine at once, and that as soon as I arrive, I'm to be given two hundred servants of my own: footmen and pages and ladies-in-waiting whom I shall have to make use of somehow. I have no idea what Joséphine did with them all, or why this emperor thinks I wish to be equally extravagant. Though, truly, I would like Collette to give me one of her four blankets. I am an empress now, so I could certainly take one without her stopping me. But I am also Hapsburg, and I would rather freeze than take something by force.

We pass through a village nestled against a backdrop of foothills and fields, and I wish I had thought to bring my charcoal and paper. I'd sketch the lonely chimneys piercing the sky, smudging the horizon with their trails of black smoke. When we reach the bustling city of Salzburg, I know exactly how I'd draw the gardens of Mirabell Palace, with their neat rows of boxwood. I am hoping we'll be breaking for lunch nearby, but the horses keeping going, rain starts falling, and Caroline never stirs. Nor does Collette, who snores. And for the rest of the day it is like this. We enter city after city where we might stretch or eat, but the carriages never stop.

When we finally reach Munich at nine in the evening, nothing can improve my mood, not even the torch-lit views of Nymphenburg Palace, with its glittering lakes and long canal. I am grateful for the thousands of people who've turned out to see me, but I can barely make out their faces through the darkness and rain. Even if I could, what would it matter? They're here for a story, to tell their children that one morning a royal coach pulled up to the Nymphenburg Palace and the wife of the Emperor Napoleon got out. She was dressed like no other woman in the world, with more diamonds in her tiara than the empress of Russia. And her dress! Well, only a queen could afford such ermine.

Once inside the palace, I have no idea how many courtiers introduce themselves to me. I have not eaten, I have not rested, and by the end of the night, I'm so tired, I don't even have the energy to weep. But as we retire to our rooms and Collette helps me undress, I wonder if this is Napoleon's plan. To wear me down so that by the time we reach Compiègne, I no longer care that he has married me without anyone's genuine permission—not mine, or my father's, or even God's.

"Would Your Majesty care for some music?" Collette asks. Her dimpled face looks innocent and sweet, but I know the truth. Caroline has sent her to my rooms to spy.

"No, thank you," I say.

But she lingers at the door, even after I am dressed in my nightshift. "Perhaps you would care for some milk then? Or tea?"

"I am not going to disappear. Or run away. I know my duty."

Her cheeks burn scarlet, and we stare at each other in the open doorway. Then she turns on her heels and goes to leave.

"Wait," I call after her, and quickly, she turns back. "What city is it tomorrow?" I ask.

"Stuttgart." She sighs. "There's to be another reception at a castle," she says, "and every nobleman in Württemberg will likely be there. More bad food and old men."

So that's why she looks so miserable every night. Not because the journey is long or rough, or because she misses her home, but because the French have finer food and men. "Thank you, Collette. I will see you tomorrow."

She hesitates. "Your Majesty?"

"Yes?"

She twists the ends of her cashmere shawl in her hands. "Did you wish to marry the Emperor Bonaparte?"

Now it's my turn to flush. I think of my family back home in Vienna, and of Adam and Sigi, whom I may never see again. "No."

She nods, as if she understands. But she has never had to make a difficult choice, this girl. I doubt she's even wondered where the money comes from for her gowns, or why men go to war in foreign lands. "I'm sorry," she whispers.

I blink rapidly. "Me too."

"How will you ever be happy?" she asks.

"I have my painting," I say. "And someday there'll be children." She looks at me as if she's never heard of such sacrifice. But a hundred queens have done this before me, and it will have to be enough.

"If there's anything I can do—"

"Sigi," I say at once. "My dog."

"I would—I truly would," she says. "It's the queen—she doesn't like pets."

Callous, miserable woman. I look up so that my tears won't start fresh, and I try to think of something—anything—to keep me from weeping. "Tell me about Metternich," I say.

I can see Collette now wishes she'd never come. "The prince?"

I nod slowly. "They are lovers, aren't they?"

Immediately, Collette steps toward the door. "You didn't

hear that from me," she whispers. Then slowly, she nods her head. "But yes, it's true."

"Is he the one who arranged my marriage to Bonaparte?"

"I—I can't say, Your Majesty."

"But if you had to guess."

Her silence is all I need to know.

The next morning we are all up at five, dressed and ready to depart by six.

I wear my new French gown, a white silk dress embroidered with silver bluebells, but my thoughts are Austrian. I dreamed of Adam last night. I think of the look on his face as my carriage pulled away from Braunau, and my heart begins to ache. I wish I could have frozen that moment in time, like a Louise Moillon painting of fruit where nothing moves and nothing ever changes.

"How long it will take before we reach Stuttgart?" Caroline asks the driver, but frankly I don't care. And even when we reach Ludwigsburg Palace and the grand reception being held in my honor, I feel indifferent. *Cake?* Why not? *Lebkuchen?* If I must. *Would Her Majesty prefer the waltz or the contra dance?* "Whichever is shortest," I say irritably.

The women around me gasp. I know what these people are thinking. *Nothing impresses this haughty new empress.* But I'm too upset to care. King Frederick of Württemberg clears his throat, and Caroline gives a high, false laugh.

"What Her Majesty *meant* to say, Your Highness, is that a shorter dance now will mean more time for others later."

"That's not what I said."

Caroline glares at me. "But it's what you *meant*." She holds my gaze so that it's understood I'm not to say another word.

I don't, and for the rest our journey to Compiègne, we are silent with each other.

Then, on the twenty-seventh of March, after the carriages have crossed the borders of France, Caroline turns to me. "*Mio Dio*, this is it!"

I sit up in my seat and look out the window of our royal *calèche*. The city of Compiègne is spread before us like a colorful blanket. Markets and churches jostle for space in the city square, and everywhere there are people—in the cafés, on the streets, in the open-shuttered windows. My heart gives a small leap as I wonder if I will ever be able to capture a scene like this on paper.

"Beautiful." Collette sighs, and I know she is looking at the handsomely dressed women in their embroidered muslin gowns. "Do they know we are coming?" Collette asks, but Caroline only points.

Somewhere in the distance a group is chanting, and as the carriages draw closer, I can make out their words. "VIVE L'IMPÉRATRICE! VIVE L'IMPÉRATRICE!" Despite the rain, the people of France have come out to greet their empress.

"Be ready for anything," Caroline says, still unaware that Paul has prepared me. "Sit straight, put your hands in your lap, and—"

The carriage jerks to a stop. She exchanges a look with Collette, and I can guess what it means. Napoleon has spotted the royal *calèche* and intends to meet me before we reach the château.

I press my palms flat against my skirts and try to remember Maria's instructions. When he asks whether he looks as I expected, I'm to lie and say, *"No, sire, you look much better."* And when he inquires how the journey from Vienna has been, I'm to smile and tell him, *"Too long for a bride desperate to meet her groom."*

My speech will be a portrait by Gottlieb Schick. An umbrella here, a potted palm there. Everything planned, the entire set prearranged. I will take my place, and he will take his, and the picture we create for this new empire will be flawless.

The door of the royal *calèche* swings open.

The Ogre of France is standing before me.

"Marie-Louise," he says, and it's as if Metternich's painting has come to life, red velvet coat and all. He has not bothered to flatter himself through art. He has the same short legs and rounded stomach from his portrait. His hair, which I've heard was once long in his youth, is cropped short just below his ears. Despite the rain, he is wearing a white cloak embroidered in gold, and his boots are far too nice for this weather. *Pomp and ceremony,* I think.

Caroline claps with joy to see her brother, and Collette begins fanning herself with her hand. But the emperor doesn't look at either of them. His gray eyes are too busy appraising me.

"It is a pleasure to finally meet you, sire." I offer him my hand, exactly as my father told me to do, and the look on the emperor's face is rapturous.

"Tell me," he says, "do I look as you expected me to?"

"No. You are more"—I lower my head in what I hope looks like modesty—"*far* more handsome in person."

I peek up through my lashes, and his smile is so wide that I'm embarrassed for him. He is forty years old, with a reputation so dark that Genghis Khan would be ashamed to own it. Does he really believe that a nineteen-year-old girl can be enamored with him?

"And your father?" he asks suddenly. "How did he command you to behave toward me?"

It takes all of my resolve not to tell him the truth. Not to say, *"He warned me about your ambition. How you can sing love songs by night and kill a thousand men by day. How nothing will stop you from taking what you want."* But I know my lines, and I recite them for my father. "To obey you in every way," I tell him.

Napoleon closes his eyes, as if my words have transported him. "Marie-Louise," he says when he opens them again, as formal as if the two of us were sitting at court, "will you accompany me to my carriage?"

Caroline exclaims, "What about—"

Napoleon shoots his sister a look, and immediately she is silent. "We will see you at the château." He holds out his hand for me, and I take it.

There are umbrellas as far as the eye can see, and every servant rushes forward in an attempt to shelter us.

"Just one," Napoleon snaps. "*One.*"

A single man steps toward us, and Napoleon nods. "Thank you, Méneval." He clears his throat. "To our *calèche.*"

He will not keep up this façade forever. At some point,

possibly even tonight, the charm will fall away, and I must be ready. Inside the coach, a handsome man in his forties is waiting. He is sitting across from a pretty young woman who pats the seat next to her, indicating where I should sit. But no one speaks, and when the door is shut and the horses take off, everyone waits for the emperor.

"My bride," he says at last. "Marie-Louise, this is Joachim Murat, the king of Naples and Caroline's husband."

I incline my head. "An honor to meet you." *How can he live with Caroline for a wife?*

"The pleasure is mine," he says. He is dressed in a white coat with gilded epaulettes, and if I'm not mistaken, he has gone to great lengths to arrange his black hair in long, tight curls. He would be laughed out of court in Austria for this. But he seems harmless enough.

"And this is my stepdaughter, Hortense Bonaparte, the queen of Holland."

I incline my head again. "Your Majesty."

"I am to be your mistress of the robes," she says quietly, and I realize with a start that my husband has commanded his own stepdaughter—the child of Joséphine—*to wait on me.*

"Oh," I say, and the three of them watch me, but nothing else comes. I am not like Metternich, who can spin his shock into pretty words. I need time to prepare my flattery and lies.

When the silence continues, Napoleon clears his throat. "All of France has been waiting for this moment," he declares. "The day when the heir of Alexander the Great took a Hapsburg princess for a wife. Look." He reaches out and with a swipe of his hand, he pushes aside the brocade curtains. "The Château de Compiègne."

It is larger than any palace I have ever laid eyes on. It looms over the horizon like a marble bird, with great glass wings and a beak of stone. Even in this pouring rain, it is magnificent.

"There's nothing like it in all of Austria, is there?"

I look up at the soaring windows. I'm tempted to lie, but I tell him the truth. "No."

"Of course not. The greatest Hapsburg emperors would be awed by this."

Such arrogance. I look to Hortense, to see what she makes of this statement, but her face is frozen in a welcoming smile.

"This is one of the emperor's three seats of power. The others are Fontainebleau and Versailles. You've heard of them, I'm sure," says Caroline's husband.

"Yes." I turn back to Napoleon. "And where does His Majesty spend most of his time?"

Napoleon's smile widens. He obviously takes pleasure in being addressed this way.

"Fontainebleau," he replies. "But you will find there's not much difference between the three." There is no time to ask what he means. Our procession has come to a stop in the *cour d'honneur*, and Napoleon is already putting on his gloves. "Your hat," he says irritably, pointing to my bonnet. "It's not straight."

I lift my hand to the fur-lined trim and can almost hear his thoughts: *Joséphine would never have stepped out into the* cour d'honneur *without checking that her attire was flawless.*

"Here, let me do it," Hortense says kindly. She unties the bow beneath my chin and sets the bonnet right. Suddenly, my heart begins to race.

"Every person in France is waiting for you," Napoleon warns. "The king of Holland, the Princess Borghese—are you ready?"

No. But this is not the time to panic. I swallow my fear and nod.

The coach door opens, and a sea of eager faces stare back at me, dripping with rain and oblivious to the weather. Someone shouts, *"Vive l'empereur!"* and the entire crowd takes up the chant. Then Napoleon laughs. "They never did that for your father, did they?"

I despise this little toad. But I smile at him like a wife and stand like a queen.

He raises my arm with his, and the entire courtyard erupts into cheers. The hundreds of dignitaries who have stood in the rain to wait for this moment press closely around us, and all of them are bidding me congratulations. "Your Majesty!" someone shouts. "Your Majesty!" A young man in heavy furs rushes forward, and he's the same one who sheltered us with his umbrella.

"Not now," Napoleon says harshly. "Where is the cardinal?"

"Doesn't Your Majesty wish—"

"My only *wish,* Méneval, is to discover whether we are officially married."

The young man looks stricken. "Yes. But in God's eyes—"

"God is for the common people, monsieur. Take us to my apartment."

Méneval glances at me as we enter the palace, and I am sure that my cheeks are the same color as his cloak. I think of Adam and the first time I invited him into my rooms. I was eighteen years old. A year before, the *comte* had divorced his wife of eleven years upon discovering her betrayal while he was at war. After this, he began walking the grounds of Schönbrunn each morning. I would find him sitting in the Gloriette, overlooking the vast baroque gardens of the palace, and whenever Sigi saw him, my spaniel would go mad with joy. Adam would humor him by throwing a stick or scratching his long ears, and we came to know each other this way.

Morning after morning I discovered what an extraordinary person he was. How his favorite painters were Francesco Guardi and Thomas Gainsborough, and how he saw himself as a soldier first but a collector second. His favorite antiques to acquire were Greek, then Roman, and finally Renaissance. We had known each other for more than a year when I suggested he visit me in my chamber. That night my ladies-in-waiting were dismissed, and I learned ways of preventing pregnancy.

When Napoleon sent his stepson, Eugène, to arrange this marriage, there were two questions that Joséphine's son never asked: is Ferdinand's sickness an inheritable disease, and has Maria-Lucia been touched? As we make our way through the palace, I wonder if Napoleon believes that I am a virgin, and if so, whether he might be angry enough to return me to Austria once he discovers the truth.

"Your Majesty understands that the entire court is waiting beneath the grand staircase," Méneval adds cautiously as we walk. "Everyone has been assembled there since noon. The Princess Borghese has just arrived, as has Madame Mère."

"They can wait a little longer." Napoleon sounds amused. He takes my arm as we reach the staircase, and together we cut a swath through the glittering courtiers in velvet hats and heavily jeweled vests. "Where is he going?" I hear someone exclaim, then a woman gasps. "He's not really going to take her—"

Napoleon spins around. "Yes. I am." The woman is shocked. "I'll be back when I have reconquered Austria."

CHAPTER 11

PAULINE BORGHESE

Château de Compiègne
March 28, 1810

"I don't believe you."

But Paul leans close to me during the final waltz and whispers in my ear. "It's true," he says simply. "Afterward she beat him at chess—"

"Not the chess," I hiss. "That she asked for it again!"

He dips me back so that I'm looking up into his great black eyes. "Her older sister probably told her what to say once he was finished," he guesses.

"She doesn't have an older sister," I snap, and as we stand face to face, I feel the blood rush to my cheeks. Napoleon has only known her for a day, and Paul has sworn she isn't any great catch. But he wasn't there for the carriage ride back, when anything might have happened between them. "He likes her. That's what he said to you this morning, isn't it?"

He shrugs. "He likes all women—for a time."

"But this one's a Hapsburg. And for all his talk about

equality and common blood, I know the truth. He wishes he were royal."

Paul doesn't argue. The music crescendos, and throughout the ballroom of the Château de Compiègne, hundreds of diamonds catch at the light. The gems dazzle from every surface: women's necks, men's cravats, the too-flirtatious Duchess of Devonshire's hair. If the gods could see us now, they would stop time so that not a single one of us would age. Osiris, both the brother and husband of Isis, could immortalize us all in our perfection.

Paul puts his hand on my back, and I enjoy the small thrill of scandalizing the members of the ancien régime. *The Princess Borghese is dancing with her chamberlain!* Then the floor begins to clear until we're the only couple dancing. I catch the empress watching us as we go by, with her pretty blue eyes and a sweet-as-honey gaze. At every formal ball, at every weekend soirée, *I* am the one who ends the dance. It has been this way since my brother first held court, and it will be this way for as long as I am the Princess Borghese.

I close my eyes, and for a moment, nothing but the music exists. There aren't five hundred guests from all across Europe to see my brother wed his second wife. I've worn my white silk dress embroidered with gold lotus flowers, and the tiara in my hair has similar diamond blossoms. In the light of the hanging chandeliers, I must shine like white fire. I search for my current lover, de Canouville, in the crowd. His pretty face is next to Napoleon's. Not surprising. My brother has always been a great admirer of beauty.

"So what else have you heard?" I ask casually.

My chamberlain hesitates. Then finally, as the music softens, he says quietly, "He advised Méneval to marry a German, since German girls are as fresh and innocent as roses."

I'm so shocked, I nearly forget that we are dancing. "He wants *innocence*?"

"For now," Paul is quick to say.

But I feel a fire in the pit of my stomach that is all-consuming. My brother, who had his way with the married Countess Walewska for the first time *after* she fainted dead at his feet, admires innocence? The same brother who enjoys spanking court women and then taking them to his chamber? The hypocrisy of it boils my blood.

When the piano stops, I face Napoleon and make my deepest curtsey.

"Very pretty." Napoleon claps, and the entire court immediately follows suit. "*Bellissima!*" he exclaims in our native Italian. He beckons me with his eyes, and Paul leads me across the floor to where the emperor is standing.

"That was very impressive," Marie-Louise says, and though we met this morning, her tone is formal. "You're a wonderful dancer."

I glance at de Canouville, who is watching me with open desire. "I've been dancing since I was a child in Corsica," I reply. "I hope you dance as well. My brother likes watching beautiful women . . . waltz."

Marie-Louise inhales sharply, and my brother gives me a thunderous look. "Come with me," he commands, and everyone steps away as if I've suddenly become poisonous.

"Tonight," I whisper in de Canouville's ear as I pass. "My apartment at midnight."

I follow Napoleon through the ballroom's double doors. He is breathing so heavily that one of the passing soldiers asks if he is well. "Fine," he barks, and the young man steps back into the shadows. No one has dared to follow us, and our footfalls are the only sound in the marble halls. My brother waits for me to enter the library first, and once the door is shut, I placate him. "It was a joke."

"I will strip your title!" he shouts. "You will be nothing more than Madame Pauline!"

He watches me in the flickering light of the fireplace, and for a moment, I am actually fearful. "My husband was a prince long before you were emperor," I say at last. My marriage to Camillo makes me a princess, not my brother's whim. Like his tender bride with *Hapsburg* blood.

"I have summoned your husband to Paris," he counters. "He's to be at my wedding on the second of April." I open my mouth to object, but he hasn't played his final card. "For the occasion, you will be carrying the empress's train in the chapel. You may be a princess"—he pauses—"but she is the empress of Rome."

"I will not carry her train," I warn him.

My brother's lips twitch upward. "Jealousy has never become you, Pauline. And you most certainly will. Or you will find yourself living in Rome with Camillo."

I search his face to see if this is an idle threat, but his gaze is unflinching. "Why are you doing this to me?" In the light of the flames, he looks younger than his forty years. I imagine him in the blue and gold *nemes* crown, an Egyptian pectoral around his neck and a crook at his side.

"It's a silk train," he says harshly, "not an explosive."

I cover my face with my hands. "I can't live with Camillo. He's a fool."

"I've had enough, Pauline."

I watch my brother walk behind his desk and seat himself heavily. He looks weary, as if this conversation has drawn everything out of him. "In four days there will be an official ceremony, and you will be standing in the Louvre with your sisters and Camillo."

"I want nothing to do with that man!" I shriek.

"Then you should have considered that when you took your vows, but he will be staying here for my wedding."

"He will not live with me in Château de Neuilly," I say flatly. My brother gifted me that house during his Spanish campaign. "I would sooner see Joséphine in it than Camillo."

"Then you will send him to Hôtel Charost!" he says angrily, referring to my property on the rue du Faubourg Saint-Honoré. "But have a smile on your face come the second of April."

He storms past me, and I can see there'll be no moving him tonight.

CHAPTER 12

LOUVRE, PARIS

April 2, 1810

It may be the greatest spectacle Paris has ever witnessed, with soldiers marching down the Champs-Élysées in a steady stream of red coats and silver carriages as far as the eye can see. It costs a fortune to put on a parade like this, and the general populace feels that another war will bankrupt this empire. Yet everywhere I look there is joy—in the faces of the people crowding the streets, in the excitement of the courtiers who will grow rich serving our new empress.

"I've never seen anything like it," Méneval says, and I suspect he has seen his share of processions in this country. We've been standing outside the Louvre for an hour; Napoleon loves pageantry. "Nothing will ever be the same in Europe after today. The daughter of Austria is marrying the ruler of an empire so vast that Charlemagne himself would be envious. What nation will challenge an alliance like this?"

I try to imagine what peace will mean after decades of revolution and war.

There would be no more public lists of the dead. No more burials of courtiers who rode out to war with their ambitious emperor simply because he wanted more land. And once there's peace in Europe, why shouldn't there be peace abroad? Why would France have need of colonies and slaves when there'll be so much prosperity and happiness here?

When we are finally inside the Louvre, we all walk to the room Napoleon has transformed into a stunning chapel of crimson velvets and silk. I take my place near Méneval in the brightly decorated pews and wonder if I am the only one who appreciates the irony that it was Marie-Antoinette, the great-aunt of the bride, who turned this palace into a public museum. Yet it was Napoleon, *liberator of the people,* who instructed the museum's director to replace the paintings in the "chapel" with tapestries depicting her great-niece, Marie-Louise—and himself. I have heard rumors that when Monsieur Denon refused, telling him the paintings were too big to remove, Napoleon replied, "Very well. I'll burn them." The next day Denon discovered a method of taking them down.

In the rows behind me, I count half a dozen—if not more—of Pauline's former lovers. There is Gréoux, who only lasted a week, and the Comte de Forbin, among many others. I wonder that Pauline doesn't blush to see them all here in one place. But that's not her way. More likely than not, she'll feel some sort of triumph to know that they are seeing her in such a glittering state.

In front of me, Madame Mère weeps softly into her handkerchief, tears of joy staining her cheeks. And as the doors are pulled open once again by a pair of armed guards, she whispers reverently, "There he is!"

The emperor appears in the dimly lit chapel wearing a shirt so heavily embroidered in gold that I am certain his arms will be sore come morning. There is a murmur of surprise as he approaches the chancel, and when he reaches the first pew, where I am standing with his mother, I can see why everyone is shocked: his shoes, which have always been the plainest of military boots, are encrusted with yellow diamonds and gold. I have never seen him dressed as he is now: in a black velvet hat and a long satin cloak embellished with golden bees. The crown jewels of France anoint his wrists, his neck, even his cap—the transformation is so complete, it's hard to recognize the man beneath the trappings.

Madame Mère watches her son, and I recognize Pauline's devotion in her adoring gaze. But it's the second empress of France who takes my breath away. She enters the salon in a gown of shimmering silver tulle. The velvet manteau that trails behind her is lined with ermine and stitched in silver thread. An intricate veil of Alençon lace covers her blond hair, and the diamond tiara that holds it in place catches the light from a hundred different angles. She is completely calm, as if the hundreds of courtiers and the Gobelins tapestries were simply not present. Not even Joséphine had such composure, but then I suppose this is the difference between a wife raised on the tiny island of Martinique and a princess raised in Schönbrunn Palace. She approaches the chancel with even steps, and when she reaches the emperor, she nods formally, as if greeting an equal.

"Like one of Botticelli's angels." Madame Mère sighs, but I can see from Pauline's face that she doesn't share this view. She is standing behind Marie-Louise in a white silk gown and carrying the bride's manteau alongside four other queens, which must certainly be a first in history. There is her sister, Caroline, the queen of Naples; Napoleon's sister-in-law Julie Clary, the queen of Spain; Joséphine's daughter, Hortense, the queen of Holland; and Napoleon's sister-in-law Catharina, the queen of Westphalia. None of the women appear particularly pleased, but Pauline is the only one whose face is set in an unsightly scowl. And when she turns to me, her expression is so unpleasant, I smile.

"How can you laugh about this?" she demands when the ceremony is over and the Cardinal Grand Almoner has pronounced them man and wife. We are on the steps of the Louvre, where the imperial carriage will arrive to take the new empress and her husband to Pauline's home. "I've turned the Château de Neuilly upside down for that woman," she whispers harshly. "And do you know what I get for it? *That*."

I follow her gaze to a tall man in white silk pants and a satin cape. Camillo Borghese. He's speaking with one of the few cardinals who came for this ceremony. Of the thirty who were invited, only eleven appeared, since the pope is still refusing to recognize this marriage. The cardinal's face looks troubled, and though he's clearly saying something of great import, Camillo has his fingers spread apart and is inspecting his own rings.

"I have to introduce him as my *husband*," she tells me. "The entire world has to know I'm married to a fool. And do you have any idea how much this wedding *fête* is costing me?"

She studies me with her great dark eyes, and I wish I could convince her that she doesn't have to live like this—from petty jealousy to petty jealousy. She was a calmer, happier woman in Haiti. "She'll be the mother of your niece or nephew someday. If you want to remain in Fontainebleau as the emperor's hostess," I say purposefully, since this is the new empress's job, "I would take care to make very good friends with Marie-Louise."

I can see the rebuttal forming on her lips. Then she looks across the courtyard to her brother and his wife. "She's a birthing cow. That's the only reason she's wanted. We have nothing in common to talk about."

The *cocher* opens the glass door of the carriage, and once we're inside, a thought occurs to me. "You should ask about her dog," I say with studied casualness. "Queen Caroline made her leave her spaniel in Braunau."

She sits forward. "*What?*"

"She said everything Austrian must stay."

"A *dog* is not Austrian!" Pauline exclaims, looking incredulous. As I had hoped, she is considering how she would feel if anyone tried to part her from Aubree. In a life filled with constant movement and loss, her Italian greyhound is the one constant that has never disappeared. Jewels, houses, lovers—all of these things have come and gone. Even Dermide, the son she named after a character in one of Ossian's Celtic poems, died when he was only eight years old. "What is the matter with her?" she says, almost to herself.

I keep my silence as the carriage rolls toward Château de Neuilly, but I can think of half a dozen things wrong with Queen Caroline.

"She will get that dog back," Pauline says with certainty. "I will see to it tonight."

"He is a spaniel named Sigi."

Pauline looks out the window at the setting sun, and her eyes fill with tears. "I suppose this could be a blessing," she says at last. "My brother's determined to get a child on her this year. If I've befriended Marie-Louise, he's more likely to listen to me when I tell him he must divorce her after she's given birth."

I sit back against my seat, and the shock on my face must be plain. "She's the daughter of the Austrian emperor—"

"And my brother doesn't belong with her!"

It frightens me how she can be so certain.

"Your Highness," I begin, and I hope my voice is calmer than my heart, "any thoughts he has of immortality are in the form of heirs, not new kingdoms. Your dream of living in Egypt—"

"I hear she's panting after some general back in Schönbrunn Palace," she says, cutting me off. The carriage stops before the torchlit courtyard of Château de Neuilly, and Pauline takes out a hand mirror to check her reflection. "So in a year or so—"

"She'll have a child and be sent back to Austria?" If Pauline has set her mind on her brother's divorce, she will needle and infer and pour a hundred different poisons into his ear until he believes the idea is actually his own. I watched her turn his mind against Joséphine.

The *cocher* opens the door, but I grab the handle and pull it shut. "Not yet!" I turn to Pauline, who is flawless in her ivory gown and pearls. "You are being very unattractive, Your Highness."

She has never been told this in her life. She is utterly still, and I'm reminded of statues in the Louvre: pale, smooth-bodied, and completely cold.

"What's to be gained here?" I demand. She stares out the window at the long row of servants helping the guests from their carriages. I lean forward, and we are so close that I can smell the faint scent of her soap. "What? Did you think he would make you queen?" When she doesn't respond, I add heatedly, "You're his *sister*."

"Cleopatra married her brother."

"That was two thousand years ago!"

"But it's what I want."

I search her face, to see if she's in earnest. Then she points out the window to the towering figure of Château de Neuilly. Pauline has turned it into a glittering fairyland, with small white lanterns hanging from the trees and torchlights lining every winding path.

"In five hundred years, this will still be standing. And the Egyptian artifacts I've collected inside will last even longer. A thousand, maybe two thousand years."

"I don't see what this has to do with—"

"I have to know that people will remember me. If you can just wait—" She reaches out, and this time I allow her to press her palm against my cheek. "You know how I feel about you, *mon ange*. You keep me calm. And happy."

"So why do you need other men?"

Her eyes expand; how can it be the first time I've ever challenged her this way? "Because they don't mean anything!"

"De Canouville?"

She blushes. "He's a child. A innocent child." But she is smiling wolfishly as she says it, imagining his dimpled face and earnest gaze.

"What about Napoleon?"

For a moment, she stops breathing. "I told you," she says, and her voice has an edge. "You are the one I want to grow old with. But in the meantime—" She pulls me close to her, then kisses my cheek briefly and leans back. "Let's entertain as we've never entertained before!"

She opens the carriage door, and outside half a dozen people begin calling her name.

"Your Highness!" two young women shout, then her lover de Canouville sees her, and the officer actually breaks into a run. "Pauline!" he cries, and when she turns to him, his eyes light up like a child's. "You put Venus to shame tonight."

"I should hope every night," she says, teasing him.

"We were waiting for your carriage door to open. Everyone was wondering what was happening." He looks over at me, and the suspicion is clear.

"Did you think I'd miss my own soirée? But tell me"—her voice lowers—"has my brother arrived?"

This is the moment the royal *calèche* comes bearing down the drive. Everyone stops, then Napoleon emerges with Empress Marie-Louise. Immediately Pauline is at her brother's side, both de Canouville and I forgotten.

"Welcome to Château de Neuilly," she announces, and for the first time since she has come to France, I see Marie-Louise's eyes widen. Musicians have begun playing Austrian music from somewhere inside, and the sound of women's laughter reaches us over the clink of glasses and plates.

"How did you find this music?" the empress asks. "It's old—very old. It's . . . wonderful."

I wonder how long it's been since I've heard one of my mother's songs. Years now. Napoleon gives Pauline a congratulatory smile. "Pauline could turn water into wine, if she put her mind to it. Shall we go inside?" Napoleon asks. "There is nothing like this château in all of France. My sister has exceptional taste."

As we cross the castle's threshold, I try to imagine seeing Château de Neuilly through a foreigner's eyes. Every surface that isn't marble is carved from polished mahogany. Magnificent cut-glass chandeliers cast a golden sheen across the thickly woven carpets. Books, thousands and thousands of them, line the walls of every room we pass. "Have you read all these?" she asks.

Pauline actually grins. "Almost."

"There are *thousands* of them."

"Her Highness is a great reader," de Canouville says proudly, though no one has thought to introduce him to the empress.

She searches our faces for an explanation, and it occurs to me that her blue eyes are larger than anyone's I've ever seen. But when no introduction is forthcoming, she clears her throat delicately and turns to me. "Do you have a favorite author, Monsieur Moreau?"

"Homer," I say. "And Your Majesty?"

She hesitates. "Genlis."

"The romance writer?" Pauline asks incredulously.

Napoleon frowns. "Why not?"

"Because you've said it yourself!" Pauline exclaims. "It's—"

"Very addictive," I say, before she can add something truly insulting.

Marie-Louise is shocked. "So you've read him?"

I shrug. "There are many more books in France than in Haiti. If I could, I would explore them all."

We have reached the salon, and a dozen people rush forward. All around us are calls of "Your Majesty!" At first Marie-Louise tries to greet each person separately, but there are too many, so she smiles politely and nods.

"Isn't anyone interested in me?" Napoleon demands.

No one in the salon is fool enough to believe that he might be joking. Immediately, the great press of women fluttering around the empress move toward the emperor. Marie-Louise glances at me, then turns to de Canouville.

"So you must be Camillo Borghese," she says, and there's a moment of tense silence.

"God no. This is de Canouville. Unfortunately, my husband could not attend this evening."

"Perhaps she forgot his invitation." De Canouville winks.

Marie-Louise looks from Pauline to de Canouville, as if this might be some kind of jest.

"The Prince Borghese has taken ill," I explain. "De Canouville is Her Highness's good friend."

"Her *very* good friend," de Canouville adds crassly, and Pauline rewards his obnoxiousness with a kiss.

For a moment, the empress doesn't know where to look, so she keeps her eyes on an Egyptian painting.

"From my collection," Pauline says.

De Canouville snorts. "She has entire rooms of this stuff. When the emperor conquered Egypt, he brought back every treasure he could find. Would you like to see it?"

Pauline shoots him a look, but de Canouville is oblivious, and the empress, who is desperate to escape the crowds, nods at once. "I would love to."

Pauline cuts through a group of admiring women to interrupt Napoleon. "Your wife would like a tour of Château de Neuilly."

So the five of us move from room to room, and Marie-Louise exclaims over all of Pauline's treasures. Her pleasure seems genuine. We visit the guest chamber, with its tub so large you could bathe an elephant, and Pauline's bed, so tiny it might be for a porcelain doll.

"You *sleep* here?" Marie-Louise has no idea how happy this question will make Pauline.

"Her Highness is a *petite fleur*," de Canouville answers. "A delicate bed for a delicate princess."

Napoleon lowers his brows, but de Canouville is already making his way toward the salon. "Feel this," he says, pointing to the blue velvet couches. "There's nothing finer in all of France. Our emperor himself gifted these to Pauline. And out there is the grotto." He opens a pair of double doors and inhales deeply of the fresh air. "Have you ever seen a grotto like this? Fountains, statues, flowers, *urns*."

Despite herself, the new empress laughs.

"Shall we take her to the Egyptian galleries?" de Canouville asks. He looks from face to face, but only Marie-Louise is smiling.

We pass through a hall filled with portraits of Aubree, and the empress halts. "Who did these?" she wants to know.

Napoleon is incredulous. "The *dog* paintings?"

"They're *wonderful*." Tears fill the empress's eyes, but she blinks them away and inspects one depicting Aubree in the grotto.

"Richard Cosway." Pauline's smile is genuine. "He's my favorite artist. No one captures Aubree like he does."

"They're very good." The empress steps closer, to get a better view. "Is she a greyhound?"

"Italian greyhound. It's a smaller breed. I can bring her out if—"

"We're here to see the galleries, not a zoo," Napoleon says shortly.

I've often thought he is jealous of his sister's dog.

Pauline's voice turns to ice. "The galleries are in here."

As we enter the first chamber, Marie-Louise seems overwhelmed. In a château filled with opulence, these galleries are the finest. The walls are covered in paintings taken from Cairo, and innumerable treasures fill endless polished-glass cabinets and wooden shelves. "I've never seen anything like this," the empress whispers.

I remember how astounded I was the first time I saw the hundreds of figurines lining the walls, some lapis, others alabaster. Oil lamps, combs, golden necklaces, and bejeweled boxes dizzy the senses. And then there are the sarcophagi. The empress reaches out to touch the painted face on a woman's coffin. Slowly, with an artist's hand, she traces the ancient features of the young doomed girl.

"That is from a tomb in Egypt," Napoleon says proudly. "Their temples," he adds, "were incredible. Unbelievable. Carved gods stood from this ceiling to the floor." He indicates their height, and when his wife is duly impressed, he adds meaningfully, "Had I stayed, I might have made myself pharaoh."

"You still could," Pauline replies swiftly.

A moment passes between brother and sister that makes Marie-Louise hesitate.

But not de Canouville. "And these?" he wants to know. He points to a pair of alabaster vessels on the tallest bookcase.

"Canopic jars," Pauline explains. "For storing your organs after you die."

De Canouville doesn't ask about anything else as we pass through the next two galleries.

I watch the empress marvel over numerous artifacts—some of which are encrusted with jewels or made of precious metals. I am touched to see that it is the artist's palette that fascinates Marie-Louise the most. The ancient wooden tray is still stained with ochre, malachite, and lapis. She touches each color, and I imagine she's thinking about the last hands that held this—a painter's hands, living more than two thousand years ago. Was he old? Young? How did he die? Did he have a family? Or was the artist a woman?

"Stunning," she says. "I have no words."

When we emerge from the galleries, a waiter appears offering wine. "For Your Highness?"

Pauline is the first to take a glass. "Always."

Downstairs in the salon, the Austrian musicians have stopped playing, and scantily dressed women have taken their place on a small stage. The actor Talma is among them, singing something I can't understand and holding up a heavy glass of wine. "Is it time?" he shouts when Pauline appears.

She holds up her own glass in an imaginary toast. "Why not?" She turns to Napoleon and Marie-Louise. "Just for you."

She has kept this a secret from everyone, including me, and I'm afraid she is going to do something so offensive that the emperor will never forgive her. She takes the stage, and my muscles tense. But the performance she gives is actually tender—a song from Jean-Baptiste Lully's mesmerizing *tragédie lyrique*. The moment she opens her mouth, Pauline becomes the temptress Armide, and as she sings of her unrequited love for the hero, every guest is riveted.

"I have not triumphed over the bravest of all . . ."

"There's no one like her in the world," de Canouville murmurs.

I am loath to agree with him on anything, but I have to nod.

"The entire enemy camp is vulnerable to me . . ."

"You're nothing more than a chamberlain to her," he warns

me. "Just remember that, *mon ami*. I am the man she *wishes* she married."

I feel a moment of intense hatred for this man, who thinks he knows Pauline. "Then I would be careful," I say spitefully. "The men she wishes she married have very short lives. Fournier got sent to Italy, and no one knows where the others have gone. Dead on the fronts somewhere."

I can see that I have shocked him, and I'm glad.

"And he alone, always invincible . . . prides himself on looking upon me with indifferent eyes."

We both look toward the emperor. Though he is holding Marie-Louise's arm, he is utterly fixated on Pauline's performance.

"He is of an age ready for loving, when one loves without effort . . . No, I cannot fail, without extreme vexation, to conquer a heart so proud and so great."

"Bravo!" de Canouville shouts wildly when it's over. "Bravo!" He holds out his hands to embrace her, but it's Napoleon she goes to.

"I didn't know you would be performing *Armide*," the emperor says, and his look is not brotherly.

"She's your favorite," Pauline says, and Marie-Louise's eyes narrow.

As the hours pass, I watch our second empress strolling from guest to guest on the arm of the emperor and wonder what she must make of all of this—the half-clothed women, the wild musicians, the suggestive lyrics delivered on stage from a sister to a brother. I do not know if she has yet realized that the serving bowls that guests are choosing tidbits from are modeled on Pauline's breasts. Marie-Louise appears to be taking it all in good grace, but I have seen my share of royalty, and I know what their pleasant exteriors can hide.

When everyone has gathered outside for their carriages, I find the empress standing alone. "Did Your Majesty enjoy herself this evening?"

Marie-Louise glances around her, and though she sees that Napoleon is speaking with his sister at the steps of the château, her expression is guarded. "My sister-in-law is very . . . enthusiastic," she says carefully.

"Yes," I reply, showing equal discretion. "The Bonapartes have a great zest for life."

"And festivities. I hear there's to be another event tomorrow, hosted by the minister of war. And after that, a fête thrown by the Imperial Guard."

I look over her shoulder at Napoleon, who is laughing so intimately with Pauline that anyone would think she was the new bride.

"Tell me," she adds, and her voice drops low. "When does he govern?"

"I expect it's the excitement of a new marriage." But I can't stop watching him with Pauline, brushing back her hair, touching her arm.

She follows my gaze. "You love her, don't you?"

I am so shocked by the question that I step back.

"My father taught me how to observe people," she explains. "He believes it is the first skill of any diplomat. Which is what every queen must be."

It takes several moments to regain my composure. "I met her in Haiti," I admit, though I wonder why I am telling her this. "She was . . . different then."

She nods as if she understands. "You're the perfect courtier. The rest of them can't see it. Thank you for warning me about Compiègne."

I study our tall, golden-haired empress and wonder if the emperor will ever know just how extraordinary his young bride really is. "It was a great sacrifice for Your Majesty to leave Austria behind."

"Yes," she admits quietly. "But I suspect that sacrifice is something you understand."

In seven years no one has ever said this to me. Not even Pauline.

"Do you ever wish to go home?" she asks.

I close my eyes briefly. "Not a day goes by that I don't think about it."

"But she keeps you here."

It's not a question, but a statement, and I don't deny it.

CHAPTER 13

MARIE-LOUISE

Fontainebleau Palace

"I am not like other men. The commonly accepted rules of morality and propriety do not apply to me."

—*Napoleon*

It is done. I am married, and though I know my father doesn't mean it when he writes, "I wish nothing but great joy for you and your husband," I still feel sick when I read his words.

From the writing table in my new chamber at Fontainebleau, I look down again at my father's letter and begin to weep. *Nothing but great joy for you and your husband.* There would have been joy if I had married Adam and stayed in Austria to take care of Ferdinand. But there was no joy in lying down for a man twice my age; a man who warned me when our business was over that he was "an emperor with great appetites" and that I should expect to see him daily, "maybe twice daily even."

I know I must write a reply to my father in the same dutiful tone, so when my husband's spies open the letter, nothing will reflect badly on myself or Austria. I reach for the quill and am about to dip the nib into the ink when my chamber door swings open and Napoleon appears. "Sire." I rise and hope my tears are not visible. He gives me a slow, meaningful smile, and immediately I know what he wants.

"Undress," he says, and the heat floods into my cheeks.

"Perhaps you would like—"

"I have told you what I'd like. Undress and bend over."

I gasp. "The bed?"

"Or the chair. You can choose."

My stomach clenches, and there's a fire in my blood that would take oceans to put out. I let my dressing gown slip onto the floor along with my chemise. Then I climb onto the bed and lie quietly on my back.

"I said—"

"Yes, I heard you. But I'm the empress of France, not some common whore."

He is still for a moment, trying to decide between respect and rage. Then he moves toward the bed. "Very well, my little German rose." He unbuttons his pants and climbs on top of me without getting undressed. The whole affair is over within the minute.

When he is finished, he rolls onto his back as if he has accomplished something great and stares at the ceiling. With Adam, I would lie in his arms, and he would kiss me tenderly, starting with the crown of my head and making his way toward my lips. Then I would fall asleep on his chest, listening to the beat of his heart.

"How does a woman know when she's pregnant?" he demands.

If I were pregnant, I would never have to tolerate him on top of me again. I could tell him any number of things, like intimacy might hurt the child. "She is tired, then sick, and finally, she stops bleeding every month. That's the surest sign."

He lies on his side so that he can face me, and I reach for my dressing gown. "I want to know within the hour you do," he says firmly. "Even the suspicion of pregnancy is enough."

"You will know as soon as I do," I swear.

He watches me dress, and there's something flat, even cold in his stare. The artist who painted his miniature portrait got it right. He is the only man I've ever met whose soul can't be found in the depths of his eyes. *"And what if he doesn't have one?"* I can hear Maria ask, but I push the thought from my mind.

I return to the desk, and he watches me from the bed. "Are you happy here, in Fontainebleau?"

It's a strange question to ask. He didn't care about my happiness last night, when he ordered me to wait naked for him in bed, and he certainly didn't have a thought for it this morning, but I must not insult him. "It's not Schönbrunn," I reply.

He raises his brows. "In what way?"

I hesitate. "What do you mean?"

"You said it's not Schönbrunn. I want to know how it's different."

I look up at the painted ceiling and try to think. "Schönbrunn is run like a ship," I tell him. "There are no excesses and certainly no pageantry." It has been one week since our marriage, and I am still exhausted from the "cele-brations."

"Nothing separates a commoner from a king except a few glittering processions and a crown," he challenges. "Our dear uncle Louis discovered that."

Uncle Louis. It takes me a moment to realize that he is speaking of *my* uncle, the husband of Marie-Antoinette. "I don't believe that. Monarchy is about serving one's kingdom," I say carefully, "not the other way around. Processions are expensive, and a good king is always watching his treasury."

"Is that what your father says?"

I turn in my chair to face him. "That is what *I* say. I was to be regent for my brother when he took the crown. Ferdinand has many . . . health problems," I add, being generous.

Napoleon is very still. Surely he's heard of Ferdinand. All of Europe knows. It isn't some secret. "And are these health problems common in your family?"

I have heard people say that my siblings' illness is the product of too much intermarriage. And it is true that my mother was my father's double first cousin. But it has always been this way for the Hapsburgs, and there has never been such illness before. "I suppose my mother was unlucky," I tell him. "Two children born sickly." *If this bothers you, perhaps you should have considered it before bringing me to France.* "My sister Maria-Carolina is epileptic and mute."

Napoleon struggles to a sitting position. He is not a young man, and his stomach has grown large. "Well, I am lucky," he says flatly, and there is not the slightest hint of irony in his voice. "The entire world will bow at my son's feet. He'll be the product of the greatest general since Alexander. Nothing will stop him."

"And if it's a girl?"

"Then she'll be the Princess of Venice. But there'll be sons," he says with utter certainty. "There might be a son cooking in there even now."

I press my lips together to stop them from curling.

"So will Metternich be regent when your father is gone?"

The question startles me. "I—I don't know." I can't imagine a time when my father isn't here. He's so young and healthy. But then so was my mother. "I suppose." Then I ask the question I've been wanting to ask since December. "He is the reason you took me for a bride, isn't he?"

The question hangs in the air for a moment. "He pushed, as every ambassador pushed," he says thinly, and now I see what Metternich has done. I wish there had been a way to warn my father of Metternich's treachery.

"But Prince Metternich wanted it more than anyone else," I press.

"Tell me about your father," he says, avoiding my question. "How does he run his kingdom?"

"Carefully," I reply. But I'm determined to bring up Metternich again. I will simply have to wait for a better moment. "His accounts are—were—always balanced." *And then you came and demanded a fortune from our defeated country.* "He meets with his subjects twice a week, without fail. There is nothing more important to him."

Napoleon studies me. "You understand what it is to run

an empire then. It is never-ending work, endless expectations, ceremonies, pageantries, *war*." Then something in his dark eyes softens. "If you behave yourself here in Fontainebleau, nothing will ever be denied to you."

Immediately, I think of Sigi.

"Pauline told me you wish to have your dog," he says.

I am shocked: both that he has read my mind and that Pauline would intercede for me. "That—that would be wonderful."

"Consider it done." He stands and buttons his pants. "I'll expect you to be ready tomorrow by six."

"For what?" I thought the celebrations were over.

"Our honeymoon. We are visiting the Low Countries," he informs me. "Have your ladies pack warm clothes and walking shoes." Then he shuts the door behind him, and this is all I am told. But what does it matter? Sigi is coming! Just as I'm about to fling myself triumphantly onto the bed, there's a knock at my door. It's Hortense.

"I am here to help Your Majesty pack," she says. I stand aside so that she can come in. She is dressed in a white gown with a shockingly deep *décolleté*. My dressing robe is more suitable for public attire. But her blue-gray eyes are innocent, and her chestnut curls are arranged around her head like a halo. It's the first time we've been alone together, and I'm not sure what to say to the queen of Holland. "Then you know about the Low Countries?" I ask.

"Everyone knows about it, Your Majesty. Half the court is going. We're to leave tomorrow by six." She adds quietly, "He never travels alone."

We sit across from each other at my writing table. I am eight years her junior, yet I was brought to France to take her mother's place and give the emperor the child her mother couldn't. By right she should hate me, yet I search her face and she is perfectly at ease, as if nothing on earth could be so normal as sitting with the woman who took your mother's crown.

"You'd think it would be awkward between the two of us," she begins.

I shift uneasily on the padded chair. This is exactly what I'm thinking and the second time my mind has been guessed.

"I hope you know I have never borne you any ill will. What happened to my mother was her own doing." When she sees my shock, she hurries to explain. "My mother knew she couldn't have more children when she married Napoleon. Things—terrible things—happened to her when she was imprisoned during the Revolution."

"I'm sorry," I whisper. "I didn't realize."

"Thousands of innocent people suffered your great-aunt's fate, including my father."

"I had no idea."

She nods. "She married him anyway, and when he crowned himself emperor, she swore to him that there would be a child."

"And when there wasn't?"

"She asked to have mine."

I sit back. "She took your *son*?"

Hortense shrugs, as if it really weren't such a great deal.

"She wanted to. But I insisted he be raised with me in Holland. It was a great fight between us," she admits.

"But you won."

"Because the emperor agreed with me. She was desperate. You have to understand, my mother loves Napoleon . . . tremendously."

We watch each other in the morning light. What type of woman is Joséphine? Is she conniving, or just a thoughtless fool willing to sacrifice her own daughter's happiness for a husband who is a tyrant? A servant comes to the door with tea, and I wait until the woman pours it before speaking. "Did you want to marry Louis?" I ask. I try to imagine having Louis Bonaparte for a husband. Even in Austria they've heard of his uncontrollable outbursts at court, and I'm relieved that he rarely comes to France.

Hortense cradles the teacup between her hands and stares at the table. Perhaps I've been too forward. After all, she owes nothing to me. I'm about to apologize when she replies, "No. I wanted nothing to do with Louis. But that's no great secret at this court, Your Majesty." She looks up from the table, and her eyes are haunted. "It was my mother who wanted the marriage. For an heir—that's what they say." She covers her eyes with her hand for a moment, and I realize she is thinking of her eldest son, who died from croup at four years old. "My mother isn't a bad woman," she swears. "You don't realize how it is in this palace. I mean—you will. I—I shouldn't be telling you these things. Let me start packing." She stands abruptly, but I reach out to take her hand.

"*Please.* I want to hear it. If I'm to be empress, I should know the way it is in France."

She takes her seat, and I press the teacup back into her hand. "It's treason, what I've said against my husband," she admits. "But he's not to be king for much longer. My brother is taking the crown from him. Louis refused to raise an army for an invasion of Russia. He said he wouldn't send innocent men 'to a fool's war.'"

So there is one country willing to stand up to him. "Where will he go?"

"Your father is offering to give him shelter." She frowns. "Your Highness didn't know?"

Shame warms my cheeks. "Napoleon has yet to speak of politics with me." I look into my teacup. "I don't hear from my father very often," I admit.

Hortense's voice is slow and suspicious. "Because he doesn't write, or because you don't receive his letters?"

Hortense gives me a long look, and I am enraged.

"I've had two letters since I arrived," I tell her. "*Two!* I have no idea how my brother Ferdinand is faring. And Maria—" Hortense reaches out to touch my hand, and I realize my cheeks are wet. "Should I confront him?" I ask her, and I don't like the hopeless sound in my voice.

"My mother tried. It never did her any good. But then her letters were often to men Napoleon suspected her of having an affair with."

"Was she?"

Hortense appears deeply conflicted. "If I am fair to Napoleon, I would say he was correct in his suspicions. Still, he loved her. As much as it's possible for him to love," she corrects herself. "He wrote her such letters—"

"Do you have them?"

She glances at me warily. "Twenty—at least."

"I would like to see them, to know if this man has ever loved anyone but himself."

She hesitates. "They are love letters, Your Majesty. Some of them are very . . . detailed."

"Did your mother ever read them to her suite?"

"All the time. There's nothing she kept private."

This is what I wanted to know.

"Does Your Highness truly want—"

I nod, and she rises. "Ten minutes," she promises. "They're locked away."

I call for more tea while Hortense is gone, and when she returns, she is holding a small leather box. She places it in front of me, and I run my hands over the carving of Venus.

"My mother asked me to keep it for her. She wanted to make sure a few letters survived in case anything happened to hers."

I open the lid and stare at the envelopes bundled inside. I glance up to be sure that Hortense still approves, and she nods for me to continue. "The twenty-ninth of December, 1795," I read aloud. That was fifteen years ago, before Egypt, or Austria, or the throne of France.

I awake all filled with you. Your image and the intoxicating pleasures of last night, allow my senses no rest. Sweet and matchless Joséphine, how strangely you work upon my heart.

Are you angry with me? Are you unhappy? Are you upset? My soul is broken with grief and my love for you forbids repose. But how can I rest any more, when I yield to the feeling that masters my inmost self, when I quaff from your lips and from your heart a scorching flame? Yes! One night has taught me how far your portrait falls short of yourself!

You start at midday: in three hours I shall see you again. Till then, a thousand kisses, mio dolce amor! *but give me none back for they set my blood on fire.*

The intoxicating pleasures of last night allow my senses no rest. I try to imagine Adam writing these things to me . . . to put them in a letter for any prying eyes to see. "Was she his first lover?"

"I believe so."

I take out another letter and read, this time to myself.

Your letters are the joy of my days, and my days of happiness are not many. Junot is bringing twenty-two flags to Paris. You must come back with him, you understand?—hopeless sorrow, inconsolable misery, sadness without end, if I am so unhappy as to see him return alone. Adorable friend, he will see you, he will breathe in your temple; perhaps you will even grant him the unique and perfect favor of kissing your cheek, and I shall be alone and far, far away. But you are coming, aren't you? You are going to be here beside me, in my arms, on my breast, on my mouth? Take wing and come, come!

A kiss on your heart, and one much lower down, much lower!

I am shocked. "Are they all like this?"

Hortense looks terribly embarrassed. "Not all. But . . . many."

"He was passionate," I point out.

"He was twenty-seven then, Your Highness, not forty."

"And now he's turned his passions elsewhere."

"Yes. To war."

"Are you not upset that your husband will lose his crown?" In the space of a single day, she'll descend from queen of Holland to a princess of France.

"I'm not the queen of Holland in any true sense," she replies. "I don't speak their language, I don't know their customs. I'm the granddaughter of a man who ran a sugar plantation. I'm not like you."

"But you were born an aristocrat," I remind her.

"No. My father liked to pretend, which is why he went to the guillotine. He was born in Martinique, the same as my mother. He was less royal than Pauline's dog."

I laugh out loud, in spite of myself. Then she covers her mouth with her hands, and we both laugh together. I like Hortense.

"Speaking of which, I hear they're bringing your *chien* from Vienna."

I stare at her. How can she possibly know this? "He *just* told me," I say, amazed.

She gives me a private smile. "Nothing is secret at this court, Your Majesty. When you discover that you're pregnant, half of France will know before the day is out."

"Is that how it was for you?"

"Yes." She takes a long sip of her tea, and an awkward

silence fills the chamber. "Even two years later it's unbearable to think about," she whispers.

My mother buried three of her children, and she told me that the loss never disappears, only the intensity of the pain you feel about it. I reach out to cover Hortense's hand with mine. "I'm sorry," I say, and I wonder if I will have just as many sorrows in seven years' time.

She wipes her eyes quickly. "The emperor disapproves of emotions. That's how men are."

I think of my father, who was sick with grief when my mother died, and of Adam, who was beside himself when Ferdinand broke his arm on a horse that he gave him, and I know this isn't true. But I don't contradict her. "And your other sons?"

"In Holland," she replies, "with their father."

She is too distressed for me to ask how this came about. So instead I say firmly, "We should do something cheerful."

"Would you like to stroll through Fontainebleau before we pack?" she offers.

I smile. "Why not?"

So we wander the halls of the château together, and the courtiers' eyes go wide when they see us: the daughter of Joséphine and the nineteen-year-old second empress of France.

"Do you think they're staring?" I whisper.

She giggles. "I can guarantee it, Your Majesty."

We stop in each major room, and Hortense is able to recall the history of every gilded chamber. There's the salon Pauline seduced her latest lover in, and Louis XIV's antechamber, where his mistress hid behind the tapestries as the queen paid an unexpected visit.

"Is there anyone at this court who has actually bedded their spouse?" I ask.

Hortense leans against a pillar and thinks. "The Gauthiers," she says earnestly. "They met when they were children and are still in love."

I stare at her, and when she realizes how her answer appears, she blushes. "Well, it's true," she replies.

"But what about loyalty for the good of your children?"

She looks at me curiously and obviously wants to speak.

"Say it," I urge her, since we are alone.

"Will you remain loyal to Napoleon?" she asks.

I think of Adam, and my eyes begin to burn. But why is she asking me this? I search her face, and suddenly she inhales. "I would never spy for him. *Never.*" When I don't say anything, Hortense continues.

"I promise you, Your Majesty, it was an innocent question. When Napoleon first told me about your arrival, I wished to be your Mistress of the Robes as much as you wished for a crippling disease."

"So not at all." We look at each other for a moment, and I believe her.

"You see, we're in similar situations," she says quietly. "We're both living at the whim of the emperor."

We continue through the richly paneled ballroom, and I think about her question. *What if Adam were here? What if I could see his face and touch his skin? Would I be loyal to my marriage?* Yes. However great the pain, I would have to turn him away. This is what it is to be a queen. My great-aunt married at fifteen years old. Her husband was a dauphin who had no interest in anything but locks—fixing them, forging them, building them. But when she met Axel von Fersen, the great love of her life, she did not begin an affair. Instead, she pined for him from afar. This was her duty to France.

I look at the paintings of the goddess Diana on the walls and wish that I, too, were mythical. Or a work of art, with no family, or loyalty, or duty to one's kingdom. I am about to ask Hortense why this ballroom is filled with images of this goddess when a sudden noise makes us both turn.

"Monsieur Moreau," I say, and Pauline's chamberlain makes a sweeping bow from the doorway.

"Your Majesties." He crosses the room and stands before us. He truly is an extraordinary-looking man, with skin of bronze and eyes of the deepest green. "The emperor wishes to see the queen of Holland in his library."

Hortense glances at me, then looks to Paul. "Now?"

"As soon as possible, Your Highness."

"I won't be long," she promises me. She hurries across the ballroom, and Paul remains, standing beneath an image of Diana.

"Do you know who had all of these painted?" I ask.

"François I, in honor of his mistress Diane de Poitiers, Your Majesty. An entire ballroom dedicated to his mistress." He turns up his palms. "*Les français.*"

We begin to walk the length of the room and stop before one of the high, arched windows that look out over the landscaped Gardens of Diana. Only twenty years ago Marie-Antoinette walked these paths. I imagine my great-aunt in her flowing chemise, and I wonder if she can see me now, dressed in a similar muslin gown with ribbons around my waist and silk shoes on my feet. An entire revolution left half a million people dead, and for what? This ballroom is just as lavish, this court just as full of greed and excess. Nothing has changed except the name of France's ruler, and now, instead of an L on the throne, there is a golden N.

"Do you believe in ghosts?" I ask quietly.

"My Taíno ancestors believed in Mabuya, the presence of spirits in the human world. But I've never seen one. I find it hard to believe in something I've never seen. And Your Majesty?"

"It's not Catholic to believe in ghosts," I say.

"But has Your Majesty ever seen one?" Paul asks.

I look up at him. He's one of the few men at this court who are taller than me. "I don't know."

"I suspect this palace would be filled with ghosts, if they exist."

I think about my poor, doomed aunt all throughout my packing, and even when we are boarding the coaches in front of the steps of Fontainebleau, I imagine that I can see her face in the mist.

"Six-thirty," Napoleon is raging. "I said six, and right now it's six-thirty!"

"It couldn't be helped," Hortense soothes him. She settles

in beside me, across from Napoleon and Méneval. "We all thought Metternich and Queen Caroline would come. But if Caroline is pregnant—"

He turns in my direction and fixes me with his steel-gray eyes. But he doesn't say anything, and I assume I'm supposed to look as desperate for a child as Joséphine was. When I arrange my features into a look of perfect blankness, his neck turns red. "Drive!" he shouts so that the coachman can hear him, and the horses pass through the gates of Fontainebleau at a gallop.

"I wish to dictate," Napoleon announces immediately.

"Certainly, Your Majesty." Méneval searches for his bag. He takes out a quill and ink, then produces a wooden writing board with paper. And for the next three hours, we are treated to a litany of things the emperor wishes to accomplish on our honeymoon. There will be visits to wells and granaries. Forts and monasteries are also on the list. Then tomorrow, at precisely four in the morning, we'll be touring St. Quentin's cotton mill. Four in the morning.

"And that is all," Napoleon says at nine-thirty.

"Have we scheduled breakfast in all of this?" I ask.

Hortense gives me a warning look, and Méneval quickly glances away.

"We do not eat breakfast while traveling."

I frown. "Does the same apply to lunch?"

"A woman should not have to eat!" Napoleon thunders. "Look at you! You're not exactly starving."

Hortense gasps, and Méneval looks as if he might faint. We ride through the morning in total silence, and when our procession of carriages stops for lunch, Napoleon shouts to the driver, "Keep going!"

But the young man is sure he's heard wrong. It's been five and a half hours since we've left Fontainebleau, and none of the courtiers or servants have eaten. "Your Majesty?"

Napoleon opens the door and climbs the steps to the driver's seat. "What is he doing?" I exclaim, and Hortense covers her mouth in shock. He's taken the poor boy's whip and is thrashing him with it.

"Stop!" I scream from the carriage. "Please, stop!"

A half-dozen men rush to see the commotion. "Your Majesty!" someone shouts, and the boy jumps from the carriage and begins to run.

"I don't want to see you again!" Napoleon cries after the boy's fleeing figure. "Do you understand?" He throws down the whip and descends the steps, eager for a fight.

A group of horrified courtiers, braving the weather, have made a half-circle around our carriage, and now everyone steps back as the emperor says, "The Duchesse de Montebello."

The old woman curtsies respectfully.

"I believe I saw you in that dress last week. I hope you plan to change into something with taste when we reach St. Quentin."

She lowers her gaze. "Yes, Your Majesty."

"Where is the Duc de Bassano?"

The courtiers look around, then a voice rises from the back of the growing crowd, and the people part to let the *duc* through. He's a tall man, with broad shoulders and a tanned soldier's complexion. He wears a green and gold cockade in support of the Bonapartes, and the ribbon is fastened to his hat.

"Exchange places with Méneval," Napoleon instructs. "We have plans to discuss from here to St. Quentin."

"Will we be stopping for food?" the *duc* asks bravely. "The men in my carriage are near dead with hunger."

There are several seconds of uncertainty: no one is certain how Napoleon will react. Then the emperor shrugs. "We'll stop in the next town."

As the courtiers return to their carriages, I search for the young man who was driving our coach, but he's disappeared. A replacement has been found and is making his way toward us. I was warned about Napoleon's temper, but still I am shaken, now that I have seen it. We take our seats, and as the carriage rolls away, Napoleon opens his window, letting in the bitter wind and rain. No one says anything.

That evening, as the carriages rattle through the streets of St. Quentin, Napoleon whistles a happy tune. "Here we are!" he announces when our long procession passes through the gates of a nobleman's *maison*. As we descend from the coaches, he begins to sing, *"Mort et convoi de l'invincible Malbrough."*

> *Marlbrook the Prince of Commanders*
> *Is gone to war in Flanders, His fame is*
> *Like Alexander's . . .*

"Dinner at seven o'clock," he says, as if he's never been in anything but a merry mood.

In the privacy of our adjoining chambers, he is similarly cheerful. "A chessboard," he exclaims when he enters my room, though I notice that he doesn't offer me a game. He gives me a slow, meaningful smile and says, "Undress."

CHAPTER 14

PAULINE BORGHESE

Aix-la-Chapelle
May 1810

"He's *bored*? His bride isn't entertaining enough for him? I can't believe it!" Paul puts down my brother's letter, and I continue to feign shock. "But how could this be? She's a Hapsburg princess. The blood of a thousand generations flows in her veins. Surely that's enough for the emperor of France."

"Shall I read you the rest now?" Paul asks dryly.

"Continue." I lie back against my wide, silk cushions and wonder that more wealthy continentals don't bring their own furnishings to these spas. What's the point in coming to take the waters of Grannus if you're going to recline on stone benches and wooden chairs?

Paul glances at two blond women floating in the thermal baths, and when they both stare back, I feel a sudden irritation. I'm here to find a cure for crippling pain, and he can't keep his eyes on the letter.

Then he begins:

I miss speaking with you, Paoletta. There is no other here with whom I can have an intelligent discussion about Arrian's account of Alexander the Great's campaigns, and their obvious implications to this empire.

The countryside becomes more tedious every day, and the farther we roam from Paris, the more eager I am to return. There's not a roadside inn anywhere in France this empress would refuse to eat in. If we could visit them all, she would consider it a successful journey.

Write to me. I don't care that you're taking the waters of Grannus. It's no excuse for silence.

—Napoleon

Paul returns the letter to me and picks up Goethe's *The Sorrows of Young Werther*. But before he can begin, I see the muscles along his jaw tighten, and follow his gaze. Captain de Canouville is striding toward us in his swimming costume, and *my God*. He smiles widely, and every woman in Aix-la-Chapelle is watching him. But I'm the one he settles down next to.

"Steam, water, the baking heat—how is it that none of this affects Your Highness? I swear, there is no vision on earth so beautiful as you." He kisses my lips, and I badly want to pull him on top of me. It's such a shame they allow children into these baths.

Paul fans himself with his book. It *is* hotter than Egypt in here. "Would Your Highness like to take a break for lunch?" he asks. "You've had nothing but soup for three days."

Because I've been shaking and vomiting. Last night I did

not fall to sleep until four in the morning. "Oh, who can eat food in this place?" I say lightly. "Do you think I'm a German, heartily eating my way through the Low Countries?" He frowns, but I turn to de Canouville. "I've had a letter," I explain. "My brother is bored. Apparently *the womb* does nothing but eat."

"The entire world at his feet, and he chooses an Austrian. Where are they?" he asks.

"Breda," Paul says.

"*Breda?*"

This is where Charles II lived in exile. It's a godforsaken place.

"And he wanted us to join him," I marvel. "Caroline, of course, found a way out of it. Pregnant," I scoff.

Paul looks at me curiously, but it's de Canouville who says, "She isn't pregnant?"

"I should hope not. She already looks like a sow."

"She *lied* to the emperor?" Paul asks.

"He isn't God," de Canouville sneers.

"That's treason," Paul warns darkly.

"And what? Her Highness is going to turn me in?"

Both men look to me, and I wish I had never brought the subject up. "Yes, my sister lied. Yes, it's all treason." I lean back against the pillows, and the cramping in my stomach is suddenly intense. "Why don't we take a walk?"

Immediately de Canouville sits up.

But Paul hesitates. "Your Highness, we've been here for three weeks, and you haven't made it farther than these baths. Do you think—"

"I'm fine," I say shortly.

"You're wasting away," he persists. He thinks these spas aren't good for my health. "How many more days can we sit here like this?"

"As many as it takes to recover," I answer.

We don't leave Aix-la-Chapelle for another two months.

"I know your brother is angry, but *this*?" De Canouville paces my suite, back and forth, until it makes me sick to look at him. "He can't be serious."

Napoleon has removed our brother Louis from the throne of Holland for disobedience, and if I don't return to Fontainebleau at once, he has promised to see to it that I will lose my title as the Princess Borghese.

"He won't do it," de Canouville swears. "He's back from his honeymoon and bored with life. It's a bluff."

"And how do you know?" I stand at my window and look out over the gold and turquoise baths. I know he misses me and needs me, and now he's proven it. "Was it a bluff when only eleven of the thirty cardinals appeared for his wedding and he swore to humiliate them in front of Rome?"

De Canouville loses some of his color. It was a slight no ruler could bear. Nineteen empty seats at the most important wedding in Europe. So the next week Napoleon summoned them all to the Tuileries, where he kept them waiting for more than two hours. When he finally arrived, it was to tell them that he didn't have time to speak and that their carriages could be found outside. But as the cardinals reached the open courtyard, their horses were gone.

An innocent accident, of course. A foolish groomsman's mistake. By the time the cardinals were able to leave, it was seven at night.

He's grown tired of disobedience.

"This time my brother isn't bluffing," I say.

CHAPTER 15

PAUL MOREAU

Aix-la-Chapelle

"Just make a hole in the ceiling above my bath and have your servants pour the milk through when I am ready. It's a slight inconvenience to you, I know, but think of the consequences to my health."

— Pauline to her brother-in-law, Jean-Louis Leclerc

The servants are in a mad frenzy of packing, gathering silk dressing gowns by the handful and shoving them into any available trunk. Embroidered shawls, muslin gowns, gauze dresses—all must be ready by this afternoon.

"The shoes," de Canouville announces, as he watches the commotion from the door of Pauline's chamber. "I count at least four pairs of slippers by the chaise."

Pauline comes from behind and wraps her arms around his chest. "They couldn't be any lazier, could they?"

"They've been working since six this morning," I say shortly.

"And what exactly are *you* doing?" de Canouville demands. He turns to face Pauline. "I will never understand why your chamberlain must be here every morning. Let alone why he's allowed a room next to your suite. We ought to be more judicious in who we allow into our circle, Pauline."

All the servants stop packing. They look from me to de Canouville.

"Paul is a friend," she warns. "And you will treat him as such."

I meet Pauline's gaze, and de Canouville catches her wink at me. *That's right. I am more than a replaceable bedroom amusement.* "Paul, would you see to it that all of this is taken care of?" she asks.

"Certainly, Your Highness."

I lift a trunk of books and step around de Canouville, who is blocking the door. His face is comically distraught, and I press my lips together to keep myself from laughing.

I carry the trunk outside, where the sun is beating down on the whitewashed courtyard and a dozen men are tying boxes onto coaches. If I *were* Pauline's lover, I wouldn't be so interested in who she's associating with. I'd be much more curious about the twelve carriages she needs for a trip to Aix-la-Chapelle, and where the money will continue to come from for such things. Someday Camillo Borghese will find a woman who loves him, and he'll look to petition the pope for a divorce. He won't care that Pauline is the emperor's sister, and if the pope still feels the same way as he does now about Napoleon, she will lose everything. The Borghese jewels, the Italian villas, her apartments in the Palazzo Borghese, and the title of *Principessa* will no longer be hers.

As I secure the trunk of books to the back of the carriage,

a shadow looms behind me. I turn, and the captain is standing too close to me, his thumb resting casually on the butt of his pistol. Two women stop to look in our direction, and the head groomsman watches us from the steps of the villa. He'll vouch for me if anything happens. I turn back to the carriage, and de Canouville asks, "What do you think you are to her, *mulâtre*?"

I clench my fists into a ball.

"Why did she take you from Saint-Domingue?" de Canouville hisses. His mustache is slick with sweat, and the heat of Aix-la-Chapelle does not agree with his coloring. He waits for me to answer, and the longer I'm silent, the redder he gets.

"No one *took* me from anywhere, captain."

"I know what you are! Your father was a Frenchman who liked to bed African whores, and you—"

Before he can draw his pistol, I have pinned his arms behind his back and pressed his face against the carriage. "I am Her Highness's chamberlain, and that is *all*. But if something should happen to me, if I should have an unfortunate accident on my horse or be shot while walking down the road, I can promise you this. The princess will not rest. She will find who did it, and there will be no mercy, not even if that man is you. If you'd like to take that chance—" I stand back. "Then go ahead and do it."

Immediately, de Canouville reaches for his pistol. The women in the courtyard gasp, and I see the head groomsmen hurry inside. De Canouville looks around, first at the faces of the horrified servants, then finally at Pauline, who's arrived on the shady steps of the villa. He lowers his gun, and his body is shaking. "I want you out of France."

"I want many things, captain, but they don't all come to pass."

"What's happening?" Pauline cries, running toward us. "What is this?" She looks at the two of us, and I realize I have never seen real fear on her face until now.

"A little misunderstanding." De Canouville replaces the gun in its holster. "I thought he was stealing."

"*Paul?*" She covers her chest with her hand and looks to me. "Are you all right?"

"Perfectly fine, Your Highness."

"It was an innocent mistake," de Canouville says, uneasily. "Anyone might have made it. Right?" He looks around him, but the faces of the servants are purposefully blank.

Pauline studies him for a moment. "Paul, I'd like to speak with you inside."

As I pass de Canouville, I refuse to give him the satisfaction of a look. Let him believe what he wants about this conversation. I follow Pauline through the painted halls to her chamber. No room in the town of Aix-la-Chapelle can possibly be more lavish than this, with its soft Persian carpets and great curtained bed. I stand before her as she takes a seat on the divan. When I don't say anything, she buries her head in her trembling hands.

"Your Highness—"

"Don't try to comfort me! You know how sick I've been these last three months."

It's true. She has made herself sick with worry and jealousy.

"I *saw* you fighting."

"He's . . . de Canouville is not an honorable man. He is a man possessed. He can't bear the thought of anyone else being with you"

She lowers her hands. "*What?*"

"I was almost killed today," I say slowly, "by a man who is willing to murder for your love. Your *exclusive* love. You may find that flattering, but I find it dangerous. And if you aren't careful, someone will end up dead."

The ride back to Fontainebleau is tense. I'm sharing the coach with de Canouville and Pauline, but she is punishing him with silence, and I have little to say. I watch her in the carriage, her black hair swept off her pale, thin face by a pearl and gemstone band, and I try to remember the girl in Saint-Domingue, who wore flowers instead of diamonds.

"Will someone please cover that?" she complains, indicating the window near de Canouville, which is letting in the full afternoon light.

He hurries to draw the curtain, then looks in her direction for approval. "Are you thirsty?" he asks, but she doesn't answer. "Would you like something to drink?"

"You know what I would like? A man who can protect me," she says heatedly. "Not someone who threatens the people I love."

De Canouville looks at me in panic, and for the briefest of moments, I feel pity. He will never hold on to her. She will slip from his grasp, just as she slipped from the countless others who have gone before him. Talma, and Gréoux, and Blangini, and Forbin. She'll grow restless and start spending time away. It's true, she has been with de Canouville longer than some, but eventually she'll grow tired of him.

And someday, if I am honest with myself, she'll grow tired of me, too.

But loving this woman is my weakness. When she goes to sleep in her small pink bed, drawing up the lace covers and calling for Aubree, she's impossible to resist. I've listened to her cry out against nameless phantoms in the middle of the night, those that come to her when she's dreaming: the men who robbed her of her innocence in Corsica, masters who abused their positions in Marseilles. I've watched her weep into her pillow until the silk is damp with tears, then suddenly wake and ask me why her pillows are all wet. She is damaged and beautiful, vulnerable and fearsome, and I can understand de Canouville's desperation to save her. But what he doesn't know is that only one man has ever held her attention.

"I am deeply sorry, Your Highness. I apologize not only to you," he says cleverly, "but to your chamberlain, Monsieur Moreau, as well." He does an admirable job of looking earnest, yet when he raises his brows in supplication, Pauline looks away.

For the next two hours, the only sounds in the carriage are the horses' hooves striking against the road. When we stop for lunch, de Canouville looks weary enough to cry. He leans against the wall of the roadside inn, and even the tempting smell of roasted lamb isn't enough to lure him inside. As I approach the door, he reaches out his hand to hold me back. Only this time there is no menace in his eyes.

"What does she want?" he asks me.

I look through the open door at the slight figure of Pauline, and before it swings shut, I think to myself, *Something she'll never have*. "Napoleon. So never speak against him. They are very . . . close."

"What are you saying?" He narrows his eyes. "You want me to believe she's infatuated with her brother? That may be what they do in Saint-Domingue—"

"It's your life, captain. Gamble it away however you see fit." I open the door, and the scents of roasted meat and wine make me ravenous.

The princess is sitting at a long mahogany table surrounded by ladies. When she sees that I am alone, she frowns. "Where's de Canouville? He isn't going to eat?"

The well-dressed courtiers look up at me. I tell them the truth. "He is pouting."

Several women giggle, but Pauline looks toward the door. "It's three hours to Fontainebleau!" She rises, and the women stare open-mouthed as she goes to find him.

"She's never done that," I hear one of them whisper. Then another announces, "She likes this one."

CHAPTER 16

MARIE-LOUISE

Fontainebleau Palace
July 1810

No woman in France has ever been happier to put her honeymoon behind her. I look up at the pale summer's sky and want to weep with gratitude. The birds, the flowers, the freshly trimmed hedges around Fontainebleau's lake . . . I link arms with Hortense, and the two of us breathe deeply of the lilacs and geraniums. Two months—*two*—traveling through an unending parade of forts and mills.

"You must be excited to see you-know-who," she says.

It's all I've thought about since returning. I've picked out which paths we'll walk, and the milliner has fashioned him a collar that says *Le Chien de l'Impératrice* in gold.

"Not Sigi." Hortense laughs. "The general."

"Who?"

Hortense lowers her brows. In the bright afternoon light, her dark hair looks auburn, and though she isn't a great beauty, she is fetching in her white muslin gown and lace parasol. "Your Majesty," she begins, "don't tell me you haven't heard? Your father is sending Adam von Neipperg to Fontainebleau to deliver Sigi. You will have a visitor from home!"

I stop walking immediately and glance around us. The Grand Parterre is filled with courtiers, strolling near the river or lounging on its banks. "How do you know this?"

"Everyone knows. Caroline told me this morning." Hortense watches me carefully. Then a sudden understanding begins to dawn. "Was he—"

"A good friend," I say swiftly. "That is all."

We continue walking, and the men tip their hats to us as we pass. *Did Maria arrange for him to come? Or my father?* Suddenly I feel hot, though I'm dressed in the lightest possible gown with nothing at all covering my arms. Adam is coming with Sigi. *My* Adam is coming with Sigi!

"Your Majesty, are you feeling well? Your color is—" She studies me intently, then her voice grows serious. "If he is something more to you than a friend, Your Majesty, do not go to meet him. The emperor will know."

"Let's walk over there," I suggest. Hortense follows me into a thicket of overgrown trees, away from prying eyes, and we sit together on the grass. "How would he know?" I ask quietly.

She leans forward. "They say he can anticipate his opponent's move on the battlefield from hundreds of miles away. There are people at this court who believe he can read minds."

"Do you believe that?" She has lived with him for fifteen years. Only his siblings know him better.

"No. I believe my husband when he says that Napoleon is

a military genius. But Louis also says educated guesses brought his brother to the throne of France. He has *educated luck.* He deduces things by watching very carefully."

"So if he saw me with Adam—"

"He will know. By the flush of your cheeks, or the motions of your hands—by any number of things you will not be able to control."

"Then he must not see us."

Hortense covers her mouth in horror. "Your Majesty, you don't understand what he can do. My mother—he divorced her without warning. For fourteen years she'd supported him faithfully, then one day . . ." She turns up her palms. "He had her painted out of Jacques-Louis David's *Distribution des Aigles,* and her monogram was erased throughout the Tuileries Palace. He gifted her with Malmaison, her château twelve kilometers away from Paris. Then, as soon as you arrived, he sent her farther away." Hortense shakes her head. "When he makes up his mind against someone . . ."

"Where has she gone?"

Hortense's eyes fill with tears. "Did you know that Prince Frederick Louis of Mecklenburg-Strelitz asked for her hand in marriage, and she turned him down for fear of having to leave France? She has been writing Napoleon letters, begging to return, but they're all sent back, unanswered."

"I had no idea," I whisper.

"When he first sent her away," she admits, "he told her it was on your request."

"*Never!*"

"I know. But he swore that you were jealous, that you had

heard of her beauty, and that you were afraid your new husband would be seduced by her charms."

First punishing her for not having a child, now punishing her for the thing she prizes most: her beauty. I think on the strangeness of our friendship: the daughter of France's first empress and the emperor's second wife. "Thank you for telling me this," I say quietly. "I'm so sorry."

She dries her eyes with the edge of her shawl. "If it wasn't you, it would have been someone else, and she would have been exiled all the same."

I look at her in the heat of the afternoon, with her thick curls hanging in perfect clusters on either side of her face, and I think that if she is ever painted, it should be like this. In a garden, surrounded by white roses and bright myrtle. It doesn't seem fair that she's known so little happiness in her life. I cover her hand with mine and promise, "It will get better."

"That's what the Comte de Flahaut tells me," she whispers.

I meet Hortense's eyes and realize what she's saying. Only four months ago this would have been unthinkable. But at this court, nothing is shocking to me anymore. "What about your husband?"

"As long as we're discreet . . ."

"And the courtiers keep their silence?"

"Everyone has secrets here," she says gravely. "It's in no one's interest to tell tales."

I think of Adam coming all the way from Vienna, and though my heart is filled to bursting, I know he is lost to me. I will never be able to carry on an affair. I am the empress of France. And whether or not I love my husband has no bearing on my conduct. A queen must be her country's moral compass, always pointing north, always steady.

But as I look at Hortense, for the first time in my life, I know what it is to be deeply, truly envious. "It never troubles you," I ask earnestly, "that you are married to Bonaparte and in bed with Flahaut?"

Hortense's cheeks burn scarlet. "Yes. But I love him, so what else is there?" She glances away. "And he is so kind to me. He loves my children." Her eyes light up. "They're like sons to him."

How will Adam treat the children I have with Napoleon? Will he be tender to them? Resentful? Or perhaps he'll never wish to see me again. It would be the sensible thing to command his heart to do . . .

"He's tall, even taller than you," she explains. "He has the most wonderfully dark eyes. He writes poetry and plays the pianoforte. He rarely comes to court, but he was at Château de Neuilly for Pauline's *fête*."

I think back to that night. I cannot recall a man fitting this description. I do not think he was presented to me. There are so many things I want to ask her: how she met him, where they spend all their time together. But just as I lean forward to whisper, a shadow appears.

I shade my eyes with my hands and look up to see Pauline's chamberlain. He's dressed entirely in white, from his billowing silk shirt to his riding breeches. In the heat of July, he looks refreshingly cool.

"Your Highness." He smiles warmly at Hortense, then turns to me. "Your Majesty. The emperor has requested you both in his study. The entire family has been called for an import-ant announcement."

I look to Hortense. "And he said nothing else?" she presses.

"Just that his mother and siblings should be there."

My heart begins to beat rapidly in my chest. Hortense rises at once and offers me her hand. Then the three of us cross the gardens toward the palace.

"It must have something to do with me," Hortense worries as we open our parasols. "He is still angry that I did not convince Louis to raise an army in Holland. Perhaps he's taking away my title as well."

But when we reach Napoleon's study, the emperor is laughing with Pauline and Madame Mère. "Marie-Louise!" he exclaims as soon as he sees me, and there is no doubting that this is a joyous occasion. "Paul, if you would please shut the door."

I look around the study, with its red and gold paneling and matching chairs. How many kings have seen these walls? My uncle, Louis XVI, certainly. I suppose a long line of French rulers once used this room as a place of refuge from the tediousness of court.

"Please, sit," Napoleon instructs, and the women in the room are given seats while the men cluster around my husband's desk. Present are Méneval and Paul, several foreign ministers, and finally Napoleon's most important counselors.

"In preparation for the pregnancy to come," he begins, "I have made a decision about the heir to my throne."

Pauline and Caroline exchange a look, and Madame Mère stares directly at me. I have had little interaction with Napoleon's mother. She is dressed almost entirely in black, and only the thick strand of pearls at her slender neck adds any color to her face. She is a hard woman. Even without the sharp cheekbones and strong jaw, it would be impossible to mistake her for anything else. But she keeps to herself, and Hortense says she is no one to be afraid of. Her only interest is Napoleon—his health, his happiness, his continual success.

"As soon as the empress conceives," Napoleon says, "our child shall be known as the King of Rome or the Princess of Venice."

Napoleon's counselors turn toward me, and I am trying to find my voice when Pauline shouts, "The *King of Rome*? Rome should belong to me!"

"And who believes that?" Caroline demands.

"It's my right!" she insists. "I'm the Princess Borghese."

"And he's the emperor of France."

"You can't do this!" Pauline rises from her seat, and then suddenly everyone is arguing.

"Silence!" Napoleon shouts, but the women's voices are louder than his. "Be silent!" he thunders, and the study goes quiet. "I have made my decision, and that is final."

I glance at Pauline. Like her chamberlain, she is dressed entirely in white, from her thin muslin gown to the small pearls in her hair. She opens her white sachet, takes out a handkerchief, and weeps theatrically into the linen. "He loves his children more than me," she accuses. "I knew it would happen."

"It's only a title," I hear Madame Mère say.

The look Pauline gives her own mother is chilling.

"What children?" Caroline demands. "The only fat on our empress's belly came with her from Austria!"

The ministers look away as Napoleon advances toward his sisters, and I'm reminded of a lion tamer driving back creatures that could destroy him with a swipe. "Leave," he commands.

Pauline clutches the handkerchief to her chest as Paul ushers his female relatives from the room. When the doors swing shut and the circus is over, Napoleon walks toward to me and cups my chin.

"There will be a child," he says with unusual tenderness. "He might be growing in there even now."

But I know that nothing has changed since our marriage in April. "Yes."

"And when he comes, he will be known to the world as the king of Rome!" There is clapping from the ministers. "There is a surprise for you waiting in the Council Chamber," he says. "Your father has sent the general Neipperg with something you left behind."

Although I already know, I'm still compelled to ask. "Sigi?"

Napoleon smiles mysteriously. "Let's go and see."

He offers me his hand, and everyone rises. A pair of guards open the double doors. "The general's come a long way to make this delivery," Napoleon remarks. "Caroline tells me you have some acquaintance with him."

I can feel the blood rush from my face. "Yes. He is a very good friend to my father."

"And to you." I wonder how much she's told him.

"The court of Austria is small," I say carefully. "We are all very close. Also, we knew each other as children."

He studies me for a moment, and I hope the lie isn't written on my face. Then he reaches out and pinches my behind. "My little dumpling." He pinches me again. "As sweet and innocent as a dove. If my ministers knew what was good for them," he says loudly, "they would all go to Austria for wives."

I wonder if he humiliated his first wife this way.

"Are you ready?" he asks triumphantly.

We have reached the Council Room. It's real. Count Adam von Neipperg has come. Not with a great army that will defeat Napoleon, but he is here, just as he promised. I stand before the door and look skyward to keep my tears from falling, then nod my approval. He opens the door, and a flash of fur speeds toward me. "Sigi!" I cry. My spaniel is beside himself, dancing at my feet, flopping on his back to show me his belly, and barking to be picked up. I scoop him into my arms and press him tightly against my chest. "Sigi," I inhale his scent. Lavender, just like the quilts at home.

"Your Majesty," a familiar voice says. I look across the blue and red Council Chamber. He is standing beside the fireplace, dressed in black, from his polished riding boots to his gold-trimmed jacket. Even his silk eye patch.

"Count Neipperg." My first urge is to run to him, to press my cheek against his coat and weep with gratitude. But I control my breathing and force myself to walk slowly to where he's standing. "Thank you for coming to France," I say, "and for bringing Sigi." Napoleon clears his throat, and I realize he's standing next to me. "This—this is the emperor."

Adam executes the perfect courtier's bow, and Napoleon nods regally. "Welcome to Fontainebleau. And thank you for delivering this gift to my wife."

I know exactly what Adam is thinking. Sigi is no gift. He was mine long before I met Napoleon, and his arrival in Fontainebleau is not an unexpected surprise; it is four months late. "The journey was my pleasure," Adam replies. "Her Majesty is greatly beloved in Austria, and this ride was a small thing to ensure her happiness."

Napoleon smiles thinly, and as he reaches out to ruffle Sigi's fur, my spaniel emits a low, threatening growl. "Sigi!" I exclaim, and he begins to bark. "Sigi, *be silent!*" I glance at Napoleon. "He's never done this before."

He turns up his palms. "Austrians," he says in jest. "There's no silencing them."

The ministers all laugh, and even Adam smiles wanly.

"Thirty years ago our unfortunate aunt Marie-Antoinette was standing in this very spot. Now here we are." Napoleon indicates the Council Chamber with its ornate fireplace of griotte marble and low-hanging chandeliers. "The great-niece of our ill-fated Hapsburg queen and the emperor of France. And soon the dynasty will continue."

Adam looks at me. "Her Majesty is pregnant?" he asks.

Napoleon puts his arm around my waist. "You may tell her father that an heir is most definitely on its way." He rubs my stomach, and I turn my head so I won't have to see the look on Adam's face..

"I've seen these things before." Napoleon is staring at Sigi. "Is it common?"

"Veronese painted toy spaniels two hundred and fifty years ago," says Adam. "Perhaps you've seen one depicted in his work. The dog isn't overly common."

Napoleon frowns, and I realize he's never even heard of Veronese. "Well, I'm sure Aubree will be delighted to have a friend," he says dryly. He turns to me. "Exchange your news. We have dinner in an hour." He retreats to the side of the chamber with his ministers, and I am left alone with Adam.

"It was very kind of you to come," I repeat.

"As promised, Your Majesty."

Not exactly as promised. He will return to Vienna while I will remain in Fontainebleau, like the birds in a Nicolas Lancret painting, trapped in a gilded cage. "How are *Vater* and Maria?" I ask.

"Well. They send you nothing but their deepest love."

"And Ferdinand?"

"The crown prince has been better," he says quietly. "He misses you. As does everyone in Schönbrunn." He holds my gaze. Napoleon and a dozen different ministers are watching our exchange.

"Perhaps I can come and visit," I say.

"Your family would like that very much."

But even as I nod, I know it will never be. "Would you like to say goodbye to Sigi?" I ask lightly.

He steps closer to me, so close that his hands nearly brush against mine. Then he scratches Sigi's ear and promises, "I won't forget you. We'll meet again soon, *mein Schatzi*."

"You shouldn't promise such things. He'll end up missing you."

Adam meets my gaze. "I hope so."

I stand on the steps of Fontainebleau and watch the carriages disappear in a cloud of dust. "There they go," I say softly to Sigi, and only the eager wag of his tail keeps me from crying.

"Are they destined for Schönbrunn?"

I turn. Pauline is dressed in a light summer gown, with pearls in her hair and around her wrists. She is carrying Aubree, who seems wary of my new addition to Fontainebleau. "Yes. I'm sad to see them go," I admit, "but I'm very thankful you interceded on my behalf."

Pauline steps forward, and Aubree buries her nose in her arm. She's a timid little dog, but perhaps someday she and Sigi will be friends. "If my attitude was ever less than welcoming in the past," she says, "I apologize. The most important thing now is Napoleon's happiness. I know we both want what's best for my brother."

"Yes."

"And you'd do anything for him, wouldn't you?" she asks suddenly. "Because there's no one like him in this world. The things he plans to do . . . the things he's already done . . ."

I watch her carefully, but she seems to be genuinely concerned for him.

"Everyone wants something from Napoleon," she clarifies. "Money, titles, opportunities. He needs the women around him to be utterly loyal." She looks at me, and her dark eyes seem to know exactly what I'm thinking.

"I will be loyal," I promise.

"I hope so. Because it would crush him to have brought home a second Joséphine."

That evening, as Hortense shares a small gelato with me before bed, I tell her about Pauline's question. "She wanted to know if I would be loyal."

Hortense puts down her spoon. "She's heard about Count Neipperg then," she guesses. "From Queen Caroline. Or maybe one of the queen's women."

My heart is racing. "What will he do?"

"Nothing," Hortense says easily. "It's only rumor."

"He won't punish my father?"

"How?"

In any number of ways. "He might remove him from the throne of Austria."

But Hortense looks doubtful. "The count was here for a few minutes, and you were not alone with him," she reassures me. "He gave you Sigi, and that was it."

We both look toward the fire, where my spaniel is curled up in his new basket, sleeping.

"Besides"—she smiles—"do you really think he'll punish you after this news?"

We're both looking down at my little belly when the door of my chamber creaks open and Napoleon steps inside.

"Your Majesty!" Hortense hides her surprise and rises. This is normally his time with Méneval.

"Leave," he says.

Hortense glances at me.

"Go," I tell her. "I'll see you tomorrow."

She leaves her gelato, and Napoleon watches me from the door. "An old friend of yours?" he asks.

I put down my spoon. "Who?"

"*Who?*" he repeats, then crosses the chamber so quickly that I can't prepare myself for what he does next. He reaches for the gelato and shoves the bowl into my face. "Do you think I'm a fool?" he rages. "Do you think I didn't see what was happening?" He pushes the bowl harder, then lets it drop to the floor. "Come on, little piggy. Keep eating. Isn't that what you do best?"

I can barely breathe. I reach for a serviette, but my hands are trembling too hard to wipe the food away. I have never been so humiliated, and by my own husband. I rise from the chair to clean myself, but his hand on my shoulder holds me down.

"You want to know why I'm eating?" I cry.

He doesn't say anything, so I tell him.

"I'm *pregnant*."

He withdraws his hand as if he's been burned, and I watch him with open hatred. "How—how do you know?"

"Because tonight was the second month that I've missed . . . because I'm certain."

"Marie—"

"Stay away from me!" I scream. I rush from my chair, but he follows me into my boudoir.

"*Ma bonne amie.* I'm sorry."

I wash my face in the bowl of lemon water the servants leave out for me each night, and I can sense Napoleon behind me as I cry. *What if this child turns out like its father? What if he's just as twisted and cruel?*

"*Mio dolce amore*," he says tenderly. "If I had known . . ."

The words make me cringe. I put down my towel and hope he can see the disgust in my eyes. "Now you do."

"I will make it up to you. Whatever you want. I promise."

But it's too late for that. What I want has returned to Austria.

CHAPTER 17

PAULINE BORGHESE

Fontainebleau Palace
August 1810

Why is it that God punishes me like this? *Pregnant!* And now my brother is handling his wife like she's made of Sèvres china, plying her with silks, and lace, and sweets. Paul told me that last night, when he was visiting the emperor in his study, she arrived, and he let her write an official letter to Russia. And when she was done, he praised her for its tact!

I look across the room to his most recent gift to me and want to tear it apart. How dare he think he can buy my forgiveness with a fur pelisse. De Canouville sees the direction of my gaze and frowns.

"Napoleon's gesture of goodwill," I snap. "From his visit with the Russian emperor. He was gifted with three. There is nothing unique about it. If you want it, have it. Use it to trim your uniform. Or your jacket. Or your undergarments." Despite the pains in my stomach, I walk to the chaise and pick up the pelisse. "Take it," I say firmly. "I never want to see it again." Besides, he'll look fetching in black fur.

I sit on the chaise and put my head in my hands. I am the one who brought this about. I convinced my brother to divorce Beauharnais. And now it is all Marie-Louise. *What does Marie-Louise want? What does Marie-Louise think? Would Marie-Louise care to answer letters in my study? After all, she has such wonderful political acumen and competence!* When I think of how Paul convinced me to apologize to her, I want to kill him.

De Canouville tenderly rubs my back. "He will never stop being your brother," he says.

"He wants me to meet him in his study tomorrow," I reply. "He wants my help decorating the child's apartments." Tears of rage cloud my eyes, and I wish I had never heard the name of Marie-Louise.

"Then it will be your style that influences the king of Rome."

But I'm in no mood for placating.

When I reach my brother's study the next morning, every courtier in France is rushing about like a headless chicken.

"Which design do you prefer?" he asks me. "The first one, with the silver armoire?"

I lean over his desk. "The third one."

"With the library?"

"You want the child to be literate, don't you?"

He takes his quill and circles the third design.

"You know," I say, "there was a time when you believed all great reputations came from the east, and that Egypt would fix your name in the records of posterity."

"Not now," he warns. "Egypt is finished. Do you understand? It was an exercise, Pauline. A three-year training for real wars. Be happy with the treasures you have. Don't live in the past."

"You didn't always believe that."

"And we didn't always believe the earth revolved around the sun."

There's no winning with him. There will always be an answer, or a quip, or some jibe. "You want this christening to look like Marie-Antoinette's christening of her Dauphin?" I ask. "You want your son—or daughter," I add provocatively, "to be dressed in the same clothes as Louis XVII?" I step back. "Then go ahead. Build nurseries in the Tuileries and Fontainebleau, but when your people revolt, don't come asking me why." I turn around, but he grabs my arm.

"You are not dismissed."

My eyes meet his, and I hope he can feel their heat. "What? Shall we plan the child's wedding, too?" I wrest my arm free and cross the chamber.

"Do *not* leave this room."

"Or what?" I open the door and slam it shut. In the hall, Marie-Louise is waiting to see Napoleon. Immediately, she rises from her chair. I look at her stomach beneath her blue and white gown. God only knows what she'll fit into in a few months. They'll have to send for a tent. "You think you're very clever, don't you?" I ask, and I can see her surprise at my sudden change in attitude. "Beating my brother at chess, embarrassing him at billiards. We came from poverty," I remind her sharply. "Some of us didn't pass our childhood in games. But enjoy this time," I suggest. "The presents, the flattery, the attention. Because six months from now, no one will be interested in you at all. And when my brother rejoins his army in Spain, don't be surprised when he takes your child with him."

She flinches, and I don't wait for her to respond.

I find Paul and de Canouville in my chamber. They are reading on opposite sides of the room. Paul, some book on fallen empires, and de Canouville—well, who knows what de Canouville reads? Probably a play. Some light piece that Talma would never touch. They both stop as soon as they see me, but only de Canouville hurries to his feet.

"Is something wrong?" He puts down his book. "What happened?"

I'm about to tell him when a knock at the door interrupts my thoughts. "What?" I snap, and suddenly Paul rises to his feet.

"Your Majesty." Paul bows, and de Canouville follows suit.

I turn to meet Napoleon's gaze and realize what has happened.

"What did you tell my wife?" he asks quietly. "What did you say to her?" he shouts. When I don't say anything, he tells me, "I am done, Pauline. I am finished with this. With *all* of it. What did you tell her?" he asks me again.

"I—I warned her that once the child comes, things will be different."

Napoleon looks at Paul, as if my chamberlain could somehow verify this statement. Then he sees de Canouville, and his whole body stiffens. I follow his eyes. It's inspection day, and de Canouville is wearing his captain's uniform. But unlike the jackets of the other men, his is trimmed with Russian fur. He looks down at his coat, and the color drains from his face.

Napoleon leaves without another word.

CHAPTER 18

PAUL MOREAU

Fontainebleau Palace
September 1810

I turn from the desperation in de Canouville's face. At seven this morning, a courtier woke me with a note from Pauline's lover asking that I meet him here in the gardens at noon.

"Alone?" I'd asked warily, and the courtier leaned close.

"The emperor is sending him away."

I had warned de Canouville. I had cautioned him against Napoleon's jealousy, but instead of feeling vindication, all I felt in that moment was pity. Now I look at the silent rows of trees and wonder how long they'll grow in Fontainebleau. When he and I are long gone from this place, those trees will still be standing. Not a care in the world. Just the grass and the rain and the sun above their heads.

De Canouville begins, "If you speak with the emperor, I swear to you, I'll be forever in your debt."

"I'll do whatever I can."

He grasps my hand and squeezes if forcefully. "Thank you. *Thank you.* I hope you know that Pauline would want it this way. You have no idea how she'll miss me. If you love her at all—you'll find a way to persuade him."

I take back my hand and keep myself from saying something truly vile. "I must go."

"But you'll tell him, won't you?"

"I said I would."

But the emperor is unmovable. The mention of de Canouville's name turns his face red.

"Imperial furs! She gave away my gift of the Russian czar's furs." I watch him pace from his mahogany desk to the empty fireplace, and though the summer's heat is choking the paneled room, he refuses to open a single window. "It's audacity, isn't it?" he asks.

"It's poor judgment for certain, Your Majesty."

He stops walking and turns to face me in my chair. "Why are you always impartial? The man hates you, you know. So why are you speaking on his behalf?"

"Because he's ignorant," I say truthfully, "and a terrible fool. But there's no real malice in him."

He looks at me as if I've spoken in my ancestors' tongue. "And you would risk my displeasure for a man like that?"

"It was a calculated risk."

He waits for explanation.

"I was gambling that His Majesty would understand I came not for the captain's benefit but for his sister's. He loves her, and this seems to make her happy."

Napoleon nods, and for a moment I think I have won de Canouville's reprieve. Then he replies, "I am always mystified by people like you." A chill goes up my back. He clasps

THE SECOND EMPRESS | 200

his hands behind him and watches me intently. This is the way his soldiers must feel.

"I do what I think is right, Your Majesty."

"Even when it isn't in your interest?" He shakes his head thoughtfully. "Do you know what my sister asked me this morning? She wanted me to take Captain de Septeuil instead." He lets me absorb this sentence before continuing. "She offered me de Septeuil's life for de Canouville's, because de Septeuil once refused to spend the night with her."

I stare at him. I have met de Septeuil. I've seen him at Pauline's *fêtes*. He is in love with his fiancée and would never abuse the girl's trust. "Perhaps she didn't realize—"

"She knew *exactly*!" he says angrily. "Why do you defend her when you know what she is? Paul, I am going to tell you a truth." He walks to the chair next to me and seats himself. If anyone saw us together like this, they would think we were old comrades, not the emperor and a servant. "She's a habit for you."

I try to understand what he's saying. "A habit?" I repeat.

"Like snuff," the emperor says. "At first it's enjoyable. Then, with enough time, it simply becomes habit. You don't know why you do it, except that you always have. And without it, life would be a little less."

I wait for him to finish. Less what? But he is waiting for me to respond. Is Pauline a habit I developed in Haiti? Do I love what she is, or what she was? I meet Napoleon's gaze. How can the same man who tossed away a loyal wife to marry a nineteen-year-old be so incisive?

He shrugs. "Think on it. Men of your age are married with children." He stands. Our meeting is finished.

"And de Canouville?"

"Will be joining de Septeuil in Spain," he says briskly. "I need two soldiers to deliver my messages to Commander Masséna. They both leave tonight."

When I meet Pauline in her apartments, the hope in her face infuriates me.

"What did he say?" She rushes from the divan, her blue silk robe trailing behind her. She hasn't dressed, and it's two in the afternoon.

"He said de Canouville will be leaving tonight."

She gasps.

"With de Septeuil, per your request." I turn away to go to my apartment, and she hurries after me.

"You have to understand—"

"What do I *have to understand*, Your Highness? That you condemned an innocent man to certain death? The road to Salamanca is a war zone. If they come back alive, you may consider it a miracle." Tears stream down her face, but the sight no longer moves me.

"*Please.*" She reaches out.

I move away. "Whatever happens to those men, it's on your conscience."

I don't return to my apartment. Instead I go to the stables, where I find the soldiers who first befriended me seven years ago. Dacian and François are unsaddling their horses. The mounts hear me first and snort. Then Dacian calls out, "Paul!"

François slaps his thighs, and a small cloud of dust rises in the air. "Going for a ride?"

"Not today."

Dacian nods. "Trouble at the palace?"

"Am I that easy to read?"

"It's the only time you're in the stables so late."

I sit on a bale of hay and watch my friends strip their horses. The earthy scents of dust and summer grass remind me of my youth. Not a day went by that my father and I didn't ride out to oversee the plantation.

"So what's the trouble?" Dacian asks. "Or can't you say?"

"The emperor is sending de Canouville to Spain."

"The princess's lover?" Dacian confirms.

"Yes."

He laughs. "So why are you upset? He's gone, and you're there. Isn't this what you've been hoping for?"

The entire palace knows. "Is there anyone who doesn't think I'm waiting for the princess?"

Dacian and François exchange looks. Then Dacian seats himself next to me and puts his arm around my shoulders. "We've known it for years, Paul. She's all you talk about. Of course, it's useless. Even you know that. She's married to a prince and has a courtesan's appetite for men. But 'the heart has its reasons which Reason knows not of.'"

I'm not in the mood to hear Blaise Pascal quoted to me. Dacian can read it in my face because he immediately amends, "At least that's what they say."

"When I met her, she was innocent."

"Really," François asks, "or in your mind? Because she had

a reputation in Paris long before she went to Saint-Domingue."

"But she was *different* there," I protest. "Tender—"

François shakes his head. "Paul, the woman has bedded half of Paris and probably has the clap. What are you hoping to gain by staying with her? You're her husband without any of the privileges that come along with that position."

"Or money." Dacian laughs, and François passes him a withering look.

I rise from the hay. "This is the Princess Borghese you're speaking about!"

"Beauty like hers can make a man forget many things," François says. "But Charles VIII died of syphilis. A title doesn't confer immortality. How often is she ill? Once a week? Twice?"

It's hard to say. Pauline is a great actress. There's no telling when she's truly sick or just wanting attention.

"And it's always her stomach, isn't it?" François asks. "She's sick with the clap, and any man who beds her is risking the same."

The stables and horses begin to blur as I let myself absorb what François has just said. *How many times did I watch women suffering from the clap in Haiti? The infertility . . . the pelvic pain . . .*

"So why is de Canouville being sent to Spain?" Dacian asks.

I explain about Pauline's gift of imperial furs, and how de Canouville had them sewn onto his military coat. Then I tell them what is truly making me sick: how Pauline asked that he send de Septeuil instead, so now the emperor is sending them both.

"I don't know who's more vindictive," François reflects at length. "The emperor or his sister."

I close my eyes. It's too much for one day. "I'm going back."

"To Saint-Domingue, or to the palace?" Dacian jokes.

"I don't know."

François stands. "Paul, you belong here."

But I never intended to stay this long. And what have I accomplished? After eight years, the emperor feels the same about slavery as he did before we met, though I have pushed him as hard as any courtier would dare to free the slaves in France's remaining colonies. I've tended Pauline through every sickness, yet her health has only gotten worse. And now, knowing what she is capable of doing to an innocent man . . .

Dacian and François continue watching me, and I tell them the truth. "I want to return to my home. To *Haiti*."

"But Saint-Domingue was destroyed," Dacian replies. "You've heard the stories."

"Yes. I know all about how the French burned my people alive in cauldrons of molasses. How they mutilated and tortured Haitian prisoners, digging pits on the beach and waiting for the tide to roll in so they would drown. In Port-au-Prince," I tell them, "the emperor's soldiers invited all *mulâtres* to a ball. Then at the stroke of midnight, he announced that the men would be put to death. They killed them right there, in front of their wives."

François and Dacian look horrified, but is it any worse than what their fellow soldiers did in Egypt, when Napoleon allowed his men two days and nights of raping and looting?

Even Napoleon himself found himself a personal conquest: the sixteen-year-old daughter of Sheikh El-Bekri, who was made to submit to him as the new ruler in Egypt. When Zenab begged Napoleon to take her with him as the French moved out, he refused, not knowing—or caring—what would become of a girl who had been dishonored in Egypt. So her fate was to be beheaded by the city's elders, and when Napoleon heard of it, he shrugged. "If they want to kill their most beautiful women, that is their choice," he said. So why is it any surprise that his soldiers massacred the blacks of Haiti?

"Before the war could finish," I tell them, "French soldiers killed my family."

Dacian is shocked. "I'm sorry." He glances at François. "I didn't realize—"

I nod. "Even the emperor doesn't know."

"You understand that you won't find the same country you left behind," François says heavily.

"Then that's what I'll go to do. Rebuild."

Both men stare in disbelief, and I know what they're thinking. Why would anyone look to trade civilized France for lawless Haiti, with its heat and dirt and cities razed to the ground? But they haven't heard the palm swifts calling to each other in the warm spring breeze. Or woken from a nap in the afternoon heat to hear the thunder drumming in the distance. My father's plantation may be gone, but there is still the land.

CHAPTER 19

MARIE-LOUISE

Fontainebleau Palace
December 1810

"Shall I read it to you?" Hortense asks. She puts down her brush. Since Napoleon gifted me this space last month, I've been teaching her to paint. But although she's a good student, she seems to tire quickly.

"There won't be any news about Ferdinand," I say wearily. "And certainly none of Adam."

"You don't know that."

But I do. Her mother might have been free with her gossip when she was empress. My father is not. She removes the letter from the open envelope and begins:

My dearest Maria,
You wrote about feeling confined, but I can assure you that
these months will pass quickly, and sooner than you know,
you will be experiencing the joys of motherhood. God blessed
me with thirteen children, and though some have returned

*to His eternal embrace, I will always be grateful for their
presence, however fleeting, on this earth. Whatever happens
in February—boy or girl, stillborn or live birth—you have
made the house of Hapsburg-Lorraine proud.*

*I sent Prince Metternich with a gift last month and was
informed that you no longer receive male visitors alone. If
this is true, I am sorry it applies to the prince. I had
believed the emperor had more sense than that.*

Hortense lowers the letter onto her lap, and we stare at
each other in silence. My father knows that Napoleon's ministers read every piece of correspondence that comes to me,
particularly from Austria.

"It's a reprimand," she says aloud.

"Yes." After announcing my pregnancy to the court in
September, Napoleon forbade me to leave the palace. Even
taking Sigi outside is now prohibited. As the future mother
to the heir of an empire, nothing dangerous—physically or
morally—is permitted. When I argued, warning him that a
prison is no place for a child to be born, he asked me which
amusements I'd miss the most. "Everything," I replied indig-
nantly. "The fresh air, the gardens . . ." So he had a winter
garden planted inside the palace. And when that wasn't
enough to stave off boredom, he ordered an artist's studio
built as well.

It's true, there are unexpected freedoms in being pregnant. I am enjoying the nights in my bed alone and the priv-
ilege to eat whatever I please. This morning I had coffee with
thick cream and rolls, and tonight I shall have almond milk

with pastries. But these are small compensations for living like a monk.

"We should stroll through the palace," Hortense says suddenly. She puts down my father's letter and claps. "Come here, Sigi!" My spaniel runs from his warm basket next to the fire and climbs into her lap, licking her cheek and barking. "He needs a walk."

I wish I could bend over and pick him up, but it's become too difficult to carry him now. I put my hand on my belly, and the small movement inside makes me smile. But what if this child is like his father? Or even worse, like her aunt Pauline? I catch Hortense watching me curiously, and I tell her, "I've been hoping for a little girl."

She fastens a lead to Sigi's collar and sighs. "I always wanted a girl. But I wouldn't exchange my sons for the world," she adds at once, "even if they're in Austria."

If only we could trade places, I think. "How long will their father will keep them there?"

"Until Napoleon orders him back to Paris," she says softly. "And that could be tomorrow, or never."

"You haven't asked the emperor to send for them?"

She gives me a meaningful look. "When my eldest son died, and I was grieving, he accused me of loving my son more than him. He will order Louis back only when he's ready."

I think of all the orders he will give for our child, and Hortense pats my knee.

"It will all go well for you," she promises. "Look how lucky you've been so far."

But I think of Adam hearing about my pregnancy in Vienna, and I don't see how I've been fortunate at all.

"And think," she adds kindly, "if it's a boy, you'll be finished." She rises from her chair, and Sigi begins to bark. "Shall we?"

We leave my artist's studio tucked in the corner in Fontainebleau, and Sigi leads us through the halls, sniffing at every passing boot, then barking when the boot's owner stops.

"There's Pauline's salon," Hortense whispers to me.

I look at the ornate double doors, and when the footmen see us, they push them open before we have a chance to wave them off. "Her Majesty, the Empress of France," a herald announces, "and Her Royal Highness, the Princess Bonaparte."

I stop where I'm standing and exchange a look with Hortense.

I have never seen Pauline's salon in this palace. Now I can see that, like her rooms in Château de Neuilly, they have been made to resemble an Egyptian palace, from the polished ebony furniture to the painted murals. There are alabaster lamps in the shape of sphinxes, and pots of incense burning on the mantelpiece. But it's not the décor that's most shocking. It's the sight of Pauline resting her feet on Madame de Chambaudoin's neck. I am dumbfounded. The Princess Borghese uses women as footstools?

Pauline stands from her extraordinary Egyptian throne. She's carrying Aubree in her arms. The dog is adorned in a gold and lapis collar. With her regal snout and wide, dark eyes, she looks like she might peer back at you from an

Egyptian tomb. "Marie-Louise," she says. "Hortense. To what do we owe this double surprise?"

I look around the room. Two dozen ladies-in-waiting are in attendance, each of them wearing Egyptian jewels.

"We thought Aubree might enjoy a visit from Sigi," Hortense fabricates. "Isn't that right?" She looks down at Sigi, whose tail wags excitedly, then frees him from his lead.

Pauline's smile actually reaches her eyes. She bends down to release Aubree, and the dogs run circles, jumping and sniffing each other.

I glance behind her at Madame de Chambaudoin. The old woman is still lying supine on the floor. "What do you think?" Pauline asks me, casting her gaze around the room. "This could be Cleopatra's court, don't you agree?"

"It's very . . . convincing," I say. I don't know any other word for what's she's done. In all the courts of Europe, this has to be unique.

"We almost ruled Egypt together, you know."

"We?" I confirm, as Hortense shifts uncomfortably on her feet next to me.

"My brother and I. Who else?"

My hand goes involuntarily to my stomach, as if to protect my child, and when Pauline sees the gesture, she narrows her eyes.

"He loves me," she whispers, so that even Hortense has to strain to hear her over the barking of the dogs. "More than Joséphine, or you, or even this child you're carrying. Nothing comes between us."

It comes to me clearly: *she is sick*. Possibly in body, but definitely in mind. Doesn't anyone else in Fontainebleau see it? How long has she been abusing old women?

"Tell me," she says, and as soon as she steps close to me, I can smell the incense on her clothes. "Does the emperor ever mention de Canouville?"

"No." I've never heard him mention the name.

She nods, as if she's trying to convince herself of something. "He does this on purpose. Sends away the people I love."

There's a haunted look in Pauline's eyes. Was it the departure of a man named de Canouville that prompted this behavior? I have never heard talk that the Princess Borghese uses women for footrests, or dresses her servants like Egyptian slaves. . . . She looks at me as if she were waking from a dream, then calls to Aubree, and her little greyhound comes running.

"We—we should go," I tell her. "Sigi!" My spaniel leaps over Madame de Chambaudoin. Hortense winces, and I can no longer keep my silence. "Why is she on the floor?"

"She likes it. Don't you, Madame?"

The old woman nods.

"And you believe that?"

Pauline shrugs. "You believe my brother is faithful to you, that your lover is pining for you somewhere in Austria." She measures my expression. "We all have our little dreams."

I am speechless. Hortense scoops Sigi into her arms, and the footmen hurry to open the doors.

"You're no different than any of us!" she calls, as Hortense and I take our quick departure. "You're a Bonaparte now, and your child will be a Bonaparte."

My child will be a Bonaparte, Pauline, when you are a royal.

"You wished to see me, Your Majesty?"

Paul stands at the door of my studio, and I nod from behind my wooden easel. "If you would like to come inside and take a seat—"

He glances behind him, perhaps because he's heard that I'm not permitted audiences alone with men. But this is important. "Shall I shut the door, Your Majesty?"

"If you would."

I watch as he crosses the room and am surprised that for someone so attractive, there isn't more gossip about him at court. According to Hortense, there was once a pretty lady-in-waiting of Joséphine's who caught his eye, and some talk that one of Pauline's women might be allowing him to visit her chamber at night. But he has never married, and after eight years of serving Pauline, there has never been so much as a whisper of their ever having been together. If he is wise, he will never allow her to seduce him. The moment the chase is over, she will be finished with him forever.

He takes a seat on the chair across from me and glances around the studio. It's a cozy chamber, with paint-spattered tables, a pair of wooden easels, and a thickly padded cushion next to the fire. He smiles at Sigi, then waits for me to begin.

"I visited the Princess Borghese this afternoon."

Immediately he looks alarmed. "And did Your Majesty enjoy herself?"

"Not exactly."

He nods slowly, as if he were expecting this.

"Monsieur Moreau," I begin.

"Please, Paul."

"Paul, there is something very wrong with her. She was using women as footstools, and her eyes—"

"Yes. She is sick, Your Majesty."

"With *what*?"

He looks at his hands in his lap and whispers, "I don't know. I've been trying to keep away from her recently," he admits. "She has done things I'm not sure I can forgive, though her illness is better when I am there."

"But was she always this way?" I press.

"It used to be only when she was under great stress. But now . . ." He lets the words die away.

"Is she taking medicine?"

"I'm afraid I can't say, Your Majesty."

"Because you won't?"

"Because I don't know. There are things she keeps even from me. But if I had to guess, I would say she is taking mercury."

As sheltered as I may have been in Schönbrunn, even I have heard about mercury treatments for diseases like syphilis and the clap. For women, it's taken by mouth, but for men, whose symptoms are often worse, it's injected by syringe into the tip of the penis. I think of the famous saying, *A night with Venus, a lifetime with Mercury*, and wonder if she's contracted some venereal disease.

"I saw the pills last month in her boudoir," he explains. "But I've never seen them before or since."

"Perhaps it's a new treatment she's started?"

"I don't know. But she's been sicker than I've ever seen her. If Your Majesty could refrain from telling the emperor, I will . . . I will return to her salon and make sure she never uses women as footstools again."

"Then it's happened before?" I ask incredulously.

"Never when I'm there. But yes."

I stare at him, trying to determine what it is that makes him stay, after so many years. Then, as if he could read my mind, he tells me, "When I return to her chambers, she'll ask me to read to her from Rousseau, and we'll discuss the principles of this country's Revolution. Tomorrow we'll read Racine. I shouldn't have left her. She is sick, Your Majesty, and when I'm with her, she feels safe. Calm."

"And her—*eccentricities*—don't worry you?"

"No. Her callousness does."

To the Empress at Malmaison.

March 12, 1810.

My love—I hope you will be pleased with what I have done for Navarre. You will see in it a new proof of my desire to make you happy. Take possession of Navarre. You can go there on the 25th of March, to spend the month of April.

Adieu, my love.

Napoleon

Joséphine to Napoleon.

Navarre, April 10, 1810.

Sire, I received this morning the welcome note. After having known all the sweets of a love that is shared, and all the sufferings of one that is so no longer—after having exhausted all the happiness that supreme power can confer, and the happiness of beholding the man whom I love enthusiastically admired, is there aught else save repose to be desired? What illusions can remain for me? All such vanished when it became necessary to renounce you. Thus the only ties which yet bind me to life, are my sentiments for you, attachment for my children, the possibility of being able still to do some good, and above all, the assurance that you are happy. Do not, then, condole with me on my being here, distant from a court which you appear to think I regret.

I can not sufficiently thank you, sire, for the liberty you have permitted me of choosing the members of my household, all of whom contribute to the pleasures of a delightful society. One circumstance alone gives me pain, namely, the etiquette of costume, which becomes a little tiresome in the country. You fear there may be something wanting to the rank I have preserved, should a slight infraction be allowed in the toilet of these gentlemen. But I believe you are wrong in thinking they would for one minute forget the respect due to the woman who was your companion. Their respect for yourself, joined to the sincere attachment which they bear to me, which I cannot doubt, secures me against the danger of being ever obliged to recall what it is your wish they should remember. My most honorable title is derived, not from having been crowned, but assuredly from having been chosen by you. None other is of value—that alone suffices for my immortality.

I expect Eugène. I doubly long to see him, for he will doubtless bring me a new pledge of your remembrance; and I can question him at my ease of a thousand things concerning which I desire to be informed, but cannot inquire of you; things too of which you ought still less speak to me. My daughter will come also, but later. In short, I find myself perfectly at home in the midst of my forest, and entreat you, sire, no longer to fancy yourself that there is no living at a distance from court. Besides you, there is nothing there that I regret, since I will have my children with me soon.

Joséphine

To the Empress at Navarre.
April 28, 1810.

My love—Eugène has informed me that you wish to go to the springs. Do not deprive yourself of anything. Do not listen to the gossips. They are idlers and know nothing of the true state of affairs. My affection for you is unchangeable; and I desire exceedingly to hear that you are tranquil and happy.

Napoleon

To the Empress at the Waters of Aix, in Savoy.
July 8, 1810.

My love—You will have seen Eugène, and his presence will have done you good. I have learned with pleasure that the waters agree with you. The King of Holland has abdicated the crown.

My health is good. I shall see you with pleasure this autumn. Never doubt my love. I never change. Take care of your health, be cheerful, and believe in the truthfulness of my affections.

Napoleon

September 9, 1810

My dear Hortense, respecting myself: I have received no letters from the emperor; but I have thought it proper to testify to him all the interest which I feel in the pregnancy of the empress. I have just written to him upon that subject.

I hope that this act will place him at ease, and that he will be able to speak to me of that event with as much confidence as I have of attachment for him. I wait impatiently for you to receive the answer from the emperor, and to receive myself the assurance that you will come to rejoin me.

    Adieu, my dear daughter; I embrace you tenderly.
    Joséphine
    P.S. Remember me to all your companions.

To the Empress at the Waters of Aix.
September 14, 1810.

    My love—I have received your letter of the 9th of September. I learn with pleasure that you are well. The empress is decidedly enciente for four months. She is well and is very much attached to me.

    My health is pretty good. I desire to hear that you are contented and happy. They say that one of your household has broken her leg by going upon the ice.

    Adieu, my love; never doubt the interest I feel in you, and the affection with which I cherish you.

    Napoleon

1811

CHAPTER 20

PAULINE BORGHESE

Tuileries Palace, Paris
February 1811

"It's happening!" someone shouts in the courtyard, and I run to my balcony. A courtier in my brother's favorite bicorne hat and black riding boots is standing in the gardens of the Tuileries Palace. When he sees me, his face breaks into a smile. "Wonderful news!" he exclaims from below. "The empress is giving birth!"

I slam the doors shut and turn to Paul. "He wants me to be present," I cry. "Even though he knows that seeing it will make me sick."

He shrugs. "Then don't go. But the emperor will send for you anyway, and when his courtier doesn't find you, he'll come for you himself."

"Aren't you upset that I'll be sick?"

"You're always sick. It won't be any different from yesterday or tomorrow."

I am shocked by his coldness. "What's the matter with you?"

He doesn't say anything, although he hands me the special juice he prepares daily for me and watches to see that I've taken it all. He is different lately. Unsympathetic to my pain and less caring. Then I realize what it must be. Napoleon has made him afraid. He thinks what happened to de Canouville will happen to him. "Paul," I say gently, and he looks away. "My brother would never send you to Spain."

He laughs shortly. "You believe that's what I'm worried about? Your Highness, I have told you. I wish to leave France."

I inhale. "Paul, don't leave me. *Please.* I need you."

"And what's different now from a year ago, or two years?"

"Just give me a year. One more year, and I'll go back with you." Suddenly, I can see myself on the island with Paul, dancing in his arms on those hot summer nights. My brother will hate to see me go, and certainly I'll miss Paris. But life was calm in Saint-Domingue; it was easy there. I've never given him a date before. "Next December we'll leave," I say.

"And why not now?"

"Because there are things that have to be done," I explain. In a year, Napoleon will be divorced, and I'll have convinced him to return with his army to Egypt. Then with Egypt as part of our empire, we'll retake Saint-Domingue. "Paul, you'll wait for me, won't you?" He has to. We'll make him king of Saint-Domingue, and I'll visit him from Egypt the way Cleopatra visited Caesar as his true queen in Rome.

But Paul is silent.

"I have plans for us both. You'll be happy, and we'll be together. One year," I repeat, and when he doesn't argue, I turn to the mirror and imagine the crown of Egypt on my head. "Destiny," I whisper, but a knock at the door interrupts the vision.

"The emperor or one of his servants," Paul warns.

It's one of his servants. The man is dressed in my brother's green livery, and when he bows, I see that his hat is embroidered with the imperial emblem of bees. "You are wanted in the birthing chamber, Your Highness."

Paul glances at me, expecting an outburst. But I have spent the last month preparing for this. "If you will wait one moment," I tell the young man with a calm I certainly don't feel. But it's important no one knows how much the arrival of this child crushes me.

I go to collect my shawl, then stop in my room of antiquities. The high-vaulted chamber is brightly lit, and a pair of heavy chandeliers cast light across the hundreds of artifacts I've collected since my brother's coronation. I walk to the cabinet where the crown of Egypt rests on a velvet pillow, a powerful symbol of immortality. I close my eyes and breathe deeply. Children do not ensure immortality. I reach out and touch the glass. If there were more time, I might take the crown from its resting place. But my brother is waiting.

When I return to the salon, the servant and Paul are both waiting for me.

"Is Your Highness ready?"

We follow the man through the halls. Napoleon has always loved this palace. It's not as grand as Fontainebleau, but everything in the Tuileries is gilded, and the poorest courtier feels like a king walking these halls.

The courtier enters first and announces our names. Then we step into the antechamber.

Thirteen years ago the same people gathered for the birth of my son in Milan. Six years later, they came together again for his funeral. I rushed to the Villa Mondragone to be at his side as fast as the horses could carry me. But all the court can remember is that I wasn't there when he was dying. That while he burned with fever, I was swimming and eating well in Tuscany. My only child, my precious Dermide, the only good thing to come of my first marriage. After his death, I cut off my hair and placed it in his coffin.

"Pauline!" Caroline calls as soon as she sees me, and we stand together in a corner of the antechamber, with its mother-of-pearl *secretaire* and large porcelain busts. My entire family is present. My mother looks so happy, she might actually weep.

"The pain started an hour ago," my sister confides. "She'll give birth before nightfall Napoleon is *in the chamber*."

But my brother hates "women's business." From the time we were children, he vowed he would never attend a birth.

"He's concerned for her well-being," she tells me. "Apparently the child is breech."

"Did he give his instructions to the doctors yet?"

"No one's heard. But if I had to guess . . ." She hesitates, drawing out the suspense. "He'll choose her life."

"Over a future king of France?" I exclaim. My mother looks over at the two of us in the corner. I glance toward the closed door and immediately feel faint. "I need a chair."

"Don't be dramatic." But my legs start to buckle, and Caroline panics. "Someone bring a chair!"

One of the servants hurries over with a fan and a stool, then helps me to sit.

"I feel hot." My breath is coming quickly. "Am I hot?"

Caroline puts a palm to my forehead and looks to my mother. "She doesn't feel well."

"You're working yourself into a state," my mother says.

"You think I'm *creating* this?"

She touches my cheeks, and I see the slight frown between her brows.

I really do feel ill. My stomach . . .

"The child is coming!" someone shouts from within. Everyone rushes to the door, and no one's concerned about me anymore. "A son!" I hear my brother cry, and then everyone begins to shout and clap. "A son!" Doctors are shouting for towels and bandages to stop the bleeding. A courtier runs to spread the news, and within moments the cannon shots begin. Twenty-two for a boy. Twenty-one if it had been a girl.

Only Paul asks if I am well. My mother is clasping her hands and praying. "A successful breech birth. It's a miracle from God."

I look up at Paul and wish he could embrace me. But in all of our time together, he has only held me once: the night my husband died in Saint-Domingue. I reach for his hand, and he lets me hold it until my brother appears.

A tremendous cheer goes up in the room. I have never seen him so proud.

"Napoléon François Joseph Charles Bonaparte has been

born," he announces. "Her Majesty will make a full recovery."

There is immense rejoicing. Even Joséphine's children, Eugène and Hortense, are congratulating their former step-father. Don't they realize this child has ruined everything for them?

Then my brother makes his way toward me. "You have a nephew," he says joyously. "The King of Rome."

"Congratulations," Paul says on my behalf. "All of France will be celebrating in the streets tonight."

But Napoleon is looking at me. "If you are ill, leave. No one must be sick around this child."

"Of course not. He's the *King of Rome!*" I can see my mother drawing close, and my sisters, too. "Will the court move to the Tuileries Palace now, because this is where his *Hapsburg* ancestors resided?"

He looks around the chamber and shrugs. "Why not?"

"Because you have always loved Fontainebleau!"

My brother's face turns red, and he turns to our mother. "I've had enough of this family!" On the other side of the wall, his new son begins to cry. He hears the sound, and his face softens. "They will not ruin this for me," he swears to Maman.

"Stay," she implores, then looks at me. "No one will speak another word."

As the chandeliers are lit and dinner is about to be served, Napoleon finds me in the Grand Salon. Hundreds of courtiers have come to celebrate, and heavy platters are filled with roasted swan and wild duck, and a dozen different vegetables are piled high in silver bowls. The room is filled with talk of the future: France will be an undefeatable empire now that the empress has done in just twelve months what Joséphine failed to do in fourteen years. Who knows how many children she might go on to produce? Three sons. Four? But there's none of the day's excitement in my brother's face.

"I must speak with you," he says solemnly in my ear, and everyone's gaze is on us as we exit the Grand Salon together. I follow him down the hall where we can talk in private, then wait for the tirade that is sure to come. Only he's silent.

"I'm afraid," he says at last.

I look around us, to see if he might be referring to some immediate threat, but he shakes his head.

"Not of someone—of some*thing*. What if my son is sick?"

I start angrily, "I wasn't—"

"Not you," he interrupts. "Because of me, or her."

I hesitate.

"Her eldest brother is plagued with seizures. A sister, too."

"Are you certain?"

"Metternich confirmed it."

"And you've always known?"

"She's a Hapsburg," he reminds me. "And our son looks healthy. But what if . . ."

He doesn't have to finish. I know what he fears. When we were children, I saw it happen in Corsica. One moment he was playing with the chickens, then suddenly he was rolling on the floor, his tongue out of his mouth, his body shaking. It's happened at least a dozen times since, and there's no telling when it will happen again. Only our mother knows about this. And Caroline. "How often is her brother . . . sick?" I ask him.

"Daily. She writes to him twice a week, but he's isn't right." He indicates his head, and my heart begins to race.

"What do the doctors say?" I ask him.

"No one knows about it."

"What about your advisers and Méneval?"

"They think I'm peculiar."

"Then wait and see. It might come to nothing."

He nods. "That's right. The Bonapartes have never had bad luck before." But he's convincing himself, and I can hear he doesn't believe it. "What should I do about Joséphine? I—I think I did her wrong. I'll tell her to return to Malmaison. And she'll want to see the child."

I look at him in the low light of the hall, and all forty years are etched in his face. *He misses Joséphine and wants my permission to let her see his child. My permission. Not Marie-Louise's.* "You're tired," I say. "Tomorrow, when you're rested and fed, none of this will seem important."

CHAPTER 21

PAUL MOREAU

Tuileries Palace, Paris
April 1811

"Look at that, Paul. Have you ever seen a grip like that on a child? Tell me the truth."

I look into the cream and gold bassinet where Napoleon II is gripping the emperor's finger and shake my head. "No, but then I've never been around children."

He laughs. Everything is a wonderful joke to him now, and in the two months since the king of Rome's birth, the emperor has put on more weight than the child. "He's carrying the next heir," I've heard courtiers joke, and I smile privately, because this is really how he looks. But whenever he's not playing with his son in the nursery, he's sitting at a table in the Grand Salon, surveying the foods he had always resisted. There's been turkey with truffles, wild boar, carp, loaves filled with jam, and trays bursting with pastries. Nothing is too rich for the emperor suddenly.

"I guess you've heard about the Russians?" he asks.

So this is why he's asked me to come. He no longer works

from his study, so now the court converses with him here. "They're defying your edict," I tell him, "which forbids trade with Great Britain."

"The Czar Alexander! Whom *I* tutored. Who was *my* friend." He steps from the bassinet and moves to the fireplace, where he begins to pace. Then he indicates a chair across from him, and I sit. "Tell me, Paul, why he is he doing this?"

I hesitate. He has a hundred advisers whom he could be asking.

"From a courtier's perspective," he explains. "I want to know."

"The embargo is crippling their economy. Their trade with Britain is exceptionally beneficial."

"More beneficial than an alliance?" he demands.

"What alliance? You signed the Treaty of Tilsit with Czar Alexander," I say brutally, unwilling to play this game, "and did not keep its terms."

His neck goes red. "And what should I have done?" he shouts. "Provide Russia with soldiers for a fruitless war against Turkey?"

"That is the treaty you signed," I say simply, telling him what courtiers are saying in the halls.

The baby begins to cry and a nurse hurries in from the next room. "Your Majesty," she exclaims, "you've awakened your son."

"Then he should get used to loud noises. Do you know what it's like on the battlefield, Madame? The cannon fire, the gunshots, the horses charging like a moving, churning river."

She lifts the baby slowly from his crib and cradles him at her breast.

"That child was born to fight," he tells her, "which is why his doting mother may only see him at night. During the day," his voice rises, "I will teach him to fear nothing!"

The tiny king of Rome begins to scream, and when the nurse takes him into the second chamber for his feeding, Napoleon turns to me. "He will be fearless, Paul. War will be for him what acquiring useless baubles is for women. He'll crave the sounds of battle; the scents of the field. A tent will be just as much a home to him as a palace."

Like father, like son.

He takes a seat next to the fire and indicates that I should do the same. "I've forbidden the Russians from trading with Great Britain, and they defy me. Now there's news that the czar is preparing his army. Clearly, he's looking for war."

He is, or you are?

"How long do you think it would take to amass an army of half a million men?"

I sit across from him while he takes out his snuff jar and opens the lid. "I wouldn't know, Your Majesty."

He pinches the snuff between his fingers and inhales. "You are very reserved on this subject," he remarks. "Why?"

"Because there are greater ills at home," I say truthfully, "and in your colonies, where slavery still exists."

"So you think I should fight slavery instead of Russians?"

"Yes."

He gazes into the fire. "You are a noble man, Paul. Your people would be proud to know that at every opportunity, you have advanced their cause, even when you knew it was futile."

"Then you are going to war."

"With an army of half a million men."

I find Pauline in the ballroom. She is exactly where I left her, sitting on a heavily cushioned chair, looking out over the empty room. She turns as soon as she hears my boots, and in the soft light of the chamber, she is like a painting, with her hair in loose curls on top of her head and her red gown slipping from her small white shoulders. It takes everything in my power not to kiss her long neck, starting behind her ears and then working my way down her exquisite body. She wouldn't stop me—she would welcome it. But I must never take the same liberties with Pauline that she allows her dishonorable lovers to take.

I join her in the middle of the room, and she looks up at me with expectation. "We are going to war," I say.

She puts a hand on her stomach, and I am sure her grimace is real. "With Russia?"

"Yes." The court has been talking about it for weeks. "He plans to raise an army of five hundred thousand men."

"When?" she asks, and I already know what she's thinking. *Perhaps there's time to convince him otherwise. Perhaps he will go to Egypt instead.*

"He didn't say, but I'd guess within a year."

She leans back in her chair and groans. "What if I don't make it, Paul?"

Though she hasn't asked me to, I sit beside her, and we look out on the empty ballroom together. "Are you really that ill?"

"I don't know. Sometimes it's so bad, I can't walk."

"Then have the servants carry you."

"And after that," she asks fearfully, "what then? I'll have to stop dancing? *Walking?*" She looks up at the heavy chandeliers and passes her hand over her eyes.

"Is it always your stomach?"

"Sometimes it's my back, or just general aches. But it's terrible pain." She lowers her hand. "You don't know . . ."

Navarre, March 1811

Sire—Amid the numerous felicitations you receive from every corner of Europe, from all the cities of France, and from each regiment of your army, can the feeble voice of a woman reach your ear, and will you deign to listen to her who so often consoled your sorrows and sweetened your pains, now that she speaks to you only of that happiness in which all your wishes are fulfilled? Having ceased to be your wife, dare I felicitate you on becoming a father? Yes, sire, without hesitation, for my soul renders justice to yours, in like manner as you know mine. I can conceive every emotion you must experience, as you divine all that I feel at this moment; and though separated, we are united by that sympathy which survives all events.

I should have desired to learn the birth of the King of Rome from yourself and not from the sound of the cannon of Evreux, or the courier of the prefect. I know, however, that in preference to all, your first attentions are due to the public authorities of the State, to the foreign ministers, to your family, and especially to the fortunate princess who has realized your dearest hopes. She cannot be more tenderly devoted to you than I; but she has been enabled to contribute more toward your happiness by securing that of France. She has then a right to your first feelings, to all your cares; and I who was but your companion in times of difficulty—I cannot ask more than a place in your affection far removed from that occupied by the Empress Maria Louisa. Not till you have ceased to watch by her bed, not till you are weary of embracing your son, will you take the pen to converse with your best friend—I will wait.

Eugène and Hortense will write me, imparting their own satisfaction. But it is from you that I desire to know if your child be well, if he resemble you, if I shall one day be permitted to see him; in short, I expect from you *unlimited confidence, and upon such I have some claims, in consideration, sire, of the boundless attachment I shall cherish for you while life remains.*

Joséphine

To the Empress at Navarre.
Paris, March 22, 1811.

My love—I have received your letter. I thank you. My son is stout and very well. I hope he will be prospered, qu'il viendra à bien. *He has my chest, my mouth, and eyes. I hope that he will fulfill his destiny.*

I am always well pleased with Eugène. He has never caused me any dissatisfaction.

Napoleon

1812

CHAPTER 22

MARIE-LOUISE

Fontainebleau Palace
June 1812

I sit at my armoire and try to breathe. It's only one appearance. Even my brother Ferdinand could manage something like this. But as my lady-in-waiting arranges my curls, and I wait for Hortense to arrive with my *parure*, I can't stop thinking about Marie-Antoinette. How almost twenty-five years ago she sat in this chamber with similar women in similar jewels, and the ministers came to tell her that France was on the verge of revolution.

Today my husband's men will announce we are at war, and is it really any different? There will be weeping in the streets. Women will find themselves without money or protectors. And when the lame come home and the lists of the dead begin to appear, the people will look to us. We will be the ones who have caused their misery.

"Ready, Your Majesty?" Hortense opens a heavy velvet box and lifts out the diamond and ruby crown. There are a necklace and earrings to match. It's a set Napoleon gifted me on our wedding night. I close my eyes while she finishes my toilette, and when I look at myself in the mirror, I frown. *Who is this woman whose husband will send seven hundred thousand men to war? Why doesn't she go to the Council Chamber and stop him?*

But I will accept the task Napoleon asked of me last night. And when the wounded come home in need of care, there will be hospitals ready. And when widows are created and left homeless, funds will be ready to take care of their children. France will not suffer as Austria did.

"It will be over in twenty days," Hortense reminds me. "That's what he's saying."

But an emperor can say a great many things that will never come to pass. I stand and study my reflection. In my red silk gown and white summer slippers, I might be leaving for a picnic on the lake. Only the crown on my head and the diamonds at my neck say otherwise. "I want to see my son first," I say.

Hortense exchanges a look with my lady-in-waiting, but they say nothing as we walk toward the nursery.

"Maman!" Franz cries as soon as he sees us. I can see his tutor is shocked that I've come during the day.

"Your Majesty." He rises, and Franz abandons his desk to run over to me.

"Maman!" he shouts again, and my heart swells with pride. At just sixteen months old, he has ten words, and two of them mean "mother."

"How is your day, sweetheart?" I ask him, squatting so we can talk face to face.

He kisses my cheek, then looks at my gown and jewels and says, "Ohhh." His lips form the perfect 0. I can feel my heart bursting. He's the most beautiful child in all of France, with a head of golden curls and sea-green eyes that look up at me with absolute love.

"How is he doing?" I ask his tutor, and the old man points to a pile of books.

"We go through them every day, Your Majesty. This afternoon is music."

"And art?" I rise.

"After the pianoforte."

"Good." He's to learn these subjects at my insistence. I feel a tug on my dress, and Franz is holding up a wooden soldier.

"You," he says, and he offers me the toy in his pudgy hand.

"I can take him?" I ask, and my son nods eagerly.

"Thank you." I bend to kiss his cheek. "I'll be back tonight," I promise. "And when I come, I'll return your soldier." But it breaks my heart to think of him in here, trapped in this room like an animal.

"We should go," Hortense presses, but I can't leave him like this.

"How much time does he have to play?" I ask.

Monsieur Laurent frowns. "What do you mean?"

"On his wooden horse. Or with his soldiers. When does he play?"

"That's what the evening is for, Your Majesty. The day is for work."

"At sixteen months old?"

"These are the emperor's instructions." He grows flustered. "I don't understand—"

But I do. "There will be new instructions tomorrow."

As we leave the nursery, Franz follows me to the door.

We reach the Council Chamber, and as our names are announced before the assembly, I look down at the wooden soldier in my hand. I take my seat to Napoleon's right and look out at the grandeur. If I live for another fifty years in the Tuileries Palace, I will never cease to be amazed by its beauty. Gilded panels of laurel and flower motifs soar toward the ceiling, where angels take flight across the painted dome. Napoleon passes me a look, and when I nod, he shouts into the room for silence.

"As you know," he begins, "our war with Russia is at its start. Tomorrow, on the twenty-fourth of June, the imperial army will march toward Moscow to defeat our enemy."

This is when I should beg him not to go, when I should risk his displeasure to be the voice of reason and warn him against this. But the thought of his anger is too uncomfortable, and the pleasure of his leaving too great. His advisers breathe furiously, and the only sound in the room is the creaking of leather chairs.

"In mere weeks," he continues jubilantly, "our empire will touch borders it's never seen." He looks around the chamber. But if he's expecting applause, he's disappointed. "In my absence," he goes on, "and in all further absences of mine in France, I am leaving the regency in capable hands."

The men shift in their seats, and I notice Pauline look to her sister Caroline.

"Empress Marie-Louise, my wife and the mother to the king of Rome, shall be governing in my place."

There's a gasp in the chamber so loud that it echoes from the walls. Then everyone begins shouting at once. I hear murmurs of, "Twenty-one years old . . . she's only twenty-*one*!"

Napoleon holds up his hands. "Silence!" he shouts, but even the ministers are ignoring him. "THERE WILL BE SILENCE!"

The room goes quiet, and all eyes focus on me.

"The commands my wife gives are my commands. The laws my wife enacts are my laws. No one shall disobey her, or they disobey me."

The regency of France has fallen to me. That the emperor should choose his young Austrian bride over all his siblings and ministers speaks loudly to the entire Bonaparte clan.

"There will be letters from me daily. If *anyone*"—and his gaze falls to his sisters—"should think to challenge the empress, she will remove them from France."

I don't remember what is spoken after this. Napoleon talks about weapons and twenty short days. But it is only when we have returned to our apartments and Hortense is holding out lemon water for me that I realize the magnitude of what has happened. *I am the emperor of France.* And the world is going back to war. It is as my father said. *"So long as there is Napoleon,"* he warned, *"there will never be peace."*

And the next morning, as I make my way to the nursery, I execute my first command. "Good morning, Monsieur Laurent."

He bows. "Your Majesty."

"From now on," I instruct him, "my son will enjoy more playtime. Half of the morning, and at least one hour in the afternoon. These are the emperor's new instructions."

CHAPTER 23

PAULINE BONAPARTE

Hautecombe Abbey, Savoy, France
September 1812

I step close to the window of the lighthouse and let the autumn wind blow in my hair. The last rays of light are fading beneath the lake of Hautecombe Abbey, and the water looks like a stretch of liquid gold. I came to this monastery after my son, Dermide, was taken by the fever. I found peace and solitude then in these walls. I hope I can find it again.

I touch the cool stones and close my eyes. My brother should be in Moscow by now. Nearly seven hundred thousand men left with him to defeat the arrogant Russian czar, but for over three months, the cowardly Russians have refused to give battle. In Moscow, however, there will be no retreat. The Russians will be forced to fight or lose the most precious jewel in their crown. So this is where I'll stay until my brother comes home.

Steps echo in the stairwell, and I know it is Paul coming to bring me my medicine. He believes the Russians have the advantage, since they know their own land and can survive the severe weather. If winter comes before this war is finished, he says, our soldiers will die of cold before anything else. *Dear God, be with my brother right now, and extend Your protection to de Canouville, who is carrying my silver locket and has not returned since Spain. If they have ever sinned against you, I pray for forgiveness on their behalves.*

"Your Highness, it's time."

Time. The Egyptians understood that we aren't given much time on this earth. From the moment they were old enough to earn, they began collecting precious items for their tombs: linens, bowls, jars for makeup, religious scrolls. Those who could afford it added expensive sandals and heavy jewels. You must greet the afterlife prepared. After all, none of us know how much time we are given. Seven months ago I promised Paul we would return to Haiti. Yet look at us now—praying like monks in Hautecombe Abbey. Of course, Paul understands that we can't possibly leave my brother like this. When we return to Haiti, it must be as conquerors. He as its king, and me as his consort.

Paul offers me his arm, and we cross the fields to the abbey together. "Any news?" I ask him. The setting sun has turned his skin deep bronze, and his eyes are almost black in the fading light.

"None. The messengers say we shouldn't expect anything for at least three days."

"Three days?" I repeat. *That's impossible!* "What will we do?"

"Wait," he says simply.

But I can't accept it. "There has to be someone who knows what's happening in Moscow."

"Yes, and they're going to the Tuileries to report to the empress."

I think of Marie-Louise in Napoleon's chair, seated like the Queen of the World in his Council Chamber, and a fire burns in my stomach. There is no one more loyal to Napoleon than me. The moment I heard he was making that child—an *Austrian*, no less—the regent of France, I packed my bags and was gone the next morning. The rest of my family can do as they please, but at least there will be one female Bonaparte with some pride. Did he really think we would all sit in that chamber while *Her Majesty* issues her commands? When he might have made me regent?

We reach the abbey, and I exhale.

"Tired?" Paul asks.

"A little."

He glances behind us, and I know what he's thinking. It's a short walk from here to the lighthouse. "Perhaps we should sit by the fire and read."

Inside, I follow him into the library, with its warm, plush carpets and crackling fire. I seat myself on the widest divan, and he takes a stool, opening *Cinna* to the page where we left off. My brother has seen this tragedy performed twelve times, and I have gone to at least half a dozen. It is a story of mercy and gratitude, of ruling prudently and watching your enemies. *He who forgives readily only invites offense.* It is the greatest line from Pierre Corneille's play, in my opinion. Yet my brother prefers, *Ambition displeases when it has been sated . . . having reached the peak, it aspires to descend.*

I hope it is not descending now.

CHAPTER 24

PAUL MOREAU

Saint-Cloud, outside Paris
October 1812

I look at the courtier, in his muddied boots and rain-drenched coat, and wonder if it was her brother who sent him, or some kind-hearted general who discovered the silver locket with her picture inside. "I'm sorry, monsieur, but I cannot be the one to tell her."

The young man loses some of his coloring, but I cannot be the one to deliver this news. "Should I . . ." He looks past my shoulder into the hall. "Do I—"

"I can take you to her. She's in the salon." He follows me down the candlelit hall, and the sound of our boots echoes against the stones.

"Does she come here often?" he asks.

He's wondering if the princess makes a habit of living in such gloomy places. "Only when she's truly ill."

I open the door to the salon, and the princess is curled up on the chaise near the fire. She's been in the same position all day, suffering from her stomach pains and nausea. But as soon as she sees the soldier, she rises.

"Napoleon?"

The young man lowers his eyes. "Your Highness," he begins. "The honorable Captain Armand-Jules-Elisabeth de Canouville has died."

She screams, and I grab her hands before she can reach for his eyes. "You're lying. He's lying! He isn't dead. Show me the proof. I want proof!"

The courtier reaches a trembling hand into his vest and produces the locket. "He was wearing this when he died, Your Highness. I'm sorry."

She grabs the jewel from his hand and forces it open. Inside is a portrait of Pauline, beautiful and vivid. "It isn't happening." She begins to shake. I take the locket from her hands and guide her to the chaise, wondering about the other man she condemned to death. Will his fiancée be given anything to remember him by, or will he die a nameless death like so many soldiers do? I look to the courtier and nod for him to go.

"*No!* Tell me what's happening on the fronts!"

The courtier looks down, and Pauline clutches her stomach.

He doesn't know how to tell her that France's Grande Armée, which arrived in Russia nearly seven hundred thousand strong, is now a little more than a hundred thousand men. Three months, and half a million men are either captured or dead. Another hundred thousand have fled for their lives. When I heard this from a soldier outside the abbey, I hadn't believed it, either.

"Your Highness," he starts bravely, "Moscow has been won—"

She looks from me, to the courtier, then back again. "So why—"

"The city has been burned by the Russians, and what remains of your brother's army is waiting for word from the czar."

"Why do you say 'what remains'?" she whispers.

The courtier hesitates. "Only a seventh of his army remains." He reaches into his coat and pulls out a letter. "From a Württemberg cavalry officer," he says. His voice is shaking, but reads aloud. "'From Lieutenant Heinrich August Vossler,'" he begins.

The ravages of cold are equaled only by those of hunger. No food is so rotten or disgusting as to not find someone to relish it. No fallen horse or cattle remains uneaten. No dog, no cat, no carrion, nor, indeed, the corpses of those that died of cold or hunger, go untouched. It is not unknown for men to gnaw at their own famished bodies. But it's not only men's bodies which are suffering unspeakably. Their minds, too, have become deeply affected by the combined assault of extreme cold and hunger. All human compassion seems to have vanished; we care only for ourselves and our comrades be damned. I have actually watched men lie down and die with complete indifference, and I've witnessed other men sit on the corpses of the fallen so they won't have to touch the snow near the fireside. Dull despair or raving madness has taken possession of many, and they die muttering, with their last breath, the most horrible imprecations against God and man.

There is no consoling her. She collapses to the floor.

CHAPTER 25

MARIE-LOUISE

Tuileries Palace, Paris
December 1812

There is snow in Paris. I look out the window of the Council Chamber, and everything is white: the benches, the fountains, even the trees. My son is outside with Sigi, so his tutor can explain the origin of ice. In three months, Franz will be two years old. Monsieur Laurent tells me that he already has a few hundred words, including *garden* and *paint*.

Behind me, the Duc de Feltre clears his throat. "Is Your Majesty ready?"

The daily meeting of the Regency Council is set to begin, and the men at the table are waiting on me. I glance one last time at the winter gardens. "Yes, I am ready."

I follow my husband's Minister of War to the long council table and take my place in the emperor's seat. In this chair, with its soft velvet arms and padded back, I learned of the deaths of nearly half a million men. Some died of the war plague, others of starvation, but most of them were blown to pieces in battle. And when all of it was done, and Moscow was burned to the ground, the wreckage belonged to my husband.

He waited five weeks to hear from the czar. Thirty-five days in disease-infested encampments, while winter crept like the specter of death all around. And when no word came, he instructed his soldiers to begin the trek home.

Reports from the march have been too chilling to comprehend. Sick soldiers abandoned on the sides of the roads, left for the Russians to mutilate and torture. Men crying for their mothers as they expire from hunger, delirious. They tell us it's twenty below zero in Moscow, and that when a soldier speaks, his breath freezes in the air. This is what my husband conjured with his lust for war. This is what I did nothing to prevent. I look around the chamber. None of these men wanted a fight with Russia. My husband took no one's counsel but his own.

"There is news, Your Majesty," the *duc* informs me. But there is always news, and it is always dismal. "The emperor of France is returning home." The Minister of War looks sheepish. "He is coming ahead of his men by sleigh."

I rise from the table. "He's abandoning our army?" *My father would sooner die than flee from his own decimated army.*

The *duc* raises his hands. "Never, Your Majesty."

I picture the scene. Napoleon, creeping in the dead of night toward a sleigh hitched to a dozen dogs. *The coward. The arrogant, selfish, coward . . .* "He sent five hundred thousand men to their deaths—"

"Not quite five hundred thousand."

"I have seen the lists!" I shout. "Every day. The missing,

the casualties, the wounded." *He is traveling across the ice by sleigh. The emperor of France!* The image is ludicrous. "What will you tell him when he arrives?"

The *duc* clears his throat. "That if he hopes to keep his crown, he will act swiftly. There is talk of a coup in Paris."

"A revolution?" My aunt's greatest error was in not believing the meaning of this word.

"I wouldn't say *revolution* . . . yet."

"And what do the people want?"

The *duc* lowers his gaze. "Their sons and husbands back."

No one speaks. I am sickened by the heartache that will be felt by the mothers and wives whose tables will be empty come Christmas. Conscription was for men from sixteen to sixty, which means there will be women in France who have lost both their husbands and their sons in Russia. It's a blood tax no house should ever have to pay. I think of my own son and could weep.

I should have done more. When Napoleon left, I should have begged him to make peace with the czar. But I was selfish, and all I could think about were the many ways my life would be better without him in France.

The *duc* hands me a paper. "We will release the Twenty-ninth Bulletin today." It looks the same as the Twenty-eighth. "If Your Majesty would care to read it . . ."

It begins with a description of Napoleon's losses. Then it details all the hardships of Russia: the muddy roads, the frozen rivers, but most distressingly, the weather. According to the 29th Bulletin, it is the snow that is to blame for Napoleon's defeat. Not ambition or greed, but the bitter cold. And then it ends: "The health of His Majesty was never better."

I look at the solemn faces in the Regency Council and tell them plainly, "He has lost his mind."

No one contradicts me.

Seven days pass, and there is no word of the emperor. I sit in my son's nursery with Hortense, and we guess what might happen when he arrives. "He will rebuild his army," she says. "There are always boys willing to fight for land and glory." She looks at Franz on his wooden horse, and tears well in her eyes. "My husband says Napoleon is all my sons talk about," she admits. "They want to dress like soldiers and play mock battles."

"They're young," I tell her. "They haven't seen bloodshed. It's different when your gun is real and it has to take a man's life." This is what my father replied when I wrote to him about Franz's love of swords. Now that I'm regent, his letters come to me once a week.

"Even your son will wish to go to war someday. It's what little boys grow up to do."

"Not mine."

But she looks at me pityingly. "We warned him," Hortense says quietly. She is dressed in a heavy blue gown, and the white fur at her collar was a gift from Napoleon. For all his greed, he has never been miserly. "Even my mother told him that building an empire was reaching too high. Why not be satisfied with France? Why did he have to try for Egypt and Russia?"

Or Austria and Poland? "What does your mother say now?"

She searches my face, and when she's sure that I'm not angry that Joséphine is communicating with my husband, she tells me, "She fears for him. She thinks Britain will smell blood and come to France for the kill. He has always hated Britain. Napoleon doesn't feel that George III is worthy to rule it."

"I've read the papers," I tell her. "They said it before my marriage, and now they're saying it again: that your mother was his talisman. That she was his lucky star, and that by casting her away, he also cast off her glow."

"Journalists," she protests. "They spin tales for a living."

"But the people believe it now, don't they?" Her silence tells me all I need to know. It wasn't so long ago that the French were angry enough to execute a queen. They are the same people today, with the same passions and resentments, only now their losses are greater. "What if the British do declare war?" I ask quietly. "Have you thought about what would happen to us?"

If riots should start, it will be up to us to plan our escape from France. Hortense's husband is in Austria with her sons, under my father's protection. My husband is somewhere between Moscow and Paris.

"We would flee," she says. "We would have to. No foreign army will deal with us leniently now."

I look at my son, with his long golden curls and rosy cheeks. Did Napoleon ever look this way? I can't imagine my husband playing quietly, petting a wooden horse and giving it a name like Jacques or Antoine. But there must have been a time when he was innocent; when he looked at Madame Mère, and she knew she would always do anything for him. But then I think of his rage when he pushed my face into a bowl of food, and of Franz unable to leave his lessons—and someday the battlefield as well—and I realize, *If it comes to it, we really will flee. Then I will take my son to Austria.*

But on the night of the eighteenth of December, a young servant comes running into the Grand Salon. Despite the war, Christmas garlands have been hung over the wooden doors, and cheerful branches of holly spring from gold vases. Madame Mère is playing cards with Caroline, while dozens of courtiers are at games of their own. There is also music, but in truth, nothing seems very merry. I am speaking with Hortense when the servant first appears. I don't see him waiting behind me for an audience, and she is the one who interrupts our conversation.

"Your Majesty." She indicates someone behind me. I turn to see a young boy in blue and gold livery who is waiting nervously to speak.

"There—there is someone who wishes to see you," he says. He looks nervously at the people who are watching him, then leans forward to whisper, "He says he's the emperor of France."

I exchange a look with Hortense, and immediately we rise. "Where is he?"

"At the gates, Your Majesty. But the guards aren't sure. No one can be certain."

I cross the salon toward Madame Mère and tap her shoulder. "Can you come with me?"

She hears the nervousness in my voice and agrees immediately.

"What is it?" Caroline demands, and when I refuse to answer, she throws down her cards and follows behind us.

An old man in a gray jacket is standing outside the gates. His beard is matted, and his shoulders are hunched against the cold. "*Mio Dio,*" I hear Caroline whisper, and Hortense is struck dumb by the sight. He is unrecognizable.

"Napoleon?" Madame Mère cries and hurries forward, but the guards step in front of her before she can pass. "Are you *certain* this is the emperor, Madame?" they ask.

"I know my own son! Let him through," she demands. "He's standing in the cold!"

The men look to me, and the figure speaks. "Marie-Louise," he says tenderly. "Don't you know who I am?"

"I didn't. But now that I hear you speak . . ."

He removes his hat, and I'm shocked at how gray his hair has become. "How is the king of Rome?"

"Almost two years old now." *And happy,* I want to tell him. *Content with his life.* But instead I add dutifully, "He misses his father."

Napoleon smiles, and now he is even less recognizable. "I will bathe and be in your apartment for seven."

He looks to Hortense and cups her chin in his palm. "I have ordered my brother to return with your sons. I want all of the Bonapartes in France."

"Why? Is there going to be war?"

"Only God knows, and we're not on speaking terms right now."

We allow the emperor of France to enter the Tuileries, and the entire palace comes alive with the news. Courtiers greet us in the halls, and there are shouts of *"Vive l'impérator!"* as we pass. Madame Mère is weeping tears of joy, and Caroline is defending her husband Murat, who abandoned the army a month ago to protect his Kingdom of Naples. Everyone is talking at once, and after months of tense silence, it is all too much.

I climb the stairs to my apartment, and though Hortense offers to come with me, I want to be alone. I have lost the regency of France. My father's letters, which have been coming once, sometimes twice a week, will no longer come to me, and Franz will return to his rigorous studies without time for play. In a single night, I have gone from captain to passenger. I know it would be a crime against God to wish that the war had lasted longer, but when I think of how little I shall see Franz now, I feel sick that Napoleon is home for good.

Inside my chamber, Sigi is sleeping contentedly near the fire. He thumps his tail as soon as he sees me but doesn't make any attempt to move. I can't blame him. It's cold. I sit at my armoire and take the silver pins from my hair, arranging the curls so that they fall on either side of my face. Would Ferdinand recognize me if we saw each other now? It's been nearly four years. My hair is longer, and my face is slightly thinner, now that Franz is almost two. I overheard a courtier yesterday telling the Duchesse de Feltre that I look ten years older than my twenty-two. I turn my face to the side and wonder if it's true.

"Marie-Louise."

I jump, then put my hand to my chest. "I didn't hear you come."

Napoleon laughs. This is a favorite trick, and I see that some things haven't changed. He crosses my chamber and holds out his hand. I take it, and he studies me for a moment before speaking. "As fresh and beautiful as I remember." He leads me to the bed, but instead of lying down, he remains seated, and I sit next to him.

"I saw our son. He has grown significantly," he says.

"Yes. Six months is a long time to be away."

"Did any of the court's men pursue you?" he asks.

I lean back. "Certainly not!"

"You can tell me," he says quietly. "Or maybe it was you. Pretty little flowers will reach for the rain when the sun is gone."

I gasp. "I'm a mother!"

"So is Joséphine," he says darkly. "That's never stopped her."

I stand from the bed. "I am not one of your soldiers," I say heatedly. "You may speak to them as you wish, but I am—"

"The empress of France," he finishes. "And you are worth more than a hundred siblings. They tell me you ruled well."

I scowl. "Was this a test?"

"Does it matter?" He pulls me down beside him. "Even my Minister of War was impressed. You saw the Twenty-ninth Bulletin?"

I stare at him. "All of France has seen it."

He lowers his voice. "What do the people say?"

"Half a million men are gone," I reply. "And there are

Frenchmen dying in Spain. Two wars with no resolution. There is despair among the people."

"What do they expect?" he demands. "The czar will not negotiate. Do you know how I had to get here?" He doesn't wait for me to respond. "By *sled*. It's one step between the sublime and the ridiculous!"

I don't need to ask what would have been sublime. Victory, at any cost.

"They burned Moscow when we reached the city. There were mountains of rolling flames as wide as a sea. Can you imagine? An entire city, burning. It was the greatest thing I've ever witnessed."

I don't know what to say.

"Aren't you glad that I'm alive?"

"Yes." *But a half a million men are dead!*

He stands from the bed. He is dressed in his robe and slippers. "I went to Malmaison before coming here," he admits. "And do you know what Joséphine said? That a million lives are worth one of me."

Then she is as deluded as you are, I think.

"Certainly, many men were killed," he explains. "But they were happy to die for France."

"In the icy rivers, screaming for their wives?" He looks stricken, but I've read the reports, I know the truth. "This country lost half a million to its Revolution," I say. "And now that same number to a war in the east. There is a darkness infusing France. Total disbelief that anything will ever get better."

"Then we shall show them that this is only a small

setback." He moves toward the door. "Tomorrow there will be a victory ball. After that, a dance every night until the new year."

He shuts the door, and immediately I am ill. I rush to my washbasin, and Sigi follows behind me, whimpering at the sounds I'm making as I vomit.

"Your Majesty!" I hear Hortense call from the door. Then I see her in the mirror and wince. "What happened?" she asks kindly. She holds back my hair as I heave, but nothing else comes. "Sit down." She guides me to a chaise, but I'm shaking so badly, it's difficult to stay still. She takes a blanket from my armoire and wraps it around me. "Something happened," she says firmly. "What did he say?"

"We're to celebrate his victory tomorrow," I whisper. "And the night after that. And all the nights until January."

She presses her hand to her stomach. "He can't mean it."

But the emperor has issued a command.

And so we dance. While Prussia declares war on France, courtiers fill the ballroom in their finest clothes. And when Great Britain, Russia, and Sweden all follow, we continue to waltz. There are no young men. They have all been wounded or killed in battle. But the old courtiers who were unfit for war partner the young women who are mourning their husbands.

When Pauline returns from whichever spa she has been hiding at, the nights grow longer. There is no stopping the Bonapartes. They will dance until there is nothing left, not even a floor beneath them.

The ministers come to me for help, but there is nothing

useful I can tell them. "What is he going to do?" they ask. "Is he preparing for war?"

But Napoleon is silent. He dines, and sleeps, and spends long hours in Pauline's lavish apartments. I know I should want to keep him away from her, but I'm grateful when I don't have to see him, even if I can no longer spend the days with my son. Then on New Year's, during the waltz, he tells me, "Your father has betrayed us and joined the nations waging war against France."

I stop dancing, but he wants to continue.

"I know your loyalty is to me and our empire. But a crushing blow will have to be dealt to anyone who rises against me. I'm sorry." He cups my chin in his palm, and my heart beats faster. Is he going to imprison me? What about Franz? Tears well in my eyes, and he wipes them away with the back of his hand. "My kind, tenderhearted empress," he says pityingly.

"What's going to happen?"

"I will have to ask something very difficult of you."

I can no longer hear the music. Even Pauline, who is standing near the Duc de Feltre and watching us speak, fades from my sight. "Yes?"

"In April, when I leave to fight your father, I will need you to be regent."

To the Empress at Malmaison.

1812

I have received your letter of the tenth of June. I see no objections to your going to Milan, near the vice-queen. You will do well to go incognito. You will be very warm.

My health is very good. Eugène is well, and conducts well. Never doubt my interest in your welfare, and my affection.

Napoleon

Malmaison 1812

You restore me to life again, my dear Hortense, in assuring me that you have read the letters from the emperor to the empress. She is very kind in having shown them to you. I feel infinitely grateful to her for the friendship she manifests for you. I acknowledge that I am all the time exceedingly anxious. Why does not Eugène write? I am compelled, in order to calm my agitation, to believe that the emperor forbids him to write, that there may be no private letters.

Goodnight, my dear daughter. I embrace you with my whole heart, and with my whole heart I love you.

Joséphine

1812

My good mother—I write you from the field of battle. The emperor has gained a great victory over the Russians. The battle lasted thirteen hours. I commanded the right, and hope that the emperor will be satisfied.

I can not sufficiently thank you for your attentions and kindness to my little family. You are adored at Milan, as everywhere else. They write me most charming accounts of you, and you have won the love of everyone with whom you have become acquainted.

Adieu. Please give tidings of me to my sister. I will write to her tomorrow.

Your affectionate son, Eugène.

1813

CHAPTER 26

PAULINE BORGHESE

Tuileries Palace, Paris
January 1813

I lie back on the chaise and look up at the ceiling of the Tuileries Palace. I try to breathe deep, but it doesn't matter. In Saint-Domingue, in Milan, in Fontainebleau—this part's always the same. I spread my legs wider and wait for him to finish, and once he lowers the blanket and clears his throat, I know he's done. He waits for me to compose myself, and when I've pulled down my dress and put on my slippers, Dr. Halle begins.

"I would like to ask an extremely personal question, Your Highness. How many lovers have you had in the last week?"

I glance at my physician, Dr. Peyre, who insisted that this gynecologist come today. I rise from the chaise, and Dr. Halle holds up his hands. "This is important, Your Highness."

"And what are you implying?"

"If you can just answer the question—"

Dr. Peyre, whose face has gone red, interjects, "If you answer his question, it will help," he admits.

I try to think. *Who knows?* "Two? Three?"

"Different men?" he confirms.

"Of course. You asked about lovers, not liaisons." The doctors exchange looks, and I take my seat. "I'm not dying?"

"No." But Dr. Halle hesitates slightly. "You have *furor uterinus.*"

"I don't understand."

"You have overused your vaginal canal."

I wait for him to laugh. And when both men appear serious, I am through. "Get out!" They jump from their seats and I shriek loudly, "Out!"

"Your Highness—"

"I won't hear another word." Paul appears at the door, and I point at the doctors. "Take them away. I don't want to see either man again."

"But Your Highness," Dr. Peyre pleads. He has been with me for ten years.

"Not even you!" I'm so angry, I'm trembling.

"What did they do?" Paul demands when he returns.

"They wanted to convince me . . . they wanted to pretend . . ." I can't even say it. I can't be bothered. What do these men know anyway? They all say something different. One is sure I have the clap, another swears it's cancer of the stomach. Now I'm a nymphomaniac. "It doesn't matter," I say. "Who is Marie-Louise's doctor? The handsome blonde?"

"Dr. Espiaud?"

"Yes! Tell him I want to see him tomorrow."

Paul hesitates. "Can it wait?"

I take a deep breath and nod. "I'm finished being probed for today."

But Paul returns with Dr. Espiaud before dinner. I wonder if any other man on earth would have done this. Perhaps de Canouville. He might have.

"Your chamberlain tells me you're in a bad way," the doctor says, speaking from the door of my salon. He is tall and blond, with the largest teeth I've ever seen. If my little Italian artist, Canova, could see him, he'd sculpt him as a god. "May I come in?"

I step back to let him pass, then squeeze Paul's hand tightly after the doctor steps inside. "Thank you," I whisper, so glad he is with me.

I can see Espiaud's surprise as he enters. The room is practically bare, stripped of its priceless furnishings; almost nothing is left except the couches and a chaise.

"Is Your Highness planning a trip?" he asks.

"The doctors tell me I should be somewhere warm. Next week I'll be in Nice."

But he casts his gaze around the room, and I know what he's thinking. A princess doesn't pack her marble urns and paintings for a simple trip to the south. The imperial family is preparing for something else.

"Where should we have the exam, Your Highness?"

"The salon will do. My chamberlain will wait outside until it's finished."

Paul excuses himself, and I take my place on the couch.

"I have spoken with Dr. Peyre—"

"That man knows nothing."

"It may be. But he's given me your history. From this exam, I will draw my own conclusions."

"You don't think it's anything serious?" I ask.

"I'd be lying if I said no. You've been in pain for seven years, and terrible pain now for two."

Yes. I used to think it was God's way of punishing me for giving away my virtue at the Clary house. "You're the prettiest girl in Marseilles," Clary told me. "You can't blame me for wanting this." So I chose to believe him and blamed myself. Then I married Leclerc and suddenly understood. It wasn't something about me—it was what all men wanted.

"If you will lie down on the couch," Dr. Espiaud says, "and pull up your gown . . ."

I do as he asks, and wait for the inevitable pain. It's only a few moments.

One . . . two . . . three . . .

He sits back and hurriedly makes notes in his book. Then he tells me to breathe and probes me again. When he's finished, I struggle to sit without wincing.

"I apologize for any pain," he says softly.

I nod, too ill to speak.

"Given what I've seen, and what Dr. Peyre has already told me, I believe there is an infection of the fallopian tubes."

I have no idea what this means. "Is it curable?

"I suggest a warmer climate, as Dr. Peyre has said, and I would refrain from any—*activity*—as often as you can. It may not be the cause, but it is undoubtedly aggravating it."

He is so beautiful, so calm, that it's impossible to believe he's a doctor. He should have been born a courtier. There's no telling to what heights he might have risen then, since beauty is as useful as money at court. "And is there anything else?" I ask.

"Yes. And this may be the most difficult of all."

I hold my breath.

"It is likely you are infected with *chaude-pisse*."

The clap.

"Dr. Peyre tells me you have been applying leeches to your groin to ease the pain. I recommend stopping this. Instead, I would avoid any unnecessary stimulation."

"What about my baths?" I ask him.

"Warm."

"Even when I bathe in milk?"

He looks at me curiously, and I explain.

"I need it for my skin."

"If Your Highness feels that this is a necessity, then yes, even warm milk."

I silently review everything Dr. Espiaud has said. There doesn't seem to be any great urgency in his voice. In fact, if I look at him carefully, he doesn't seem terribly worried at all. Certainly I'm in pain. But perhaps he's right. If I am careful and limit myself to one lover, it might go away.

"Does Your Highness understand what I am saying?"

"Yes. I shall have to be more prudent," I tell him.

"Even in Nice."

Colonel Augustin Duchand will be there. I will restrict myself to his attentions alone. "But what happens if I become sick?" I ask.

"You will need to find a physician."

"But Dr. Peyre will no longer be serving me." I turn my head to the side. "Would you like to travel with my suite?"

He hesitates. "I have obligations here, Your Highness. I am paid—"

"Whatever the empress is paying, I will double it."

He blinks. "That is generous . . ."

"Triple." His blue eyes widen, and I smile. "We leave in seven days."

When my brother hears of my new doctor, he bursts into my chamber. "Where are you going?" He looks around the room. Everything has been packed. Even the heavy rugs, which I can't expect to use in Nice, are gone. I look into his eyes, and I know he is thinking of Corsica. Twenty years ago we fled our home with nothing but the clothes on our backs. Now the Bonapartes are fleeing again, only this time we'll be wearing silks and fur. He stands before my new jewelry box and reaches out to touch the mother-of-pearl. "This is new."

"I had it commissioned from Michelot last month."

"Fifteen thousand francs at least."

He has an merchant's eye for prices. "Fourteen. Everything is in there," I tell him. "The emerald *parure,* the Haitian pearls. Every state bond you gave me has been turned into jewels."

He looks away. "That it should come to this . . ."

"We are Bonapartes," I say. "What are a few diamonds if they can buy you an army?"

"I heard you sold your properties as well. Three hundred thousand francs. That's everything, everything, Pauline. What do you have left?"

"My titles. I will always be the Princess Borghese. I will never be homeless as long as there's Camillo."

He takes my hand, and I know he has never touched Marie-Louise this way, with such tenderness and affection. "I will miss you."

"You *will* defeat them," I say.

"Of course. But it will be long and bloody."

I put my arms around his neck and lay my cheek on his shoulder. He smells like fire. "Why did you make her regent? Her father is a traitor. She could give away Paris."

"The thought wouldn't even enter her mind."

"How do you know?"

"Because she does what she's told, even if it means visiting her son's nursery only once in the evenings. She'll be loyal to me."

"And what about Nice?"

"I'll visit as soon as circumstances allow."

"By March?" I ask.

"Even sooner."

But fate is a wild horse that has slipped her reins and cannot be commanded by the Bonapartes anymore. While I wait for Napoleon on the warm beaches of Nice, Paul brings me chilling news from Paris. Holland has fallen to the nations allied against us. Then Switzerland follows, and then Spain. With every trip Paul takes, I become more tired and ill. By the end of October, it is not necessary to go to Paris anymore. The entire world has heard what has happened at Leipzig. My brother lost Germany, and there is no more empire.

"You have to eat something, Your Highness."

"I told you, I'm not hungry."

Dr. Espiaud looks to Paul, but neither of them can force me to eat. I lie back against my pillows and close my eyes. "Your Highness—" But he had my answer an hour ago.

I feel a soft pressure on my bed and am sure it is Paul. He will tell me he too has lost a home. That he knows what it is to lose one's family to war. But he will never understand what it is to win an empire and then watch it torn to shreds by hungry nations.

"Paoletta," a familiar voice says softly. I can't tell if I am awake or dreaming. "Maria Paoletta, open your eyes."

I obey. *Napoleon?* "Napoleon," I whisper. We embrace for so long I can hardly breathe. I scramble from the covers. "Is that an *Austrian* uniform?"

He looks back at Paul, who understands his meaning and leaves. "It was the only way I could come here. The people are marching against me in the streets, calling for a return of the Bourbons. Haven't you seen the white cockades?"

"I haven't left this villa in days."

"Are you sick?"

"With worry. You have nine hundred thousand men, and only half of them are truly loyal. Why are they doing this to us?"

"There is no *us*," he says quietly. "The Allies say they're fighting me, not the French."

"And if they invade Paris? Do you think the Russian Cossacks will remember that when they find beautiful women alone in their houses?"

"Then God will have to protect them. I have done what I can for this nation." He rises from the bed, and I grab onto his arm.

"Don't go!"

"The army is waiting, Paoletta."

"Then they can wait until tomorrow. Please. Just for the night." He looks down at my robe, which has fallen open. "I don't know when I'll see you again."

He breathes heavily. "One night."

Napoleon to General Savary
Dresden, June 13, 1813

I want peace which is of more concern to me than to anyone else . . . but I shall not make either a dishonorable peace or one that would bring an even more violent war within six months.

Napoleon to Count Metternich
April 1813

I cannot take the initiative: that would be like capitulating as if I were in a fort: it is for the others to send me their proposals [for peace talks]. If I concluded a dishonorable peace, it would be my overthrow. I am a new man; I must pay the more heed to public opinion, because I stand in need of it. The French have lively imaginations: they love fame and excitement, and are nervous. Do you know the prime cause of the fall of the Bourbons? It dates from the French defeat at the Battle of Rossbach.

Napoleon to Marie-Louise
1813

Peace would be made if Austria were not trying to fish in troubled waters. The [Austrian] emperor is deceived by Metternich who has been bribed by the Russians. He is a man, moreover, who believes that politics consists in telling lies.

1814

CHAPTER 27

PAUL MOREAU

Tuileries Palace, Paris
March 1814

We are the only horse and carriage on the road, and the still-
ness of the countryside is terrifying. Even when French
warships arrived in Saint-Domingue, the villages didn't empty.
The coachman has warned us to keep the curtains closed,
but as we ride, it's impossible not to look. Shop after shop
has been completely abandoned, their windows shuttered
and their doors boarded up. On the farms, not a single person
can be found.

"Have you ever seen anything like it?" I ask.

"During the first days of the Revolution," Dr. Espiaud says.
"The emperor laid waste to the cities outside of Moscow.
Pillaging . . . rape . . . and now the Russians are coming for
revenge."

I close the curtain and sit back. I fled Haiti to avoid the
ravages of war, and now it's followed me to France. Is it a
mistake to go to Paris? When the Russians will arrive is a
mystery: we might beat them by weeks or a single day. But

Pauline wants news, and more important, Dr. Espiaud needs medicine from the Tuileries Palace. The doctor won't tell me what the princess is suffering from, but I know. And now she is frighteningly thin, and her great dark eyes stare out from a face that is paler than marble. Her ladies say it's nervousness, but I no longer agree with this convenient fiction.

I was up with Pauline all night. She wanted to count the money she raised for her brother—all the funds she garnered from selling her jewels. I keep seeing her trembling fingers going through the money, counting it again and again and again. The coach stops suddenly, and Dr. Espiaud scowls. He opens the curtain, and as far as the eye can see, horses and coaches are crowding the road, jostling for space as their owners rush to get out of the city.

"Are they here?" a woman shouts from one oncoming carriage.

Espiaud shakes his head. "We're coming from Nice."

"You're going the wrong way!" someone else shouts.

When we reach the city, it's a mad crush of wagons and horses. Thousands are fleeing, and it appears that anyone with means has already left. Women in the streets are begging others to help them escape, and I recall the desperation in the women's eyes as the French descended on Haiti. I watch an older man lean out of his carriage and promise a pretty girl a seat—for a price. She will pay either inside the coach or once the soldiers come, he tells her. When she accepts, he offers her his hand. No one knows what the Russian invasion will mean. If the Austrians are with them, marching under the Hapsburg flag, then Paris may be spared. But if the Russians come alone, there will be no mercy.

From the gates of the city, it's three hours before we reach the Tuileries Palace. And inside, the chaos is even greater. Servants are running from room to room, shouting out orders and carrying trunks.

"Where is the empress?" Dr. Espiaud asks.

A servant stops for long enough to point down the hall. "With her Regency Council, monsieur, deciding whether or not to flee the capital."

We hurry to the Council Chamber. The ministers have not bothered to shut the doors. So we stand outside with a dozen courtiers and listen as Joseph Bonaparte shouts about what can be salvaged of the Bonaparte empire. Nine months ago he was Napoleon's anointed king of Spain. Then he lost the Battle of Vitoria against the British. "There is no one more loyal to Napoleon than me! But to ask the empress to stay in this palace is the equivalent of murder."

"If the empress flees, what will that tell the people?" the Duc de Feltre argues. "We might as well wave the white flag!"

"What other color do you propose?" Joseph challenges. "Do you see my brother's army marching toward this city? Are there reports it's even close?"

"It's a risk we cannot take," the Duc de Cambaceres says. "Talleyrand?"

I am shocked. There is no minister in France *less* trustworthy than Talleyrand. Every courtier knows he has had dealings with both the Austrians and the Russians while claiming to be working solely for the good of France. No one is certain who Talleyrand supports, aside from Talleyrand. But behind every change of government in France in the past twenty years has been this man.

The Regency Council waits for him to speak. Then finally he says, "The empress of France must stay. When the Austrians arrive, she will negotiate favorable terms for this city with her father. Until then, seal the palace."

Napoleon's brother grows red in the face. "I tried reason," he says heatedly, "but no one will listen." He pulls from his pocket a letter and holds it up for the council to see. "From the emperor himself." He hands it to Talleyrand. "If you would."

The old minister reads it aloud from his seat:

If the battle is lost and no hope remains for saving my capital, the empress of France, along with my son, the young king of Rome, must repair to Château de Rambouillet and wait for me there. They must not, under any circumstances whatsoever, let themselves be taken by Allied soldiers. I would rather see my son's throat cut than imagine him brought up as an Austrian prince in Vienna.

Marie-Louise looks aghast, and Talleyrand wipes the sweat from his brow. The Duc de Feltre asks, "So what does Your Majesty think?"

"Who in here would like to be the one to disobey the emperor's orders?" the empress asks.

The men look down. Even Talleyrand won't meet her gaze.

"I am willing to remain in this city," she says. "This is my duty to France and her people. But there is a higher duty," she adds cleverly. "The duty of a wife to her husband." Obviously she wishes to flee Paris. Why would she stay in the same city that took her great-aunt's life?

"Then it's settled," Joseph announces firmly. "The imperial house moves to Château de Rambouillet."

Now the chamber is silent. The council is trying to comprehend the enormity of it. Napoleon reunited their country after she was torn by instability and civil war. He forged an empire from scraps, and no one, not even the emperor of Austria, could defeat him. For ten years, Europe has echoed his name. And now it has turned to dust.

"We leave tomorrow morning," the empress says. "Whatever happens, God be with each of you."

She rises, and I realize that both Hortense and her husband, the former king of Holland, are in the room as well. We stand back to let the members of the Regency Council pass, and when the empress appears, Espiaud steps forward. "Your Majesty!"

It takes the empress several moments to realize she's seeing the former court physician. "Dr. Espiaud? What are you doing here? The Russians are on the march. I don't know if the Austrian army will be with them." She hurries down the hall, and we try to keep pace. "Bring whatever you can." Then she stops to look at me. "Now is your chance. I hope you take it."

CHAPTER 28

MARIE-LOUISE

Château de Rambouillet, southwest of Paris
April 1814

Everywhere I look, courtiers are hurrying to fill the imperial carriages with as many of their belongings as they can fit inside. Groomsmen, chamberlains, mistresses of the robes—all of them are fleeing to Château de Rambouillet.

I wait for Méneval to clear a space in the coach for me and Franz. When at last he motions us inside, I tell my son, "Take Sigi into the carriage." He is old enough now to follow my instructions, but his small brow still creases.

"Aren't you coming?"

"Yes." Nothing could keep me in Paris after hearing Napoleon's letter to Joseph. *I would rather see my son's throat cut than imagine him brought up as an Austrian prince in Vienna.* I look at Franz, and an overwhelming desire to protect him consumes me. What sort of ruthless father could wish for his own son's death, whatever the circumstances? Even after all his petty cruelties, I would have remained in Paris as his loyal wife, but there is no forgiving that letter. I hope he returns to Paris to find the palace empty. More than that, I hope the Bourbon flag is snapping triumphantly in the breeze.

I wait to see my son safely inside the carriage, then search for Hortense. "Beauharnais!" I shout, looking above the heads. "Beauharnais!" But there are people moving everywhere. Children are standing close to their mothers, while men carry trunks in and out of the palace. I search every carriage, but none of them are carrying Bonapartes. At last I find her standing away from the caravan, holding both of her sons by the hand. Her husband is shouting something, but she's shaking her head.

"Your Majesty," Louis Bonaparte says when he sees me. "You must instruct my wife that her place is with the court in Rambouillet."

"Why would you not join us?"

"My mother has already fled to Navarre." Hortense bows her head. "With your permission, I would like to take my children there."

I feel a tightness in my chest as I realize this may be the last time I will ever see her. I reach out and gently take her hand. "Certainly."

"To *Navarre*?" Louis is beside himself. "I forbid—"

"What do you forbid?" I demand. "She is free to go."

He looks from me to Hortense and back again. Then he shouts for his trunks to be unpacked and placed in a separate carriage. "I will wait for you in Rambouillet," he says, his voice tight. "If you don't come, consider yourself unmarried."

I feel the lightness in Hortense's soul when he disappears in the crowds. Then she turns back to me. "Will you . . . will you be safe?"

"If we can outride the Russians and find my father. He promised to come for me. I trust him." We look back at the Tuileries Palace. In the morning light, it has a golden hue. The Minister of War told my Regency Council that Napoleon's generals mutinied before the army could reach Fontainebleau. They simply refused to fight. I guess men will do that when they've had enough.

"Where do you think my stepfather is?" she asks, softly.

I squeeze her hands and lean in to whisper, "It's over. Go and be with your family." After eighteen years, she is finally free of the Bonapartes.

She begins to weep. "I will write."

I embrace her tightly. "Me, too." When I look over her shoulder, I see a handsome man is waiting for her. The Comte de Flahaut.

As the caravan of more than a hundred carriages pull away from the palace, my son asks,

"What will happen now, Maman?"

I look down at my son, and my heart swells. "I don't know," I say truthfully. "But you will meet your *grandpère*," I whisper into his ear. His letter came this morning with Talleyrand, and I've read it more than a dozen times since. I touch the small white envelope folded in my pocket; simply knowing it's there gives me strength.

I look across the seat at my traveling companion, and

Méneval is watching me curiously. I have known my husband's secretary for more than five years, yet this is the first time we've been alone together. I wonder what he makes of his twenty-three-year-old empress, a woman who convinced the entire court of France to abandon Paris and take shelter within the Château de Rambouillet, held by the Austrians.

"How will the Allies treat him?" he asks.

"With more leniency than he deserves," I say truthfully. "He's an emperor. They won't wish to make a martyr of him."

"And you?"

I look out the window at the frenzy of horses and carriages. Women are already wearing white cockades on their breast, the symbol of Bourbon rule. "I will no longer be the empress of France. I know the Bonapartes will hope my father will restore me to the throne so I can replace what they have lost. But he will not."

He is quiet for a moment, wondering what this will mean for him. "So where will Your Majesty go?" he asks.

I smile sadly. "Home." Where I'll be the woman who was once a regent of the first French empire. I'll think of the palaces I've left behind, and the court that was once mine to oversee. I will have nothing when I return to Austria, perhaps not even my title. And when my son's father remembers me, it will be as a traitor. But for all of these losses, I pray there will be gains.

I look down at Franz, and when I touch his blond curls, he leans back into my hand. "How long until we get there?" he wants to know, and I tell him it could be hours.

"Three?" He holds up five fingers.

I hold up ten.

When we reach the gates of the Château de Rambouillet, there is gunfire in the distance, and Sigi barks wildly. Méneval moves back the curtains of our carriage. "There's a flag," he says quickly. Then he stares at me, disbelieving that this has really come to pass. "It's red and gold."

Yes. With a two-headed eagle! The Austrians have come. I hear the driver telling the guards that the empress of France has arrived with her suite. Then the gates are thrown open, and Méneval exhales.

"Calm yourself, Sigi," Franz says, and I can hear Monsieur Laurent in his words.

The carriages roll in a long procession toward the torchlit courtyard. As soon as the horses stop, I tell Franz, "I want you to stay here and watch Sigi. Maman will return in just a few moments."

I open the door, and before a single courtier can disembark, I am already searching. There are hundreds of soldiers, possibly thousands, all dressed in red and gold. A man with a white mustache comes up to me, but I don't recognize him as someone from my father's court.

"Your Majesty, the Empress?" he asks.

"Yes."

"Someone has been waiting." He steps back, and I see him. He is in uniform, with high black boots and white riding gloves. In his great feathered hat and long black cape, he looks like a true emperor. I run to him, and I don't care that it's undignified to embrace the emperor of Austria in front of so many men. "*Vater!*" I cry, and he takes me to his chest. "You came." I weep. "You came."

He strokes my hair. "Maria Lucia, my Maria Lucia. It was a promise."

"Maman?"

I turn to see that Franz has left the carriage. He is looking up at me with his great blue eyes, a perfect miniature of my father. "This is Franz," I say, making the introduction. "After his grandfather."

My son executes a bow, exactly as he's been practicing for more than an hour, and my father sweeps him off his feet.

"Franz!" he exclaims, and my son looks at me.

"It's all right." I laugh. "This is your *Grossvater*."

My son wraps his little arms around my father's neck and kisses his cheek. He looks like a Hapsburg king in his grand-father's arms. And while my father hoists him into the air, I search the men behind him.

"He's waiting for you inside."

It's been four years since he arrived with Sigi, and five years since he told me he'd come for me one day. I follow my father and son across the courtyard while the rest of my suite unloads their carriages. We enter the palace and pass through long halls until we reach a chamber filled with tables and maps, and there, by the fireplace studying a chart, is Adam Neipperg.

He's more handsome than I remember, dressed in his military uniform. I pause at the door and wait. "Maria!" He leaps from his chair, and when he sees my father, he bows respectfully. "Your Majesty. I'm sorry. I didn't see—"

My father waves his hand. "You should know that you were the first person my daughter asked for," he says.

Adam looks at me, and all the tenderness we once shared is there in his face. He crosses the chamber and peers at Franz. "Welcome to Rambouillet," Adam tells him.

"Thank you, monsieur."

Adam looks at me. "Exactly like his mother."

Franz points to Adam's black eye patch and asks, "Does it hurt?"

"Not at all. It's a small sacrifice to serve one's country," Adam tells him.

"Can I have one?" My son is enchanted.

My father laughs. "Let's hope not. It caused a great deal of pain for the count when it happened. Shall I take you into the nursery?"

"No!" Franz cries.

But I nod. "If you would." I lean over and kiss my son goodnight, and he buries his face in my father's chest. When they're gone, I turn to Adam. "It is real, isn't it?" I ask.

"Yes." He steps toward me, and he's standing so close that I can smell the heady scent of his cologne.

He reaches out and draws me to him. "I've waited five years for this moment, Maria, and nothing—not even the emperor of France—can stop me from doing this." He kisses me deeply, passionately, and he's right. The emperor of France does not stop him. I do not stop him, either. I close my eyes and think of François Boucher's painting *Fountain of Love*.

I lie on the chaise while he locks the door and blows out one of the candles. Then he comes to me, and we share the kind of night I've never even dreamed about these past five years. I whisper to Adam of all that haunts me, of all that I've done, of all the ways I am no longer the same woman he knew. Then he puts his hands on me and reminds me of who I was, of who I want to be, and how we shall live our lives together now.

When the clock in the hall strikes twelve, we rise from the chaise. I watch him dress and am surprised that I've forgotten how lean he is, his muscles battle-hardened and ready. He helps me into my long silk gown, kissing my neck and promising me things Napoleon never promised Joséphine. Then he leads me through the halls to my chamber. When I invite him inside, none of the guards make any motion. Before Napoleon—and France and Metternich's duplicity—there was Adam. He was my choice as well as my father's.

On the bed, we undress each other for a second time, and when he reaches out for me, the last five years of my life drift away like a fog. I place my head on his chest and listen to the comforting rise and fall of his breath. His heart is beating quickly. "It's strong," I tell him.

"It plans to keep going for another thirty years, at least. Are you ready for that?"

I roll on top of him and hold him close. "Test me."

I can't remember when we fall asleep, but the next morning I awaken to the sound of bells. Adam is gone, and I'm sure the lady-in-waiting who has come to help me can smell his cologne on the sheets.

"You're father is waiting in the Grand Salon, Your Majesty. Apparently there is news."

I change as quickly as possible—a pale blue dress with heavy silver embroidery—but there's a knock at my door before I can leave. The lady-in-waiting announces my father.

"His Imperial Majesty, the Emperor of Austria." She takes her leave, and I rise from my armoire to greet him.

"The Bourbon flag has been raised above the Tuileries Palace. Napoleon has abdicated."

I think immediately of my son, who will never again be the king of Rome, and of the Bonapartes, whose stars have finally fallen. "What does it mean?"

"Czar Alexander has gone to Fontainebleau with a treaty. If Napoleon accepts, he will remain an emperor."

I gasp, but my father smiles.

"Over the island of Elba," he adds. "He will return to Italy, where he belongs."

I walk to the window overlooking the lake and am surprised to see that Adam and my son are feeding the ducks outside.

"In all of this," he says quietly, "you've never once asked what will happen to you."

I look up. His blond hair is now completely white, and fine lines have begun to form at his brows. "Franz is free from his father's ambition. That's all that's important."

He sighs, and I can hear the heartache of these past five years in his voice when he replies, "I have made sure you will keep your imperial rank. For the rest of your life, you will be known as the Empress Marie-Louise."

"Maria-Lucia," I correct, and he nods.

"You will also be made the Duchess of Parma."

I want to be sure I understand him correctly. "I won't return to Austria?"

"You may remain in Austria for as long as you want," he assures me. "But someday, *mein Liebling,* you belong at the head of a nation."

I hear my son laugh and look down to see him chasing the ducks. It's the most innocent scene in the world; a child playing in a garden, the bright April sunshine gleaming from his hair. But he won't be a child forever. *What will his inheritance be? How will he take his place in the world?* "What if Napoleon doesn't sign? He told his brother he would rather see our son's throat cut than in the hands of his enemies."

"He will sign," my father says, disgust in his voice. "The Bonapartes will not trouble Europe again."

CHAPTER 29

PAULINE BORGHESE

Villa Lozère, southern France

"My destiny is the opposite of other men's. Other men are lowered
by their downfall, my own raises me to infinite heights."

—*Napoleon*

Because it's impossible to believe, I sit in the salon of the
Villa Lozère and ask Paul to describe it again.

He leans forward, then puts his head in his hands. "I've
already told you twice."

"I want to hear it again!" I tighten the silk robe de
Canouville bought for me, and shiver.

"He signed the Treaty of Fontainebleau," he repeats. "I was
there. I know he signed it."

"And Paris is filled with Cossacks?"

"Yes."

Then it's the first foreign army in Paris since the Hundred
Years War. I close my eyes and can hear Paul sigh.

"Do you know when you and I were supposed to leave
France?" he asks quietly.

God, not this.

"Two years ago," he says.

I open my eyes. "And the world has descended into war since then!"

"Europe has. Not Haiti." He rises, and I panic.

"Where are you going?"

"To prepare for your brother's arrival. And unless you would like to greet him in your robe, I suggest you do the same."

"You can't speak to me like this!" I shout. "I'm the Princess Borghese. You love me." But he's already gone. "You owe everything to the Bonapartes!" I scream after him. *And if not for me, you'd be at the bottom of some nameless grave with your parents.*

I go to the armoire and wonder if maybe I really should greet him in my robe. What does it matter anymore? The Bonapartes have fallen, just as our most bitter enemies predicted. Who will see if I'm dressed in a batiste gown or a silk robe now? He's the emperor of Elba! In Europe, I hear they're rejoicing in the streets, and this morning some ungrateful traitor left a British newspaper on my doorstep. It was open to a cartoon of my brother on a mule, and beneath it was a poem:

> *A lesson to mortals regarding my fall:*
> *He grasps at a shadow, by grasping at all.*
> *My course it is finish'd, my race it is run,*
> *My career it is ended just where it begun.*
> *The Empire of France no more it is mine.*
> *Because I can't keep, it I freely resign.*

He should have punished French dissidents harder. Robespierre would never have allowed such freedom of the press. It obviously wasn't enough to exile the likes of Madame de Staël or to ban Tacitus. I reach for my simplest muslin dress and a few pearls for my neck. I study myself in the mirror when I'm finished, and don't recognize the woman I've become. She's so small and thin, with nails that are bitten down to the quick. When did that habit start? Probably when de Canouville died.

I take up my white shawl and fasten it around my shoulders. If only Napoleon had marched on Egypt instead. In Egypt, I would have made a magnificent queen. I reach for my *réticule. How did it come to this?* There's the sound of a horse and carriage outside, then a small commotion as soldiers shout in German. I pinch my cheeks to give them some color, then bend double with pain.

This will not be our last meeting. I will *never* agree to abandon my brother to some island in the Tyrrhenian Sea. But as I descend the stairs, my confidence falters. He is dressed in a stained green uniform, with faded epaulets and blue pantaloons, his hair uncombed, his beard unshaven . . .

"Paoletta," he whispers.

He is standing with Paul. Behind them is assembled every courtier who came with me to Villa Lozère. I take the last steps slowly, and when he reaches out to embrace me, it is all I can do to remain standing. We weep in each other's arms. How pitiable the Bonapartes have become. He smells of snuff, and I imagine I smell heavily of wine. The angels themselves would weep if they could see us. "Let me go with you," I beg him.

"You will return to Italy," he says bravely, "and you will take Maman with you."

"What is there for me in Italy?" I cry.

"Camillo."

"He is at Château de Neuilly, searching for the Borghese family paintings and jewels."

Napoleon raises his brows. "Will he find them?"

I smile through my tears. "What do you think?"

We look at each other in our miserable states, and there is something almost comical in our wretchedness. For more than a decade, we ruled the world. No family rose higher than the Bonapartes. And then came Russia—frozen, powerless, meaningless Russia. "What will I do without you?" I ask, and my tears come fresh.

"Write. Perform."

"Then in six months," I say, "when everything is settled, I will come to Elba and bring Maman."

He hesitates. This exile is real, and it won't last for a week, or two months, but a lifetime. "Six months then," he replies, and I hold him tighter. My God, what will we do without him?

"Have something to eat," I encourage, but he looks back. Soldiers have filled the hall, and I can see them outside, surrounding the villa.

"No," he says sadly. "It's an eight-day trip from Paris to Fréjus, and my ship is waiting." He is trying for humor, but I can't bear it. "I will come to the port."

"Absolutely not. Pauline, they are rioting. It is Marseilles all over again."

When the Revolution came to Corsica, our little island had been ruled by the French for only twenty years—it wanted no part in the French king's execution. Corsican leaders declared the island's secession, and they accused our family of not loving Corsica enough. We were too French. So we fled to Marseilles, where different horrors awaited. For a year we watched the guillotine at work, and no one was safe from the anger of the mobs. *This is what happens when a government fails,* Napoleon said. Now it is his government failing.

"I know what it is to be in danger," I tell him, "and I am coming."

I do not wait for a reply. I return to my room and gather what I can. Paul helps me pack a small trunk. "I want you to sell everything," I tell him in the privacy of my chamber, "exactly as we planned. Even the paintings."

"And if they ask—"

"I have as much right to them as Camillo."

He lifts my trunk and moves toward the door, but I step in front of him. There isn't the same look of adoration in his eyes as he once had for me. "Have I changed?"

He watches me carefully. "How?"

"Do you think I've lost my looks?"

He narrows his eyes and moves to step around me, but I won't let him.

"You can be honest!" I exclaim. "I know you don't see me the same way—"

"Because you're *not*."

I inhale. "What do you mean?"

"Have you changed? Yes. From a wide-eyed girl in sandals and flowers to a woman in diamonds and furs."

I hold up my hands. "There's not a single diamond on my body!"

"Maybe not today. But how about yesterday, and all the days before that?"

"But it isn't my looks?"

He breathes deeply. "You can't help it, can you?"

"What?" A German soldier appears in the doorway. It's time to leave, but I want to know what it is that I can't help.

"Your selfishness is unbearable," Paul says, and the soldier steps aside to let him pass.

I look at the young German. There is definite admiration in his gaze. *Selfishness?* There is no greater act of kindness than this! Even Hortense would agree.

I join my brother downstairs. Once I've retrieved Aubree, he escorts me into his coach. This will be the last time I will ever ride in an imperial carriage. I look up at the pale silk lining and run my fingers over the velvet cushions. The long procession of military carriages roll out the gates, and my brother looks tense. "Prepare yourself" is all he says.

We ride through the streets, and nothing seems changed to me.

The women have white cockades on their breasts, and the men have pinned their support on their hats. The country is calling for Bourbon rule; they are afraid and want to find comfort in the past. And then I see it. In the park, where a great equestrian statue of my brother once stood, there is now a pile of rubble. They are breaking his statues and destroying his monuments.

"*Vivent les Alliés!*" a woman shouts as we pass, and people all along the roads take up this chant as they recognize our carriage. "Down with the tyrant!" someone screams, and a rock hits the side of the coach. Aubree buries her head in my neck.

"They have turned," my brother says with resignation. Another rock hits the carriage.

"A small mutiny. Nothing to worry about. The Allies won't let them hurt me. They want to see me impotent on Elba."

When we stop in Millau, more than a hundred men surround our carriage, and even my brother is cautious.

"TYRANT! TYRANT!"

Napoleon opens the door. He steps out and shouts loudly, "The tyrant!" and there is sudden silence. The men exchange looks, then one steps forward.

"You are the Emperor Bonaparte?"

"I am."

"The same emperor who sent our sons to be murdered in Russia?"

My brother takes off his hat and bows his head. "I mourn for those men. Every one of them."

"You left Moscow like a dog in the night!" someone shouts.

"To defend my kingdom. What would you do with your sons dying upstairs and your wife about to be ravaged below? Whom do you choose? The dying, or the living?"

He steps forward, and the crowd of angry men step back.

"I walked with vanity and ambition once. But those devils

did not ride with me into Russia. I went east to teach Czar Alexander a lesson, because a man who will trade with the British would just as soon ally himself with them against us!"

He mounts a stone bench and declares, "For every man, woman and child who has died under my reign, I am sorry." He touches his heart. "Deeply, deeply sorry. But they have not died in vain. Cossacks are marching down the Champs-Élysées, but Paris will survive. Prussians are in the streets, and Austrians are in Fontainebleau, but no foreign army can take away France's spirit. I forged this nation in the fires of revolution, and even Russians in the Tuileries can't keep us from our destiny!"

The men cheer, raising their hats in the air.

I have never seen anything like it. He is magnificent.

"We are the finest nation in the world," he adds passionately, "and without me, France will continue to be great. She will never forget her dignity and pride." He leaps from the stone bench and demands a horse from one of the Austrian soldiers. "I will ride these two days to Fréjus," he tells them. "A leader should ride willingly to his fate."

There are actually tears as we leave, and one of the men hands the emperor a Bible. "For your journey," he explains. "May God keep you safe."

The rest of the journey to the coast is the same. There are dozens of angry, threatening mobs, and as the Allied soldiers watch in awe, my brother charms them all. When we finally reach the port, thousands of people are waiting at the pier, all wearing cockades in my brother's blue and gold.

Napoleon climbs into my carriage, and Aubree leaps into his arms. She has never done this before. I put my hand to my mouth to keep from crying out

"I suppose this is farewell," he says.

"Six months," I remind him. He doesn't protest; he simply hands Aubree back to me. I look out at the large British frigate that will take him to Elba. Her name is *The Undaunted*. "It isn't the end," I tell him. "Look at these people."

The pier is so crowded that the soldiers are having difficulty keeping order. The women want to catch a glimpse of their Bony—that's what they call him here—and the men want to lay eyes on a tragic hero.

I reach for my *réticule* and hand him the heavy silk purse. "I want you to have these," I say. "It's enough to buy an army."

He tries to hand the Borghese family jewels back to me, but I refuse to accept them. "When you are alone, sew them into the lining of your coat. You don't know what might happen."

He takes a letter from his pocket and hands it to me. It's addressed to Joséphine. "I wrote it in Fontainebleau," he says.

I read the letter and my hands begin to tremble.

My head and spirit are freed from an enormous weight. My fall is great, but it may, as men say, prove useful. In my retreat I shall substitute the pen for the sword. The history of my reign will be curious. The world has as yet seen me only in profile—I shall show myself in full. How many things have I to disclose; how many are there of whom a false estimate is entertained. I have heaped benefits upon millions of

*ingrates, and they have all betrayed me—yes, all. I except
from this number the good Eugène so worthy of you and of
me. Adieu, my dear Joséphine. Be resigned as I am and
never forget him who never forgot and who never will forget
you. Farewell, Joséphine.*

Napoleon

P.S.: I expect to hear from you at Elba. I am not very well.

"'I am not very well,'" I repeat. His eyes fill with tears, and
my heart beats wildly. I have never seen Napoleon cry, not
even when we were children. He opens the carriage door and
offers me his hand. The cheer that goes up at his reappear-
ance is deafening. The soldiers escort us to the docks, where
he once stood after all of Egypt had fallen.

"Goodbye, Paoletta." His presses my hand to his heart. "Tell
Maman I love her."

He walks the gangway, and I weep while the frigate's
cannons fire twenty-one shots: a salute to the man who once
ruled an empire.

CHAPTER 30

PAUL MOREAU

Villa Lozère
May 1814

The art dealer shakes his head and gives a low whistle, walking around the collection for a second time. It takes up the entire salon of the Villa Lozère. "These are rare." He takes a slow drag on his pipe. "Very rare. The Princess Borghese left them with you?"

"You saw the letter," I say sharply. "It's written in her hand."

He strokes his dark beard and considers the collection: marble statues, paintings, Grecian urns, and alabaster vessels carved in ancient Egypt. These last are Pauline's most prized possessions. Monsieur Dion sold her some of these works, and now he will buy them back again.

"And what is she hoping to receive for all of this?"

I hand him a second letter. This one is sealed by her initials in wax. She intends to go to Elba—an island eighteen miles wide and twelve miles long—and if I know Pauline, she is hoping she can incite him to fight again. But to do it, he'll need money. She can't see a cause that's already lost.

He opens the letter and makes a noise in his throat. "Is she mad? This is an outrageous sum!" I don't respond. "Fifty thousand livres? She can't be serious."

"Her Highness rarely jokes."

He looks over the collection again, this time running his hands over a marble Isis. With fifty thousand livres, Pauline could change the face of Saint-Domingue. The poorest sections of the island could be rebuilt, and every child given schooling in some trade. But instead this money will be squandered on Napoleon's brutal wars. It will be used to fund death instead of life. "Fifty thousand livres then," Dion repeats, thinking I will haggle. But this isn't my collection, and soon it won't even be my concern. I have my own money with the Eubard Banking House. When I retrieve it, I'll be returning to Haiti.

He takes out his pipe and seats himself on her best chaise. "You must have seen quite a show as Her Highness's chamberlain."

"Front-row seat," I reply.

He laughs. "She's an eccentric, isn't she? Milk baths in the morning, a different lover every week. I hear she wants to join her brother on Elba. I guess that's why she's selling."

He doesn't expect me to reply, and I don't.

"Tell me something," he says, and I know this will be an invitation to violate some confidence or another. "Did the emperor really say he'd rather see his own son killed than raised by Austrians?"

But I don't see how this is any great secret. "Yes."

He takes out his pipe and thinks. "Where does that kind of ambition come from?"

I sit on the opposite chaise. "I believe they were born with it, monsieur."

"The entire family? Or were they fashioned that way by their father or Madame Mère?"

I imagine Madame Mère, stalking the palace halls in black, and can't imagine her molding young children into fierce political warriors. But her husband died of cancer when Napoleon was sixteen. Perhaps after his death she became something different. "I believe the father was a desperate gambler," I say. "He left them utterly penniless. It was the emperor who had to support his family."

"Poverty can drive a man to many things." He looks back at the handsome collection of treasures waiting to be sold, and there is conflict in his face. "She took great care of these antiques, didn't she?"

"They're her passion."

"And she's willing to give it all up for Napoleon?" he asks me.

"That, and much more."

CHAPTER 31

MARIE-LOUISE

Tuileries Palace, Paris

"The Allied powers cannot take from me hereafter the great public works I have executed, the roads which I made over the Alps, and the seas which I have united. They cannot place their feet to improve where mine have not been before. They cannot take from me the code of laws which I formed, and which will go down to posterity."

—Napoleon

From a distance, the parade might actually be a carnival. I can see children dancing in the streets and women laughing beneath the warm afternoon sun. The people are overjoyed by the man who will take Napoleon's place on the throne of France. They have a new Bourbon king, the grandson of King Louis XV. They believe he will save them from endless wars and death. He has signed the Charter of 1814, agreeing that under his reign there shall be freedom of religion, freedom of the press, and chambers of both deputies and peers to vote on taxation. There is nothing more for me in France.

My father holds out his arm for me to take, and I look one last time on King Louis XVIII. *May this throne bring you more joy than it ever brought me,* I wish for him.

I take my son's hand, and we walk as a small Austrian procession through the halls of the palace. I look down at Franz, and my heart aches. He was born here, and Paris is all he's ever known. I bend down to kiss his cheek and feel a selfish delight that he looks nothing like his father. In Schönbrunn, he will be received with great joy. When the people see him, there will be no reminder of the emperor who killed nearly four hundred thousand of our people.

"Farewell, Your Majesty." The courtiers bow deeply to me as I pass. Some of the women are weeping. I stop before one of my ladies-in-waiting who is particularly distraught and promise her tenderly, "Her Royal Highness, the Countess of Provence, will be a lovely queen. My father has told me about her. She is a good woman, and her crown has come unexpectedly."

In the courtyard outside, Monsieur Laurent is waiting near the imperial carriage. He has brought something for my son. As soon as Franz sees him, he runs to his tutor and embraces his leg. "Will you come to Austria?" he begs. He doesn't understand that we are moving between countries, not palaces.

"I'm afraid that isn't possible, Your Highness. But I brought something for you." He hands my son a package wrapped in silver tissue. "Open it."

Franz tears at the package, and inside there's a wooden duck with a working bill.

"Do you remember what this kind of duck is called?"

My son thinks for a moment, then nods. "A mallard."

Monsieur Laurent looks misty-eyed, then rubs the head of his pupil and sighs. "A very good trip to Vienna, Your Highness. Don't forget Monsieur Laurent back in Paris," he says.

My son hurries over to show me his gift. I thank Monsieur Laurent for everything he's done these many years. "I thought, when I met you, we would have great battles. I was wrong."

Adam comes up beside me, and Franz holds up his duck. "From Monsieur!" he exclaims.

"Very nice." Adam makes a great show of inspecting Monsieur Laurent's gift. "Does he have a name?"

Franz purses his lips and thinks. "Simon?"

"Simon the Duck," Adam repeats admiringly, returning the new toy. "Would you and Simon like to get into the coach?"

My son runs off, and Adam holds out his arm to me. We will be returning to Vienna with an escort of more than seven hundred soldiers. In two months, my father will follow with the rest of his army. "It's a long journey," he warns as I step into the carriage.

"Yes." Five years ago I undertook it under very different circumstances, not knowing if I would ever return. Now, I think of the improbability of it all: Napoleon's invasion of Russia, his decimated army, the sixth Allied war against him— and this one successful.

A soldier brings Franz and Simon to the carriage, and I think of all of the men who sacrificed their lives for my husband's throne. *My throne.* Yet if not for so many French deaths, I would not be going home. How does anyone make sense of this? Of feeling joy at the cost of so much misery?

"Is there anyone else you'd like to bid goodbye?" Adam asks me.

"Only my father."

He approaches the imperial carriage with its high glass windows and golden trim, and I pass my hand through the window. He came. Just as he promised he would.

"Keep her safe," my father tells Adam firmly. "I don't plan to lose her for a second time."

Adam draws a heavy breath and smiles. "Me neither."

A whip cracks in the air, and my father squeezes my hand. *"Auf Wiedersehen."*

"Auf Wiedersehen!" my son calls as the carriage rolls away.

I sit back against the velvet cushions and look out on Paris for the last time. We pass by Napoleon's unfinished arch at the head of the Champs-Élysées, and my son points to it eagerly.

"Look, Maman!"

Yes. In all fairness to Napoleon, he took a city ravaged by war and created something truly beautiful. Not just in this arch, which is celebrating his victory over Austria, but in the Pont d'Austerlitz, the Palais Brongniart, and Rue de Rivoli, whose construction isn't finished. Though it was all meant to glorify himself, he succeeded in what he came here to do—fashion something eternal.

CHAPTER 32

PAULINE BORGHESE

Villa Lozère
November 1814

At first I don't believe him.

"This is your money from Monsieur Dion," Paul says, "and the letter to verify how much he paid."

"Do you think I'd accuse you of theft?" I cry.

He shrugs. "I don't know."

I glance around the salon and realize that the trunks I thought he'd packed for Elba were really packed for his return to Haiti. But when I try to imagine life without Paul, it isn't possible. He has always been here. He won't abandon me. "Please, just come with me to Elba," I beg.

"I'm sorry, but I'm finished."

"Why?" I weep.

He lifts his two trunks and moves toward the door. "Because I've already waited two years longer than I promised. Because slavery is still a blight on this empire. Because I want to go home. Good luck, Your Highness—in everything." His eyes are cold. "I had planned to leave on your return from Fréjus."

He pauses. "But I wanted to see if once your brother's dreams of conquest were over, you could finally lay yours down."

"*Please* . . . I can change."

"But you won't." He steps around me and walks through the door. Outside, a hired *berline* is waiting. I cling to his arm.

"Paul, I need you!" *For thirteen years we've been together.*

"Then come to Haiti."

While my brother needs my help? "I can't."

"I know. You're a Bonaparte. Your ambition is far too great for that."

"You have no idea about ambition!" I scream after him, and he pauses in the drive. "If not for my ambition," I say, "you would never have made it out of Saint-Domingue alive. Your neighbor told you it was the French who killed your family, didn't he?" Paul turns around. His look is murderous, but I don't care. I've protected him long enough. "It was your own people. They killed your mother the same as they killed your father and brother!"

He shakes his head. "That isn't true."

"When my brother received the news, I had him keep it from you. Ask the people who witnessed it," I challenge him. "Going back to Saint-Domingue without protection is a death sentence. I would have made you its king—"

"What?" he cries. "Over an island that lost a hundred and fifty thousand people in the name of *freedom*? And you think— even if it could have been accomplished—I would have wanted that?"

I am dumbstruck by his ingratitude.

He leaves me in the doorway and whistles to the *cocher*. "Ready?"

The man tips his hat. "At your command."

"Wait!" I call, but he is no longer listening. "Please," I beg as he shuts the door. Then the carriage drives away, and I sink to the floor. "Paul!" I cry, and my greyhound comes running, afraid that I am hurt. She curls into my lap and looks up at me as I weep.

On the voyage to Elba, I am numb. The world is gray and colorless without Paul. I miss his wit, his perceptiveness, his laugh. . . . But he'll come back. If only my brother had reconquered Saint-Domingue and made Paul its king. The island would have made the perfect home, and we would have been untouchable; safe. But when he learns what truly happened there, he will return to France on the next ship. He may have received the news that his family died, but he has no idea how barbaric his people are.

"We are almost at Elba, Your Highness. Would you like to come see?"

I follow Madame de Montbreton, the youngest of my twenty-five ladies-in-waiting, to the railings, and catch sight of the island of Elba. In the warm autumn light, it's pretty to behold. But it's no place fit for the emperor of France. From the Roman Empire to this tiny isle. Six months ago, Portoferraio welcomed my brother with cannons and a parade. Today the little port is still excited, thronged with people who have come out to see the arrival of my ship. I search the faces, but no one familiar leaps out. Somewhere in those crowds is my brother. And with him is my mother, who has kept the title of Madame Mère. She arrived three months ago to comfort my brother in this terrible exile, and she has sworn never to leave his side until death.

As we draw closer to the dock, I open my *réticule* and take out my mirror. I pinch my cheeks and wipe a stray hair from my brow. And as the ship is moored, I smooth my skirts.

"There he is!" Madame de Montbreton exclaims. I follow her finger to a distant figure on the pier. It's true. There is no mistaking him, though he has gained weight since. He is dressed in his favorite hat, with white pantaloons and a crisp military jacket. I hurry to the gangplank, and my women step back, allowing me to be the first to disembark. There are hundreds of people waiting on the shore, but he is the only one I have eyes for. Napoleon meets me midway on the pier. I run into his arms, embracing him as tightly as my black dress will allow.

"Paoletta," he says tenderly, then draws back. "Why are you wearing this? When we arrive, you will change into something lively."

"Of course, Your Majesty." His eyes meet mine, and nothing has changed. "Where are you living?" I ask.

"In the Palace of Mulini." His brows raise. "You'll see."

Our mother steps forward and embraces me warmly. "Paoletta." Her lower lip is trembling. "*Mio Dio,* you actually came."

"Of course."

"None of your siblings have."

"Then they're not worthy of being called Bonapartes," I say.

My brother escorts us to the imperial carriage, and in a long procession of wagons and coaches, we make our way through the narrow streets. "So tell me the news," Napoleon says. But this isn't the time. How do I tell him that our new king has made Hortense the Duchess of Saint-Leu, or that her brother, Eugène, has taken his family to Munich? Has he heard that his wife has taken his son back to Austria? That Joséphine . . .

My mother complains, "They tell us nothing on this island!"

I look out the window of the carriage, and there, perched on a rugged cliff, is the Palace of Mulini. The carriages stop, and Napoleon offers first my mother, then me, his hand.

"Welcome to the Palazzina dei Mulini," he announces, and I can hear the sarcasm in his voice. The *Palace* of Mulini is a two-storied villa overlooking the sea. From the courtyard, the entire harbor can be seen, and all seven of the ships that comprise his navy.

"There's the Piazza Cavour," Napoleon points out, "and the Piazza della Reppublica. The Medicis fortified this island," he tells us. "Those walls are almost four hundred years old. Alonso will show you to your chambers," he tells me. "Tonight, at seven o'clock, we dance!"

I follow the young chamberlain through the ancient villa. "How old is Mulini?"

"Almost a hundred years," he says proudly. "It was build for the Medicis in 1724."

I had ancient Egyptian tiles in Château de Neuilly in better condition. I recall my beautiful home in Paris, which now belongs to our new king Louis XVIII. I imagine him enjoying its winter gardens, and strolling through the chambers, and I feel sick. But I have come to Elba to be a spark of light. I cannot sink into despair.

"These will be Your Highness's rooms," Alfonso says. "Your trunks will be delivered when—"

"I will need them now."

He hesitates. "Your Highness?"

"The emperor has commanded me to change my dress, and I must do so at once."

"Of—of course," the young man stutters. Immediately, he is gone. I go to the window and look out over the placid Tyrrhenian Sea.

"What is it you were waiting to tell me?"

I gasp. "Napoleon."

He strides into the room, silent as always, and seats himself on the leather chaise. For a crumbling villa, the furnishings are well done. I suppose that's something. I open the window to let in the sea breeze and wonder how I should tell him.

"If it's terrible, just tell it to me at once. I don't like guessing."

I sit on the other end of the couch and nod. "Then you should know. Joséphine is dead."

He is still for what seems like an eternity, looking at the empty wall and breathing deeply. Then he covers his eyes and rises from the chaise.

"Where you going?"

"There will be no dancing tonight or any other night!"

"Wait!"

But he puts out his arm to stop me from following him.

"It wasn't a painful death," I say. "Fever."

He turns to me in the hall. "July?"

"August."

"Three months after my exile," he realizes, and puts a hand on his heart.

He loved her in a way he has never loved me.

For three days, even my mother can't reach him. Then, on the fourth day, I hear a creaking in the hall, and slowly someone opens my door. "Napoleon!"

He hasn't bathed since we met. His hair is entangled and his face is unshaven. But there's a fierce determination in his eyes. "Paoletta, I have a son," he says. "And I have the jewels in my coat. The Allies have left me with this small toy kingdom. But even toys can be dangerous." He puts his lips to my ear, and a chill goes down my back. "I need you," he says, and I close my eyes.

Portoferraio, February 26, 1815.

To General Lapi,

I am leaving the island of Elba. I have been extremely satisfied with the conduct of the inhabitants. I confide to them the safety of this country, to which I attach a great importance. I cannot give them a greater mark of confidence than in leaving my mother and my sister in their care, after the departure of the troops. The members of the Junta, and all the inhabitants of the island, may count upon my affection and upon my special protection.

Napoleon

1815

CHAPTER 33

PAUL MOREAU

Paris
February 1815

"Would you like to sell the trunks as well, monsieur?"

I look at the empty boxes and smile. "Everything."

The owner glances up at me in surprise. "You don't look like a man who's fallen on hard times."

No, but then I dressed this morning with care. A red velvet coat with black breeches and boots. A black hat with a white ostrich plume on the side. "I have been very fortunate these last few years, monsieur. I am hoping the hard times are long behind me."

He smiles as if he understands, then hands me the price he's willing to pay for all of my possessions. There is enormous freedom in selling it all. It's a liberating feeling, which after all these months arranging my departure, is as heady as wine. Besides, what would I do in Haiti with a mahogany walking stick? Or a box made from mother-of-pearl?

"Acceptable?" he asks, and I look down at the price.

"Acceptable," I say, and it is done. I am free.

I wander the streets of Paris for one last evening, passing

through the Boulevard du Temple with its countless shops and dimly lit cafés. Tomorrow my coach will leave for Le Havre, and from there a ship will take me to Haiti. I wonder if anyone here will remember my name in twenty years, or whether I'll simply be remembered as the Princess Borghese's black chamberlain. If I could choose, I would have them speak of me as the courtier who returned from the riches of Paris to the riches of his father's land. I can employ two hundred workers when I return. And now that I am thirty, I feel old enough to inspire a nation.

I make my way to the Café Procope and listen to the men argue politics. Voltaire, Rousseau, Benjamin Franklin, Thomas Jefferson—some of the greatest thinkers in history have sat in these chairs. I raise my hand to the woman to order coffee when a sound like shrieking echoes outside. The patrons freeze in Café Procope, and then we rush to the door, where men are running through the streets. "What's happening?" I shout, and a newsboy answers.

"He's escaped! Napoleon. And he's marching with an army into Paris!"

There are shouts from behind me, and the café's owner closes his doors. I run to my room in the Hôtel de Crillon, and as word spreads, the city descends into chaos. Women and children are begging for coaches, screaming at drivers to stop, while men are locking up their homes and their shops. "It isn't true," a woman tells her friend, but when a cannon sounds in the distance, no one is in doubt.

"He's making his way to the Crillon," people are saying. When I reach the Place de la Concorde, I see that it's true.

Thousands of Parisians have filled the square, and I push through the crowds to see for myself.

He is standing on the balcony, dressed in his familiar black and gray. He raises his hat above his head, and the people around me cheer wildly for this man who, eight months before, was shouted down in the streets. Then someone steps beside him into the light. I catch my breath. She has never been more beautiful. She is dressed in white silk, with pearls in her dark hair and diamonds at her throat. She takes his hand, and she is absolutely radiant.

"I have returned," Napoleon shouts, "for the people of France, and I am here to serve the greatest empire in the world!"

The sound in the courtyard is deafening. The lamps cast a golden sheen on the emperor, and from below, he appears like a gilded statue.

"From this day forward, no man shall live in tyranny. As emperor," he begins, and I hold my breath, "I abolish the slave trade to make all men free."

All around me, there is wild celebration, and tears blur my vision as I realize what he's done. After thirteen years, he listened.

"Furthermore," he continues, and the masses grow silent, "whether it is under my rule or that of my son, there shall never be tyranny in France again!"

Fireworks burst with perfect timing in the air, and from inside the Crillon music begins to play. He holds Pauline's hand above his head in triumph, and I realize what he's doing. It's a show. There's a different stage with different lines, but he's freed the slaves not on any great principle of his, but because freedom is a suitable theme for this act.

I turn from the spectacle and make my way across the Place de la Concorde.

With a single word, I could be back in the Tuileries Palace, watching over Pauline as I have these thirteen years. I could be eating at the finest banquets and dancing beneath the glittering chandeliers in Fontainebleau. But whatever happens for the Bonapartes in France, I will not be here to see it.

CHAPTER 34

MARIA-LUCIA, DUCHESS OF PARMA

Schönbrunn Palace, Vienna

"I wanted to rule the world and in order to do this I needed unlimited power . . . I needed world dictatorship."

—Napoleon

There is shouting in the hall, and although I can't tell one voice from another, I am certain the men are my father's generals.

"What is it?" I sit up in our bed, and immediately Adam is dressing. He opens the door, and although we can never be married unless Napoleon dies, none of the soldiers are shocked to see him. All of Austria knows what he is to me, and what he's become to Franz.

"There is news from France," says General Leiberich.

"King Louis XVIII?" Adam asks. I hurry to find my robe, and when I reach the door, I hear, "There is no longer a king of France, lieutenant. Napoleon has taken the Tuileries Palace."

It isn't possible. It is unthinkable. "There must be some mistake," I say.

"He waited until the Allied ships were gone," he explains. "Then he disembarked at Cannes and collected soldiers as he went. He has an army of more than six thousand men."

Adam wraps his arms around my shoulders. "You're going with Franz to hide outside Vienna." Boots echo in the hall, and my father appears with Franz in his arms. I reach out and take my son in my arms, smoothing back the hair from his forehead as he cries. "Shhh . . ."

"Your Majesty is welcome to join us in council," General Leiberich tells me.

I look to my father. "Shall I return him to the nursery?"

"I want him with me so the men remember what they're fighting for."

Adam waits for me to dress, and I think of Henry Fuseli's *The Nightmare*. How the woman is asleep on her bed, her arms flung above her head so that her long neck is exposed. In the grips of her nightmare, she is helpless, while above her an incubus lies in wait. *He will come for me. I know he will.*

Adam holds up my coat, and I slip my arms into the winter fur. When I turn to face him, he takes me by the shoulders. "He will never find you, Maria-Lucia. I promise."

"He doesn't have to, Adam. He only has to imprison my father. Do you think I could remain in hiding if that happened? And he will come for us first," I warn. "I have his son—"

"Listen to me!" There is something in his voice that is utterly compelling. "The Allies will rise up and defeat Napoleon. His army is weak. We will crush him."

I nod, and he takes my arm. We walk the dimly lit halls to my father's Council Chamber. Six years ago I was called to this room for a similar purpose: to talk about a man who would decide my fate. Now, as I take a seat between Maria and Adam, I wonder if anything has changed. I look around the chamber, and once again every person of importance has been assembled except Ferdinand. In the crown prince's place is Metternich, and we purposefully avoid each other's gaze.

"By now," my father begins solemnly, "there is no one in this room who doesn't know that the emperor of Elba has escaped. What we propose is to form a Seventh Coalition against the man who now claims the crown of France."

Everyone begins talking at once, and my father holds up his hands for silence.

"On March first, Napoleon landed at Cannes with more than eight hundred men. These were soldiers he trained during his nine-month vacation on the island of Elba, which the British saw fit to give him while writing the Treaty of Fontainebleau."

General Leiberich stands. "We warned the Allies, telling them that an island off the coast of Italy would never be safe."

"But our voices were outnumbered," my father adds, "which is why he escaped. He began at Grenoble, where few soldiers put up any resistance. But when he reached Laffray, he came across a battalion of the Fifth Regiment of the Line. Apparently the men were ready to shoot, but Napoleon opened his coat and stepped toward them, shouting, 'Let him that has the heart kill his own emperor!' Despite the king's instructions to cage him like a wild beast and bring him to Paris, there was no further resistance throughout France, and in Lyons they paraded him through the streets."

The men in the chamber shake their heads, but this is the Bonaparte gift—theatrics, showmanship—and I have come to believe that it is as necessary to a ruler as his army or treasury.

"What about the king's soldiers in the Tuileries?" Metternich asks.

"By the time he reached Paris," my father replies, "the king had escaped. They stand with Napoleon now."

"So what does this mean for Austria?" Metternich asks.

My father says grimly, "We are at war."

CHAPTER 35

PAULINE BORGHESE

Château de Chantilly, north of Paris
June 1815

I look at the brilliant swaths of cloth laid out on the floor of the château and decide I want them all: the yellow silks, the rich velvets, the airy muslin. "Make me one in everything," I decide.

The tailor stares at me but doesn't object. After all, we are restored. The Bonapartes are once again the greatest family in Europe.

"And where shall I have them delivered, Your Highness?"

I smile at my lady-in-waiting, who's been told to pack everything by tonight. "The Tuileries Palace."

The dream of Egypt isn't dead. My brother has regained the throne of France despite every Allied soldier who stood in his path. The gods have given him a second chance, and this time it shall not be squandered. As for those who betrayed us after his star fell—let them reap the same ruthlessness they have sowed.

I think of Marie-Louise fleeing to Austria with my brother's son and want to rip that traitorous woman limb from limb. My brother can say whatever he wishes—*She was following her father's orders. She was obeying the Allies.* But I know the truth. She fled into the arms of her two great loves—Count Neipperg and Austria. I asked him once how he could ever think to make her regent. I even warned him that she would give away Paris. *The thought wouldn't even enter her mind*, he replied. *She'll be loyal to me.* So where is she now? Where is the king of Rome?

"Come," I instruct my lady-in-waiting, who is seventeen and hoping for an important position in this new court. And why not? She is pretty and competent, and her family never hoisted the Bourbon flag—not once—after Napoleon was sent to Elba. She follows me into the lavish chamber that the Duc d'Aumale has furnished me with. The Bonapartes will not forget his hospitality in these uncertain times.

"I wish to compose a letter to my brother," I say. I lie on the bed while she dips her quill in the ink. "Ready?"

"When you are, Your Highness."

"I want him to know that I will choose my new suite upon my official arrival in the Tuileries Palace. Not a single lady should be chosen for me, and I will not entertain any woman who abandoned me after his downfall."

The girl turns a little pale, and her quill hesitates above the paper.

"Write!" I exclaim. I don't care that her friends are among the women who shall never be invited back.

She does as she's told, then waits for me to continue.

"I also want him to know that Paul . . ." I take a ragged

breath. What? Paul left me for a handful of dirt and memories in Saint-Domingue? That in the end, he abandoned me like everyone else? "That Paul . . . is not coming back," I conclude.

The girl glances at me. "Monsieur Moreau is gone for good?"

"It would appear that way," I snap. Although there was one moment, on the balcony of the Hôtel de Crillon, when I could have sworn he was standing there, watching me with my arms raised above the crowds. It's not impossible to think he might have heard Napoleon announce that the slave trade throughout the French Empire was henceforth abolished. If he was anywhere in Paris, then surely he would have gone to the Crillon to hear my brother speak.

I imagine the look on his face when he heard the news. It's what he'd been waiting for, why he persisted in quoting Rousseau to my brother long after Napoleon warned him that France's colonial slaves would never be freed. But as a prisoner on the island of Elba, my brother realized the value of freedom.

If Paul was here now, we would be speaking of this. He would bring me my medicine, then we would read together from *Cinna*, or Racine, or his favorite—*The Social Contract*. "Man is born free, but he is everywhere in chains."

"Is there anything else you would like me to add, Your Highness?"

I lie back on the pillows and think. "Tell him not to worry. We will retrieve his son, even if it means destroying Austria."

CHAPTER 36

PAUL MOREAU

Haiti

"Bondye Bon"
—Haitian proverb meaning "God is good"

I see the glow of the houses before anything else, and as the ship sails into the harbor of Port-au-Prince, I watch the dawn break over the sleeping city. It has been thirteen years and forty-seven days, but I am home.

The captain shouts that the ship has docked, but I wait at the rails to see the sun rise over the forested hills, and when the light touches the farthest reaches of the bay, I pick up my leather bag and disembark.

Everything is familiar and foreign, all at once. I recognize the smell of the charcoal fires on the shore, and the scent of cooking fish, snapper or kingfish. Even the heavy rolling mist looks like an old friend. A coachman recognizes from the quality of my dress that I'll be needing a carriage, and I pay him to take me to the Moreau house.

"I'm sorry, monsieur." He speaks to me in French, the language of our nation, despite our freedom from their tyranny. "I don't know of any place like that."

"It was a farm," I say, "just outside the city. White farmer, black mistress—"

He scratches his head. "There were plenty of those types before the war. They're all gone now," he says regretfully. "What have you come here for?" He glances at my dress and laughs. "Not many Haitians on this island like you."

"I've been away for some time. I'm hoping to return to my family's farm."

The coachman looks profoundly sorry. "I hope you don't expect to find anyone alive."

I lower my head. "No."

He nods. "There might be a building, but that's all there'll be."

I climb into the coach and watch the city of Port-au-Prince wake up. She has been nearly razed to the ground, and on every corner there is evidence of her destruction. But my people are rebuilding. For each burned-out building, there is a brand-new shop. And the roads, which were almost destroyed during the war, have been repaved.

We pass the church where my father took me to school, and the courthouse where my mother received her freedom. Then we stop at a house with a white sign at its front, and I shout through the window, "This is it!"

He opens the door, and I read the black lettering: *Maison Moreau.*

I pay the old coachman and blink back my tears.

"No shame in crying," he tells me. "If we don't cry for the dead, then what will we cry for?"

Every house on my street has been abandoned. Where there were farms, now there are weeds and fallen trees. I step onto the porch where my father taught me how to carve leather and wood, and make my way into the house that sheltered me for more than seventeen years. Every piece of furniture is gone, looted by the French or by impoverished Haitians.

"Hello?" I call, but there is no one. Even the rats are silent.

I stand in the doorway to my father's salon and can't believe what has happened. In thirteen years, the room has managed to shrink. What had seemed like a palace is really just four small walls covered in paper.

I turn from the salon and make my way to my old chamber. The bed is still here! Not a bed, but a cot, with strings for a mattress and an old wooden frame. And they left my armoire. I carved it with my father when I was eleven years old. I go to the cabinet and open the doors, and there, like some ancient treasure from Egypt, is a woman's comb. I take it out and hold it in my palm, flat and cold like the woman it belonged to.

I wonder where she is and what she's doing now.

I sit on the bed and remember the captain's words on the ship: "*The emperor has won the Battle of Ligny. Only God and His angels can stop that man now.*" But I don't know. Love can inspire men to great feats. And Marie-Louise is deeply loved. Her father won't give up so quickly. Nor, I hear, will Count Neipperg.

The Empress Marie-Louise once asked me if I believed in

ghosts. *"I find it hard to believe in something I've never seen,"* I told her. But perhaps ghosts aren't meant to be seen. Perhaps they are meant to be felt.

I walk to the back of the house and stand in the empty fields. The dry weeds look golden in the soft morning light, and the palms sway gently in the early breeze. For all the kingdoms the Bonapartes conquered, they never had riches like this.

CHAPTER 37

MARIA-LUCIA

Schönbrunn Palace, Vienna

*"There is no immortality but the memory
that is left in the minds of men."*

—*Napoleon*

"I won't leave."

"You must, Your Majesty!"

"Under whose command?" I ask. Metternich watches me furiously, but he will never have power over my movements again. I look around the Council Chamber, crowded with faces I remember from my girlhood, and none of them dare to challenge me. I turn to Metternich. "You may have convinced Napoleon that I would make a fine bride in order to further your interests," I say. "You may even act as my brother's regent when I am gone. But you are finished controlling my destiny. I have a son, and it is my duty to keep him where I believe he is safest."

The prince turns red with indignation. "And what, exactly, are these *interests* of mine, Your Majesty?"

"I'm sure your banker could tell us. Napoleon desperately

needed a royal bride, and you were kind enough to provide him with one." I savor my reply. Then I rise from the council table, and the men rise with me. "If the British lose this battle," I tell them, "I will leave Vienna. But until it is done, I remain at Schönbrunn."

There is stunned silence as I leave the Council Chamber to find Maria with Sigi and Franz in the gardens.

"What happened?" she asks when she sees my face.

I sit beside her next to the little pond and watch my son with the ducks. "Metternich wants us to flee," I say quietly. "He believes this battle is a turning point."

"Where is it being fought?"

"In the Netherlands, at Waterloo. He says it may decide this empire's fate. There are two hundred thousand men."

I don't sleep. I pace the floors, thinking about Adam somewhere to the south and my father with his army in the north. But there is no word on Saturday, before the battle's begun, and nothing on Sunday, despite my prayers in the church. Five days pass before Austria's given any word.

And then he comes.

I open my chamber door, and Adam is there, dressed in Austria's bright red and gold. For several moments, I am too afraid to ask. Then he smiles widely, and I begin to weep. He pulls me into his embrace, and all the strain of these past six years is lifted. I will never have to fear Napoleon again . . . Franz will never be taken . . .

"He lost the Battle of Waterloo," he says. "Fifty thousand men dead. He will be banished to the island of Saint Helena to live out his days."

I close my eyes and exhale. "And France?"

"Has been restored to the Bourbon king."

So it is true. The world will never know Bonaparte rule again. I lead him inside, and we stand at the window overlooking the lake. Someday I will paint a scene of this moment, and I will call it *Liberation*.

MARIE-LOUISE, DUCHESS OF PARMA

Parma, May 1821

I know by the way the boy walks across the field that his message is urgent. It isn't anything in his face, unlined by worry and still supple with youth. It isn't even the way he walks—his steps steady, his eyes focused. It's something in the way he holds his letter, as if the content were so searing, he can't even bear to touch it.

He passes through the heather, and I admire the way the sun gleams in his hair, bronzing the tips of his dark curls. When he reaches my easel, he isn't sure whom to approach. The father of my two youngest children, Count Neipperg, who is bouncing his son and daughter on his knees while I paint, or me, the Duchess of Parma. He looks from one of us to the other, then decides the message is best suited for me.

"From His Imperial Majesty, the Emperor Francis."

I glance at Adam, but my husband frowns. My father's health is well, and there's no reason to believe there's political upset in Austria. I break open the seal and skim the contents. "It's happened," I whisper. I walk to where Adam is sitting on a blanket and show him the news.

The first line is all he needs. He puts down our children, who are four and two, leaving them with Sigi. Then he rises to comfort me, squeezing my hand. "Six years."

"Does Your Majesty care to respond?" the boy asks.

I shake my head. "No. Not now." I sit down at my easel and take a few moments to comprehend what has happened.

Napoleon is dead.

Never again will there be a night when I lie awake with Adam, wondering if the Bonapartes will return to seek vengeance on our family. Month after month, year after year, my husband's shadow has loomed across the ocean to darken our lives. Today he is my husband no longer.

I look at my beautiful children, Albertine and William, who will never have to know the despair of always sleeping with one eye open. But my joy is not complete. For as relieved as I am, my eldest, Franz, is without the father he was born to now.

Adam raises my hand to his lips, then places it tenderly on his heart. "Austria can sleep well tonight."

"And Parma," I say, since this is our home now, nestled between the Kingdom of Sardinia and Tuscany. "Do you remember that Francesco Guardi painting?" I ask him.

"In Vienna," he replies.

"There were ships being tossed by the waves. Dangerous, but beautiful somehow."

"Yes." He loves paintings as I do.

"The sea is finally calm."

AFTERWORD

NAPOLEON

A year after signing the Treaty of Fontainebleau, Napoleon was exiled to Saint Helena, a remote island half the size of Elba located in the Atlantic. This time only thirty people accompanied him. He arrived with more than two thousand books and spent much of his time reading plays and dictating his memoirs to General Bertrand. One of his recollections was the fact that he had "never loved . . . except perhaps Joséphine, [and only a little at that]." He also regretted his marriage to Marie-Louise, particularly after news arrived that she was living openly with Adam Neipperg in her new Duchy of Parma.

All these regrets did not stop him, however, from forging new relationships with women. Even on the island of Saint Helena, he managed to seduce Madame de Montholon, his dearest friend's wife, resulting in the woman's separation with her husband on her return to France. But Napoleon's days of romancing did not last long. The island—cold, damp, and infested with both mosquitoes and rats—did little for Napoleon's health. He began to complain of stomach pain and experienced severe vomiting and chills. When he was diagnosed with hepatitis, he began to use leeches and large doses of calomel, making him even sicker.

On May 6, 1821, six years after he arrived on Saint Helena, the former emperor of France and self-proclaimed successor to Alexander the Great died at fifty-one years old. Reportedly, his last words included, "Joséphine," just as Joséphine's last words were, "Bonaparte . . . Elba . . . the king of Rome." An autopsy performed by British doctors concluded that the emperor had died of stomach cancer. Since his death, some historians have argued that Napoleon was poisoned, citing the high levels of arsenic found in his hair and the numerous enemies he had made both on and off the island (one of them being Monsieur Montholon). Still others have suggested that the arsenic found in his hair was the result not of poison but of a coloring known as Schalers Green, which contained copper arsenite and could be found in the wallpaper on Saint Helena. In a comprehensive article published in 2011 by Dr. Alessandro Lugli et al., called "The Medical Mystery of Napoleon Bonaparte: An Interdisciplinary Exposé," the authors present convincing evidence that in the last six months of his life, there was no dramatic rise in arsenic levels in Napoleon's body, which would certainly have occurred had he been poisoned.

Whatever his final cause of death, Napoleon's burial took place on the island, far from the empire he ruled and the family still plotting for his return back home. In 1840 the

French king sent his son, Prince François, to retrieve the emperor's body so it could be interred at Les Invalides in Paris. His tomb remains there to this day.

MARIE-LOUISE

Once it became clear that Napoleon's exile to Saint Helena would be permanent, Marie-Louise settled in Parma with her lover, Adam Neipperg, and their first child was born in 1817. Although much of Europe frowned on their relationship, a second child was born to them in 1819, and on Napoleon's death two years later, Marie-Louise and Adam Neipperg were married. They went on to have one more child. This was clearly the happiest period of Marie-Louise's life. "Were I not to commit the sin of pride," the Duchess of Parma said, "I could say I deserve it, because God knows all I have suffered in life." Marie-Louise died at the age of fifty-six and is buried near her father and eldest son, Napoleon II (who died of tuberculosis at twenty-one), in the Imperial Crypt.

PAULINE

After her brother's banishment to Saint Helena, Pauline and her mother moved to Italy, where Pauline's husband, Camillo Borghese, was living happily with his mistress. On her arrival at Camillo's home in Rome, Pauline ordered that her husband's mistress be thrown out, and when Camillo refused, she appealed to the pope for help. When the pope instructed the hapless Camillo to return to Pauline, there was nothing for him to do but bid farewell to the woman who had been his companion for more than ten years.

There is strong evidence that during the last years of her life, Pauline was taking medication for venereal disease. At the time, one of the most popular medications for both syphilis and the clap (also known as gonorrhea) was mercury. Today we know that taking mercury can lead to mental deterioration and eventually madness. In fact, the term "mad as a hatter" was coined after hatters working with mercury were seen to develop dementia. It's possible that some of Pauline's more eccentric behaviors stemmed from mercury poisoning. If this is true, then she was suffering mentally as well as physically.

Yet throughout her many bouts with illness, it was Camillo who tended to her, much as Paul had before his return to Haiti, and slowly, a grudging respect developed between Pauline and her husband. Although her health continued to deteriorate, Pauline hosted daily parties at her home, and her legendary beauty seemed to be unaffected. Recalling her afternoon with Napoleon's famous sister, the Irish novelist Lady Morgan wrote, "The day before we left Rome, we breakfasted at the Villa Paolina, with a circle composed of British nobility, of Roman princes and princesses, German Grandees and American merchants. . . . It is the most hospitable house in Rome. . . . No lady was ever so attended by Cardinals as the beautiful Pauline."

But the news of Napoleon's death on Saint Helena came as a devastating blow to Pauline. After years of writing letters to the British prime minister, she had only recently received permission to visit her brother on his remote island in the Atlantic. Now it was too late. Suffering from cancer of the stomach, she succumbed to her illness on May 18, 1825, four years after Napoleon's death. With her dying breath, Pauline instructed her ladies-in-waiting to be sure her hair and makeup was done after she expired.

As for Paul, who served her so faithfully for thirteen years, his fate is unknown. But after his dramatic escape from Elba, Napoleon did indeed abolish the slave trade. It was one of the emperor's first acts during his one-hundred-day return to power.

HORTENSE

With the final fall of the Bonapartes in 1815, Hortense was exiled from France for supporting Napoleon after his escape. When her lover, the Comte de Flahaut, requested her hand in marriage, she refused, afraid that divorcing Louis Bonaparte would mean losing her beloved sons. It must have been a terrible choice for Hortense, since in 1811 she had secretly given birth to their son, the future Duc de Morny. But her refusal meant she was free to take her sons to Switzerland, where she settled near Lake Constance and proceeded to write her memoirs. Hortense died in 1837, fifteen years before her son, Charles-Louis-Napoleon, became Emperor Napoleon III.

BONAPARTE FAMILY

The fate of the Bonaparte family is not as dismal as it might have been, given Napoleon's exile and death. While Pauline hosted extravagant parties in her Italian villa, Madame Mère moved to the Palazzo Rinuccini (thereafter called the Palazzo Bonaparte) in Rome, where she decorated her apartments with portraits and busts of her beloved son. Although she cut a gloomy figure in her black mourning clothes, she was surrounded by servants and grandchildren, both of whom helped to alleviate the pain of her son's downfall and subsequent death. "Twenty years ago," she would tell her grandson wistfully, "whenever I entered the Tuileries, drums were beaten, soldiers presented arms, and crowds flocked around my carriage. Now people peer at me from behind curtains." She died in 1836, at eighty-five years old.

Caroline Bonaparte, who was responsible for insisting that Marie-Louise leave Sigi behind when she first entered France, died at fifty-seven. Her eldest son, Achille Murat, would later become the mayor of Tallahassee, Florida.

HISTORICAL NOTE

It's hard to believe that only eleven years after the execution of Marie-Antoinette, and the death of nearly half a million people during France's Revolution, the same country that had adopted the motto *Liberté, égalité, fraternité* went on to crown Napoleon Bonaparte emperor. The political and social chaos left in the wake of the Revolution facilitated Napoleon's rise to power, and his unbelievable conquest of much of western Europe forged a legend out of this young general from the island of Corsica. But the legend of Napoleon and the reality were very different. Even today, with well over two hundred thousand books written on the Bonapartes, few people realize just how extreme some of the Bonaparte siblings truly were.

In my attempt to recreate the last six years of Napoleon's reign, I relied on the thousands of letters that have been preserved from his court, some of which are included in the novel. I also used (although far more judiciously) the memoirs of Marie-Louise, Hortense, Mademoiselle Durand, Monsieur

Montholon, and Napoleon himself. Although many scenes in this novel may be hard to believe, even the most outrageous aspects of this book were taken from primary resources.

Take, for example, the character of Pauline, who actually owned serving bowls that were modeled on her breasts. Numerous letters attest to her use of ladies-in-waiting as footstools, and although there is much speculation concerning her relationship with Napoleon, reliable sources credit her with saying that she wanted to "do as the Ptolemies did . . . divorce my husband and marry my brother." Her obsession with Egypt was very real, and her desire to rule alongside her brother made the courts of Europe extremely uncomfortable. The Austrian diplomat Prince Metternich seemed to think that an illicit relationship existed between them, while Pauline herself commented many times that she and Napoleon were intimate. Even Joséphine suspected that brother and sister were having an incestuous affair. In 1805 she apparently witnessed something that distressed her so much that she burst into a room where the secretary general of the Council of State, Hochet, was chatting with the Comte de Volney. When they asked her what was wrong, she told them, "You don't know what I've seen. The emperor is a scoundrel. I have just caught him in Pauline's arms. Do you hear? In his sister Pauline's arms!" In a family like Napoleon's, it is not inconceivable that such a relationship might have existed. As Prince Metternich recounted, "Pauline Bonaparte was as beautiful as it was possible to be. . . . She was in love with herself alone, and her sole occupation was pleasure."

In fact, France's imperial court had become so scandalous

that the gossip made its way to Austria, and from the very beginning, Marie-Louise was vehemently opposed to Napoleon. Before her marriage she told a close friend, "I pity the unfortunate woman on whom [Napoleon's] choice falls," later adding that, "to see this creature would be worse torture for me than all the martyrdoms." However, once her marriage was announced and it was clear that her father's regency was at stake, Marie-Louise's rhetoric softened. She decided that she was ready to make this "painful sacrifice," however much heartache it would eventually cost her. But what she didn't realize—and what even her father's ministers couldn't have prepared her for—was just how erratic Napoleon would turn out to be.

There is no doubting the fact that Napoleon was a military genius. He took a country utterly devastated by war and built an empire that stretched from the Pyrenees to the Dalmatian coast. Yet this same man who created the Legion of Honor to promote advancement solely through merit was also obsessed with court etiquette and securing titles for himself. And while he may have had many admirable qualities on the battlefield, they did not extend to his personal life. He slept with his future mistress, the Countess Walewska, for the first time while she had fainted at his feet. Another of his mistresses, a Comédie-Française actress named Catherine Duchesnois, was instructed to meet him next door to his study. After making her wait for more than an hour, he sent word that she should "get undressed." When he finally appeared, the matter was "all dealt with in three minutes." This attitude toward women and sex makes his treatment of

Marie-Louise on their wedding night unsurprising. When he was finished, he advised his secretary Méneval to marry a German. "They are the best women in the world: sweet, good, naïve, and as fresh as roses."

He also enjoyed publicly insulting the female members of his court. To Germaine de Staël, who possessed an ample bosom, he famously remarked, "You evidently nursed all your children yourself." And according to Louis-Antoine Bourrienne, these kind of comments were typical. "He seldom said anything agreeable to women, and frequently made the rudest and most extraordinary remarks. To one he would say, 'Good heavens, how red your arms are,' or to another, 'What an ugly hat!' Or he might say, 'Your dress is rather dirty. Don't you ever change your clothes? I've seen you in that at least a dozen times.'"

Among his less admirable qualities, Napoleon was unbelievably selfish as well. In one of his letters to Joséphine, he reprimands his wife over Hortense's grief, telling her that Hortense is "not being reasonable" in mourning the passing of her son. "She does not deserve our love," he went on, "since she only loved her child." It was this attitude that probably explains his remark, after the tragedy in Russia, that "a man such as I does not concern himself much about the lives of a million men."

If I have been harsh in my treatment of Napoleon, it's because I believe the evidence warrants it. There was a callousness in his personality that neither experience nor age ever tempered. His treatment of Pauline's lovers in the book is accurate, as was his treatment of his secretary, Méneval. Even in the end, when misfortune might have prompted personal revelation, his greatest regret was that he "did not terrorize [France] upon [his] return from Elba."

While I tried to remain as close as possible to the known facts, in several places I have altered the history to fit the story. For example, I have Marie-Louise leaving for Austria in May, while her actual departure was on April 23. Similarly, the timeline for the extensive wars that Napoleon waged on his neighboring countries was changed. And while all the letters found throughout this book are authentic (some have been condensed), there are three exceptions: the letter from Napoleon to Joséphine in Chapter 14, the letter from Napoleon to Pauline in Chapter 19, and the letters in Chapter 25. The most significant change I made, however, was to Adam Neipperg's marital life. Unable to divorce his wife, the Italian contessa Teresa Pola, Adam separated from her instead. Teresa died in 1815, while Marie-Louise was still legally married to Napoleon. The emperor's death six years later allowed Adam and Marie-Louise to marry.

Given the wealth of information available to us about Napoleon's family, it was no small task to sort through the research and decide which memoirs seemed the most plausible and which letters should be included in the book. But among these many resources, a few stand out as being indispensable: Flora Fraser's recent biography *Pauline Bonaparte: Venus of Empire*, Steven Englund's *Napoleon: A Political Life*, and Robert Asprey's *The Reign of Napoleon Bonaparte*. I should also note that the quotes at the beginning of the chapters are real, the sources ranging from letters to nineteenth-century memoirs.

GLOSSARY

auf Wiedersehen—German for "farewell"

batiste—a soft, opaque fabric

berline—a French carriage

Bis wir uns wiedersehen, meine Liebe—German for "Until we meet again, my love"

calèche—French for "coach"

canard—French for "duck"

cocher—French for "coachman"

cour d'honneur—French for "three-sided courtyard"

Der Menschenfresser—German for "The Ogre"

fête—French for "party"

fleur—French for "flower"

Grossvater—German for "grandfather"

La Vestale—title of an opera composed by Gaspare Spontini in 1807, to a French libretto

Leberkäs—a German dish similar to sausage

Légion d'honneur—Legion of Honor, an order established by Napoleon Bonaparte recognizing both civilians and soldiers based on merit

Les Deux Billets—title of a French ballet

Les Français—French for "The French"

manteau—the long train of a dress

mein Liebling—German for "my darling" or "my favorite"

mein Schatzi—German for "my treasure"

mes chéries—French for "my dears"

mio Dio—Italian for "my God"

mon ange—French for "my angel"

mulâtre—French for "mulatto," a child born of one white parent and one black parent

parure—a set of matching jewelry, often composed of a crown, a necklace, and earrings

pelisse—a fur jacket

post-chaise—a fast-traveling carriage

réticule—purse

Schnuckelputzi—German slang for "cutie pie"

soirée—a party

Spätzle—a German noodle dish

Vive l'impératrice—French for "Long live the Empress"

ACKNOWLEDGMENTS

I would like to thank the many people who helped make this book possible, beginning with my amazing editor, Christine Kopprasch, who endured more delays than any editor ever should (and for which I am profoundly sorry). It's been such a pleasure working with you, and any author who finds him/herself under your guidance is a lucky author indeed. To Heather Lazare, who originally purchased this book for Crown, I am always in your debt. To Dan Lazar, who is truly a fantastic agent, I am extremely grateful. And to the many wonderful people at Crown who have worked so tirelessly behind the scenes: my copy editor Janet Biehl, my publicist Dyana Messina, my production editor Cindy Berman, Jonathan Lazzara in marketing, Chris Brand in art, and Publisher Molly Stern.

To my research assistant, Ashley Turner, you are absolutely invaluable.

And finally, to all the friends and family whose support I

could not do without, particularly in 2010: Carol Moran, Amit Kushwaha, Allison McCabe, Christopher Gortner, Cayman Jacobs, Tracy Porter, Cathy Carpenter, Julie Nelson, Jennifer Gonzalez, Julia Glick, Tracy Carpenter, Jill Rawal, and Aryn Conrad (who gave this book its title). Thank you.